In memory of my mother
Sybil Tope
who died just as the final pages of this book were
being written

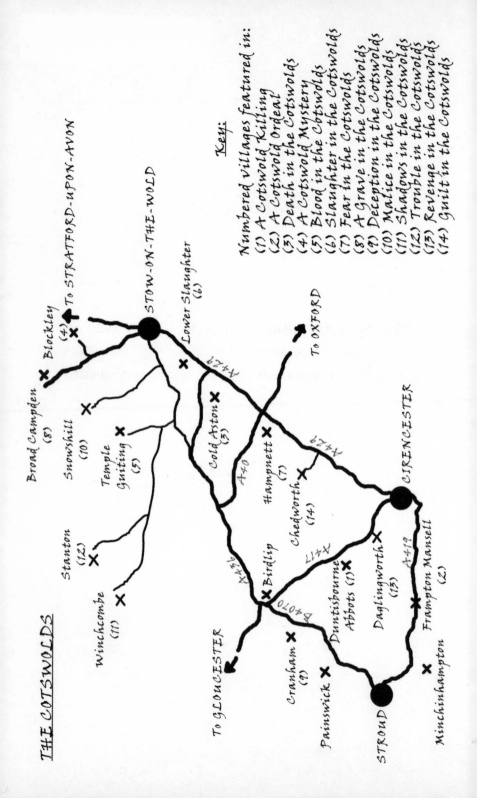

Author's Note

While the pubs, villages and towns in these tales are all real, the houses, hotel and garden centre have been invented, or enormously changed from the originals.

Contents

A Cotswold Casebook

REBECCA TOPE

Allison & Busby Limited
12 Fitzroy Mews
London W1T 6DW
allisonandbusby.com

First published in Great Britain by Allison & Busby in 2016.

A CIP catalogue record for this book is available from
the British Library.

First Edition

ISBN 978-0-7490-2004-0

Typeset in 12/17.2 pt Sabon by
Allison & Busby Ltd.

Paper used in this publication is from sustainably managed sources.
All of the wood used is procured from legal sources and is fully traceable.
The producing mill uses schemes such as ISO 14001
to monitor environmental impact.

Printed and bound by
CPI Group (UK) Ltd, Croydon, CR0 4YY

Contents

Introduction

Although I have written perhaps twenty or thirty short stories over many years, the prospect of a collection of them was initially both daunting and thrilling. Would readers be put off by this sudden change of format? Only time will tell. But gradually I recalled some quite brilliant stories I had read and enjoyed, by Celia Fremlin, Roald Dahl, Saki, Piers Anthony, and others. Most of them were at least as memorable and delightful as any novel I had read. Then I remembered hearing Chaz Brenchley (a master of the short story) say a writer has more space and freedom in a story than in a novel. I wasn't sure what he meant until I began writing these tales. Now I understand – I think.

As a reader of short stories I am aware of the effort demanded to engage with a new world and new set of characters, time after time. It is, perhaps, one of the factors that puts people off them. But here I have cheated. All the stories in this collection feature Thea

Osborne (now Slocombe) or Drew or someone close to them, set in the Cotswolds villages and towns that feature in my series of novels about Thea and her house-sitting. The world will be familiar to existing readers, and for anyone coming to them for the first time, it has a consistency that I hope will reduce the resistance.

Perhaps it should also be said that while Thea's world has a geographical accuracy, there are quite a few chronological anomalies in these stories when related to the novels.

There is also a minor element in the stories that might be called a game. Each story refers in some way to one (sometimes more than one) of the Cotswold novels. Either a character from it, or the place in which it is set, or something subtler. Here and there I have altered details of events or characters in order to avoid revealing too much of the plots in the novels. The key is at the back of the book.

In Guiting Power

Guiting Power was unlike most other Cotswolds villages in its openness. Few of the usual narrow lanes and high hedges were included in its bounds. There were swathes of grassy bank, buildings set back as if trying to create more space for travellers to pass through, or for people to congregate together. Nobody hid away behind cluttered front gardens or high stone walls.

Drew had only been there once before, but he recognised it right away. There was a squareness to the buildings, including the church, and a serenity conferred by the big old trees standing watch over the village. The origins were Anglo-Saxon, and he fancied he could still feel the presence of those people.

He was there to meet a woman Thea had known a few years earlier. She had sent a card when the Broad Campden burial ground had first been opened, wishing them well and reminding Thea of their shared history.

'I live in Guiting Power now,' said the note. 'Come and see me sometime.' And she had added address, phone number and email.

'She really means it, doesn't she?' said Drew. 'When did you last see her?'

Thea had to concentrate in order to remember. 'Must have been when I was in Lower Slaughter. I met her in a pub when I was out for a walk. I wonder why she's moved.'

'Interesting name – Ariadne.'

'She chose it herself. She was Mary originally. She got very cross when Phil kept forgetting she'd changed it.'

'Phil knew her?' While Drew felt no hint of jealousy towards his wife's first husband, he did have some difficulty with Detective Superintendent Phil Hollis, with whom she had been involved for a year or so.

'In the dim and distant past. I'm not sure I want to renew my acquaintance with Ariadne. She was terribly *intense*. And I don't think she really liked me very much.'

'So why has she gone to all this trouble to remind you of her existence?'

'Good question.'

'We should acknowledge her, at least. It sounds bad, I know, but the more supporters and friends we can keep hold of in the Cotswolds, the better it is for business. We absolutely have to have at least one funeral a week if we're to survive.'

'I can see that. I'm not sure Ariadne's likely to be of much use to us, but you never know.'

So he had carefully added the details to his database of contacts, and emailed the woman to thank her for the note. He signed it 'Thea and Drew'.

Within an hour he had a reply: 'Great to hear from you. The burial ground sounds wonderful. Just my sort of thing. Can I draw your attention to my own new business? More of the same, actually, but better organised. Original hand-knits. Homespun yarn. See the website.'

In an idle moment, Drew looked at the website and found pictures of gorgeous jumpers, capes, scarves, and a whole lot more, none of it with prices attached. It took him barely ten seconds to decide to get something from it for Thea's forthcoming birthday. Which explained his visit to Guiting Power, where Ariadne had most of her stock.

He found the house – a classic stone building set well back from the road – and walked up its front path wondering how the woman Thea had described could possibly afford such a place.

'Hey, you must be Drew!' chirped the person who opened the door. ''Arry – your man's here!' she called over her shoulder.

There were voices and music coming from a number of directions on both floors. Two small children sat at the top of the stairs, watching him. A large black and tan dog strolled down the hallway, only mildly interested. There was an impression of a large disorganised house full of good cheer and noise, which was as far from his experience of the usual contents of houses in Cotswold villages as you could get.

'Come in,' the woman on the door urged him. 'The kids and dogs escape if we leave it open for long.'

He crossed the threshold with a strong sense of walking into an alternative dimension. A flurry at the far end of the passageway announced another person. She trotted towards him, pushing her sleeves down and fumbling with cuffs as she went. 'Come in,' she echoed. 'This is so nice of you.'

'Not at all,' he said stiffly.

'Have you got time for coffee? You're sure to be busy, I know. But you'd be very welcome.'

He gave her a thoughtful inspection. Solidly built, her hair tied up in a vivid scarf, clothes sprinkled with fibres and fluff, she had dark eyes and a wide mouth. 'You're Ariadne, I take it?' he said, still sounding like a Victorian undertaker in his own ears.

'Oh, yes. Sorry. I should have said. How's Thea? I've heard a few stories about her since we last met, but I never expected her to take up the funeral business. Bit of a change from house-sitting. But then, nothing lasts for ever, does it? Things change. You're married, right? Fancy that!'

He could see her mentally comparing him with Phil Hollis, who he remembered had been a friend of hers.

'I thought one of your jumpers . . .'

'Yes, that's right. So nice of you. Although I have to say they've been taking off rather well just lately. I saw *two* people wearing them in Cheltenham on the same day last week. The high spot of my career so far.'

She led him into a large square kitchen, which while untidy was perfectly clean. The window sparkled and he could see no hint of a cobweb. In one corner there was a dog basket, containing a shaggy animal and a child even smaller than the ones on the stairs. 'Okay, Mimsy?' Ariadne asked carelessly.

There was no response, but the dog raised its head minimally.

'We're fostering,' the woman explained. 'It's working pretty well. Mimsy does most of the work,' she laughed. 'The little ones adore her.'

'Good for her,' he said faintly. He cast his mind's eye back to the hallway. There had been no stair gates. Were you *allowed* to foster children without using a stair gate?

'It's all approved by the Social Services,' she went on, reading his mind. 'They're so desperate for people that they'll turn a blind eye to a lot of things. The kids mostly love it here, and nobody's broken a leg up to now. We've got so much *space*, you see. It would have been a crime to waste it.'

'Who else is here?'

'There's me and two other women living here permanently. We all have a bit of income of our own, and with the fostering money we just about scrape along.'

'But who owns the house?' He looked around again, trying to calculate the value of the property.

Ariadne laughed. 'Everybody asks that. The answer's a bit complicated. It all goes back a long way, but technically, I'm afraid we're probably squatters.'

'Gosh! Surely the Social Services don't like that.'

'They don't know. We told them it belongs to Gabriella – which is almost true. She's Italian and came here when she married an Englishman. But now he's gone off to Panama or somewhere, and hasn't come back. The house is in his mother's name. So there's the answer to your question. It's really hers, but she's pretty well forgotten about it. I think we'll be fine as long as she keeps occupied living the high life, as she does. She knows we're here, and the house is being used and maintained.' Her smile contained a hint of triumph, perhaps at arranging matters so cleverly.

Drew wasn't at all sure he wanted to hear all that. The idea of anyone wealthy enough to forget about such a house was very hard to swallow. It sounded like wishful thinking to him, with the owner liable to come back and evict the lot of them at any time. 'Let's see the jumpers,' he said. 'I need to be somewhere fairly soon.'

'Oh. Right. Sorry. Through here, then.' She opened a door close to the dog basket and ushered him through.

It must have been a pantry originally, he supposed. It was fitted with shelves on three sides, that would have held jam, cold meat, tinned food, condiments – anything that needed to be kept cool and close to hand. Now it was home to a bewildering display of handmade items. Not just Ariadne's knitwear, but three shelves of pottery and two more of jewellery, mostly fashioned from twisted and curled wire. He moved slowly along, as if in a shop, admiring the work, and also the imaginative use of the space. 'Phew!' he said. 'You've been busy.' He fingered a pretty little milk jug, painted in blues and greens. A perfect present for almost anybody, he thought. Turning it over, he read the name scored on the bottom, *Gabriella Mallon*.

'We have stalls at fairs and markets and all that. I've got one tomorrow.'

'All this *work*,' he sighed. 'How do you keep up with it?'

'Iron discipline,' she said. 'Gabriella has her pottery studio in the garden. I use my bedroom for the spinning. Helen uses hers for the jewellery. She doesn't take as much space as me and Gabby. We have a rota for the kids. It all works well enough.'

'How many kids?'

'Five.' She smiled. 'One's at school full-time, but we keep the rest here with us. No sense in paying for a nursery when we're quite capable of doing it ourselves.'

'And they're all fostered?'

'All except Harriet. She's Helen's own child. She's the one in the dog basket.'

With a bemused shake of his head, Drew began to

examine the jumpers on the shelves opposite the small window. What was Thea's best colour, he asked himself. Blue, perhaps, or grey. They both seemed somewhat dull, and his eye was caught by a soft-looking garment in a shade of purple he thought might be officially fuchsia or magenta. It had white shapes scattered over it, with sequins sewn into the middle of them. 'That's nice,' he said, pointing to it.

'Mmm,' said Ariadne. 'Not sure it's quite right for her skin.'

His eyes widened. What was wrong with Thea's skin? Was there something he'd never noticed? His gaze fell on another jumper in orange and brown and yellow. 'How about that?'

'Far too big. She'd drown in it.'

'Well, you choose, then. It sounds as if you remember her pretty well.'

'I do.' It was said darkly, hinting at a lot more significant an encounter than he had gathered from Thea. 'She'd look great in this.' She grabbed a lacy-looking pink thing and flourished it, letting it unfold and fall from where she gripped its shoulders.

Drew accepted that he was out of his depth. He suspected his impulse had been a misguided one. Was it not famously risky to buy clothes for other people? 'You think so?' he said doubtfully. 'How much is it?'

'Seventy-five pounds. It's my own design.'

'Oh,' he said faintly. No way could he even begin to afford it. He had imagined something roughly a third of that price. Surely she couldn't be getting sums like that at her market stalls? Was she deliberately trying to rip him off? 'Too much, I'm afraid. We've had to tighten our belts quite a lot since starting up here.'

'Pity,' she said with a shrug. 'So it'll have to be a hat or scarf or gloves, then. I've got a few things around twenty. Not much under that. It's the handmade thing, you see. It adds value.'

Twenty pounds sounded a lot for a hat that might only be worn on very cold days. Similarly gloves. And he was sure there was something feeble in giving a scarf. Thea already had quite a lot of scarves. 'I'm very much afraid I've been wasting your time,' he said regretfully. 'I'm really sorry.'

Her reaction startled him. 'No, no. I *wanted* you to come,' she said urgently. 'Never mind the jumpers. It was lucky for me you had the idea of buying something. Otherwise I'd have had to think of something else.'

'What?'

'The email I sent you – remember? I knew Thea had a birthday coming up. I never forget a birthday, even if I want to. I thought you might get the idea of buying something for her.' Her voice lowered, and she glanced through the open door into the kitchen. Nobody but the child and the dog was in there. 'Listen,' she went on. 'We're going to need a quiet little funeral one day soon. It's all rather awkward. Embarrassing. We don't want any publicity. Nobody's to come to it. Your set-up sounds perfect. Legal, but very discreet.'

Drew's first thought was that one of the foster children had expired, and needed a hushed-up burial. Then he chastised himself for being overdramatic. Nothing of the sort could possibly be happening. 'Who died?' he asked starkly.

'Nobody yet. The person's very ill. We'll contact you when the inevitable happens. It won't be very long.'

'There has to be some official paperwork,' he warned her. 'Doctor's certificate. Next of kin. All sorts of things.'

She sighed. 'Don't give me that. All we need for you is the death certificate. The registrar wants the other stuff, not you. Why are you being so suspicious?'

'That's what I meant – the registrar. And you must admit it sounds a bit odd.'

'It's not odd at all. We all approve of woodland burials without the church stuff. Here you are, married to my old friend Thea, and everything's going to work out nicely.'

'All right. Yes. Of course. Just give me a call when the time comes and we'll take it from there. Sorry about the jumper. I've wasted your time.'

She was still holding the pink thing. Now she thrust it out at him. 'Take it,' she said. 'Call it advance payment on the burial. It's perfect for her. I'll wrap it if you like.'

He stepped back, his hands at his sides. Something wasn't right and by accepting the jumper he would be colluding in a transaction that his guts told him he would regret. But it *was* very pretty. Feminine and cuddly, he could absolutely see Thea wearing it in the evenings, snuggled against him on the sofa. The size looked perfect, too.

'Go on,' she urged. 'You know you want to.'

'Well . . . Thank you,' he muttered awkwardly. 'Though I'm not sure how to square it with my books. The accountant is sure to query it.'

She blew out her cheeks scornfully. 'I bet people pay you in kind all the time. As I understand it, that woman in Broad Campden paid you with a *house*.'

'No, she didn't. Is that what people are saying?' He was appalled at the idea.

'More or less, yes. Why does it bother you?'

'I don't know.' He thought about it. Looked at in a certain way, it was true that Greta had done something of the sort. 'It was less commercial than that,' he began. 'She just *liked* me.'

'Right. Fine.' Ariadne appeared to lose interest. The child in the basket stirred and whimpered, and its canine nursemaid jumped up as if stung.

'I should go,' he said. 'Let me know when you need my services.'

'Oh, I will,' she said.

He wrapped the jumper carefully, wishing he could report his unsettling experience to Thea. But it would be impossible to explain why he had gone to Guiting

Power without revealing the secret of her birthday present. He went over it many times in the next few days, marvelling over the numerous children and the creativity in every room. Where did everybody *sleep*, he wondered. There must be bunk beds and shared rooms, and long waits for the bathroom.

And who was the person on the brink of death? Despite many encounters with the dying, he found this a very unusual situation. He would go to hospices and private homes to talk to people about their own funerals, on a regular basis. He had been approached countless times with vague enquiries as to how his business actually worked in practice. But this was both more and less definite than usual. Ariadne knew someone who was dying and who presumably wanted a natural burial. But who and where was this person? The situation in the big stone house seemed too full-on to allow very much outside activity, and certainly not the kind of full-time care that a dying person required. Even if in hospital or a care home, there would be a demanding schedule of visiting. Nobody left a loved one to die unattended and unvisited if they could possibly help it.

He worried away at it for days, wishing he had asked more questions. He had met either Helen or Gabriella at the front door – nobody had told him which it was. One of them might well have a parent at the end of life, although Helen, at least, had to be rather young for that, if she had a small child. He did his customary automatic calculations. Perhaps if Helen was in her early forties, having left motherhood late, and her own parents had done the same, then it would all fit. As for Ariadne herself, he realised he knew nothing whatever about her background, except that she had been friendly with the Hollis man for much of her life.

And yet, it had not sounded like a dying parent. There would have been no need for secrecy, surely, if that had been the situation. Perhaps a detested stepfather needed to be kept at bay, or a cousin laying claim to the family jewels? He recalled a funeral at the undertaker where he had first worked, at which half the family had to be excluded. It involved barefaced lies and left a very nasty taste afterwards. His boss, Daphne Plant, had herself been uneasy about it, 'But they're paying us to do what they ask,' she'd shrugged.

On the evening before Thea's birthday, events began to unfold. The phone rang and Drew heard Ariadne's voice, with its low notes and West Country vowels. She could probably have been a remarkable contralto singer, he thought, with the right training.

'It's happened,' she said. 'Even sooner than we thought it would.'

'All right. Give me the name. Where's the body now? Has the death been registered?'

'Hang on. I told you, didn't I, that it wasn't going to be straightforward. We need a day or two to get all that done.' Her voice had dropped to a whisper.

Apprehension, suspicion, resistance all swirled together inside Drew. Alarm bells were ringing loudly. After dealing with hundreds of deaths, he was highly sensitive to the range of emotions that would come his way. Ariadne was completely outside that range. The hushed voice might be explained by listening children. Difficulties with paperwork were not unusual. But there remained several aspects that did not fit with anything he had encountered before.

'So where's the body?' he asked again. 'Do you want us to come and remove it now?'

'Oh, no. Tomorrow will do. She's here, quite safe and sound.'

An earlier thought gripped him again. Was it one of the children? Had there been some awful abuse that resulted in a child's death? Had they somehow covered it up? Was Ariadne capable of something so appalling? He took a long, slow breath and told himself not to be such a fool.

'She?'

'That's right. Her name is Jennifer Alice Millingham.'

'A doctor has seen her, right?' He had written down the name, noting the initials with a faint smile.

'Yes, yes. Drew, this is all quite legal and normal. You sound very peculiar about it. What's the matter?'

'Nothing, I hope. But getting the basic facts from you is like pulling teeth. You've got a dead woman there, with a house full of children. Is she someone's mother, or what? Has she been laid out? Orifices and all that? Do you know what happens otherwise? Is she in a bed?'

'Oh, Gabriella's seen to that side of it. The children aren't bothered. She's nobody they know. At least . . . well, they don't *care* about her, anyway.'

'All right. Well, we'll come tomorrow morning, then. Is ten o'clock convenient for you?'

'Fine. Who'll be with you?'

'My assistant. He's called Andrew. We've got a van specially modified for the purpose.'

'I'm sure you have,' she said lightly. 'See you tomorrow, then.'

He had to tell Thea. He could keep back the existence of her birthday jumper, with luck. Even if he had to deliver it a few hours early, that wouldn't be a disaster. He went to find her in the kitchen, where she and Timmy were doing a big jigsaw. It took up half the table, and had been there since just after Christmas.

'That was your friend Ariadne,' he said. 'She's got a funeral for us.'

Thea looked up, her expression blank. 'Has she? Who died?'

'Somebody called Jennifer Alice Millingham.'

'Is it her mother? I can't remember her ever mentioning a mother.'

'I think not. It sounds very odd, but she insists it's all perfectly normal. Andrew and I are doing the removal tomorrow morning.'

'Oh. Well, that's good, isn't it?'

'I hope so.'

To his frustration, nothing more was said. He went into his office at the back of the house, and consulted his file covering the legal requirements for a death. He knew that it was the usual practice for a doctor to view a patient who had died, and that almost everybody assumed it was an essential part of the process. The strict, but minimal, requirements were that all a doctor had to do was give the cause of death, on a form that was then taken to the registrar. It was this person who really held the line against murder, fraud or other criminal behaviour. If this Jennifer Millingham had been ill, visited by a GP and cared for by a competent, trusted relative or friend, then it was possible that the GP would issue a certificate simply giving the cause of death when this caring person told him – or her – that the patient had died. Drew had a hunch that this might well turn out to have been what happened in this instance.

If so, it would be a first for him. Every doctor he had ever met would regard it as a clear, ethical duty to see the body of a patient. But the law did not insist. He realised that he was rushing ahead; that Ariadne had not overtly stated that the dead woman had been uninspected by a doctor. It was just an implication that grew stronger the more he thought about it. He found an unambiguous line in his file: *Thus, there is no requirement in English law for a general practitioner*

or any other registered medical practitioner to see or
examine the body of a person who is said to be dead.

It was followed by pious recommendations that
any responsible doctor should turn out not only to
examine the body but to do anything possible to
console and advise the relatives.

Which left a certain degree of responsibility on the
shoulders of the undertaker, he thought ruefully. A
responsibility at the very least not to bury someone who
was actually not quite dead, despite the paperwork all
being in perfect order.

The jumper was received with something less than
rapture. 'Pink?' said Thea. 'I never wear pink.'

'She said it would suit you. Hold it up. It *does* suit
you. It looks great.'

Thea looked down at herself doubtfully. 'Does it?
It feels nice, I must say. Where did you get it? Is it
handmade? It must have cost a fortune, if so.'

He swallowed back the explanation he'd been about
to give her. Would she approve of the transaction
whereby her birthday present had been accepted in
part payment for a funeral? 'Don't ask,' he said. 'But
I can tell you it's one of Ariadne's. I went there last
week and chose it. She's got a big house in Guiting
Power, with two other women. I've been dying to tell
you all about it.'

She was pulling the garment over her head, and
standing in front of the mirror over the fireplace. 'It

is nice,' she said. 'Just not what I would ever have bought for myself. It'll take some getting used to. I never see myself as a pink person.'

'Good,' he said.

'What were you telling me just now? You went to Ariadne's house? Is that the same house you've got to go to in a minute to collect a dead woman?'

'Yes. Remove, not collect,' he added, for the fiftieth time.

'Sorry. I can never see why that matters.'

'I suppose it doesn't, really.'

'She's an odd person. I can't imagine her living with other people – she was very solitary when I met her. Eccentric.'

'She's that, all right. So are the others, I imagine. They've got a whole lot of foster children. Little ones. And dogs. And no stair gate. We had a stair gate until Timmy was at least three,' he remembered. 'A real nuisance it was, too.'

'I don't think there's any law about it,' she said mildly.

'Yet.'

'Foster children? Now that really is odd. I thought they were only given to people within their own area. Something about consistent community experience – some jargon like that. So they can keep the same friends and go to the same schools. Of course, it can't possibly work.' She made a slightly sneery face; one that Drew had seen before and didn't like.

'It's a good aim, though, don't you think? I suppose the children in Guiting Power might have people in Oxford or Stratford – somewhere within reach, at least. Poor little things,' he sighed.

'I suppose so. It all sounds a bit mad. Is the dead person in the same house as a lot of little kids, then?'

'*Yes*. That's what I'm trying to say. The authorities would go crazy if they knew.'

'They would. Well, you'd better go and sort it all out, then. The sooner the better.'

'I've got a few minutes. You like the jumper, then?'

'I love it. Thanks ever so much for it. It's gorgeous. Tell Ariadne she's got magic in her hands. I wonder if she used a natural dye for the wool. I think she spins it all herself, as well as knitting it.'

'I'll ask, if I remember. Ah – there's Andrew now. See you later.'

In the van, he explained some of the story to his employee. Andrew Emerson had been a farmer until very recently, the funeral business a late change of career. Repeated bouts of tuberculosis in his cattle had finally driven him out of business. He still got up with the sun, spent every possible moment outdoors, and made anxious predictions about the weather. His face was rugged and grooved, but some of the worry lines were smoothing out as he relaxed into his new life. He had turned out to be extremely good with the families during the funerals, treating them all as equals, offering a light but sincere understanding of their grief. He conveyed a sense of everyone being in this together, life proceeding somehow or other without the lost relative or friend. Drew was delighted with him, while worrying at times that there would not be enough income to sustain his salary.

'What's your real problem with this, then?' Andrew asked Drew now. 'How's it different from usual?'

'Where do I start? All I've got is a name. I don't know how she's related to anyone in the house – or even if she is. I keep coming up with unlikely explanations, and none of them is very reassuring. She could be an obstructive social worker, threatening to take the kids away. Or a rich old aunt. I know I've seen too many murder victims for my own good, and this can't possibly be another one – but suddenly it looks all too easy to cover up foul play, if you've got a lazy doctor on side.'

'Lazy doctor?'

'I checked the law again last night. It's not a legal requirement for a doctor to examine a patient after they've died. If he'd seen her within the past week or so, and knew there was a life-threatening illness, he could issue a certificate of the cause of death without seeing her again.'

Andrew thought this over. 'That seems okay to me. The important bit is the life-threatening illness, isn't it? If a person was murdered, they wouldn't have been ill beforehand, would they? So ill that the doctor wasn't surprised when they died.'

'Ill people can be murdered,' said Drew. 'If there was a proper plan in place, there could be ways of convincing the doctor that it was worse than it was really.'

'Come on, Drew. That's really over-egging it. You've got far too much imagination.'

'I expect I have.' He drove on, past Stow-on-the-Wold and turning right onto the B4068 that meandered westwards towards Naunton, before the turning up to Guiting Power. He was still very unsure of the way all the many Cotswolds villages linked together, remembering brief visits to Thea in a number of them when she'd been house-sitting. Some had been hard to find, leaving images of deep, dark lanes and large, shady trees, to be abruptly followed by wide, sweeping plains, without hedges or woodland for a hundred acres. It was more like this latter landscape on the final stretch. Beside him, Andrew was commenting on their progress. He knew people across the whole region, and was related to several of them. 'That's where my cousin Raymond lives. Letting his fences go, look. Sold off all the stock a couple of years back, so not much need to keep the fences sturdy. Seems a shame.' He sighed. 'He'll be growing rape or linseed, most likely.'

They were in good time, arriving ten minutes early. 'Shouldn't think they'll mind,' said Andrew.

They were ushered into the house by Ariadne and a woman she introduced as Gabriella. Small children were much in evidence, apparently in good health and clean clothes. Drew corrected his notion of them as waifs and strays, dressed in Dickensian rags. The house was warm and music was playing in a back room. 'She's up here,' said Ariadne.

The body was of a woman who had evidently lived a long time. White hair, sunken mouth above an unusually long chin, and thin mottled skin. 'Who *is* she?' asked Drew, his fascination only increased by the reality before his eyes.

'Jennifer Alice Millingham. I told you,' said Ariadne. 'Everyone called her Jammie, for obvious reasons.'

'Have you got all you need for the registrar? They ask about fifty questions, you know. Birth certificate, marriages, divorces, National Insurance. The whole works.'

'Not all that, no. But enough, probably. Not your problem, really. Just so long as I get the death certificate, you're covered, aren't you?'

'Yes, but . . .' He bent over the body. At least she was definitely dead, he concluded. Had been for a while.

'Listen, Drew Slocombe. She was a homeless vagrant. We met her a year ago and she used to come here to get warm and have some food. She was nice with the kids, and when her dog died, we let her bury it in the garden. There really isn't any mystery to it. We haven't got much paperwork for her, admittedly. But the doctor knows about her. She had a very damaged heart, and some kidney disease. He was surprised she lived as long as she did. We promised her she would have a decent funeral. She'd a bit of money stashed away to pay for it. I can't imagine we'll have much trouble with the registrar when we tell the whole story, can you?'

She left the room without waiting for a reply. Drew and his colleague set about wrapping the body, preparatory to carrying it downstairs. 'Not a murder, then,' muttered Andrew.

'Seems not.' The simple explanation was slow in dispelling Drew's suspicions. 'Although . . .'

'What?'

'Well – has she been up here dying for the past week or more? This looks like one of the main bedrooms. The house isn't big enough for them to spare a whole room like this. There are five children living here.'

'Can't see the problem. Kids can double up. There must be sofas downstairs.'

'True.'

'Come on, mate. It all makes sense to me. People are kinder than you think, when it comes to something like this. She's clean enough, look. They've done a good job on her.'

'All right. Let's get her down the stairs, then. We can't refuse to take her now.'

Andrew stared at him. 'And why would we? I don't get it. What are you so bothered about?'

'I don't know. There's *something*, I know. It just isn't right. I feel it in my gut.'

'*Double Indemnity*,' said Andrew, confusingly.

'What?'

'The boss man at the insurance company. Edward G. Robinson. He can feel a scam in his gut. Something like that. Turned out he was right, of course. But real life is different. Guts are not reliable.'

'I expect that's true. Come on, then.'

They kept the body in the cool room until Ariadne turned up two days later with the death certificate all signed and sealed and legal. 'It wasn't quite as easy as I hoped,' she admitted. 'But we got there in the end. The registrar phoned the doctor, who convinced her it was all okay.'

The burial was arranged with more expedition than people in Britain had come to expect. Drew deplored the lengthy delays that had become the norm, and made it one of his key selling points that he could easily perform a funeral within three days of a person's death. 'There really isn't as much to be done as they tell you at big undertakers,' he would tell his customers. 'And because we never do embalming, it's in everyone's interest to get on with it.'

Ariadne was more than happy to endorse this approach, and a small gathering assembled in the field on a blustery afternoon, to bid farewell to Jennifer Alice Millingham. A very young copper beech tree was standing by to be planted at the head of the grave. 'I got it for two pounds at the Moreton Garden Centre,' said Ariadne. 'It was in the bargain corner. I'm sure it'll grow perfectly well.'

'It will,' Drew promised. 'I'll put it in when you've all gone.'

A month later, Thea and Drew were going through the small pile of accumulated newspapers that somehow built up on the corner of the dining table of its own accord. Local news was a minor passion with Drew, who maintained that it helped him with the business. He needed to understand connections, changes, who the important people might be. Thea liked to spot familiar village names, as well as very occasional references to people she had met.

Two items caught their interest. First Thea, then Drew, exclaimed aloud before reading out the piece in question.

Thea's had the headline, 'Well-known local character found dead.' The text then explained, 'A homeless woman known to all as Jammie, has sadly been found dead in an outbuilding near Stroud. On investigation, police learnt that she had left the area around Bourton and Naunton, where she had been in the habit of spending the winter months. A witness reported that she had been told by Jammie that she had been paid to relocate to Bristol, but that she had so disliked the change of scene that she was returning to more familiar parts. Police say there is no suggestion of foul play.'

Drew read an article that had a photo attached. 'Wealthy widow's whereabouts in question,' said the headline. Then, 'Mrs Barbara Mallon, widow of the successful entrepreneur, Jack Mallon, has been missing since the New Year. Friends have informed the police, although it is thought that there may not be any real cause for concern. Mrs Mallon was known to travel widely, often with little preparation. She has a son who lives in Central America. However, the police would like anybody with information as to her whereabouts to contact them.'

The picture showed an elderly woman with white hair and a long chin. It was a face that would remain in anyone's memory. It was not, however, the face of a vagrant called Jammie. Instead, it was the wealthy owner of the house in Guiting Power, whose death, if made known, would lead to considerable difficulties for its occupants.

'Oh dear,' said Drew.

With Slaughter in Mind

Toni was disappointed not to be offered accommodation at the hotel when they agreed to employ her as part of the catering staff for the summer. She had not yet passed her driving test, and home was forty miles away. 'I can't do it, then,' she told the man interviewing her.

'Why did you apply for something so far from home?' he wondered.

'I thought it would be good experience,' she said, sounding feeble in her own ears. 'I'm going to university next year, and wanted to see what it was like, fending for myself.'

'You're only seventeen,' he pointed out.

'I know I am. That's why living in sounded a good idea.' How to explain the feelings of claustrophobia and frustration that had been building up for months, living with six other people? 'I'm actually quite capable of looking after myself,' she asserted. 'And I've got an aunt living not far away.'

'You could stay with her, then,' he suggested.

'I could ask her, I suppose,' she said doubtfully. That was not at all the plan. It would be too much like being at home, with young children getting in her way. Toni had had enough of children, at least for a while. She wanted to get out into a world full of adults, and learn some of the quirks of human nature. She was intending to study psychology once she got to university, and life in a hotel seemed to her the ideal source of material to analyse.

'Well, we really would like to have you here until September. It's booked solid, and it's never easy to find the right people for the work. You strike me as unusually bright and energetic for an English girl. It's mostly the Poles and Ukrainians who get the jobs, because they try so much harder. That's fine, but the guests really like a chat sometimes, and I think they'd go for you.'

'That sounds ominous,' she said with a little smile.

He laughed. 'Sorry. Bad choice of words. We take care of girls as young as you, don't worry. Everything's perfectly respectable here.'

'I don't think I can take the job,' she said regretfully. 'Not if I can't live in.'

He scratched his thinning hair. 'Well, maybe I can do a bit of juggling. Phone me this evening, and we'll have another little talk about it.'

'Okay, then.'

*   *   *

She went back to where her mother was waiting outside in the car, and explained what had been said. 'They really want me, but they don't think I can live in. So I said that wouldn't work. And he said I should stay with Thea and Drew, but I don't really want to. Anyway, they're ten or twelve miles away, so that's not going to work, is it? I'll be working evenings a lot. How would I get back there?'

Jocelyn rolled her eyes. 'I *said* it was a mad idea, coming up here like this. Especially Lower Slaughter. It's got so many bad vibes for the family. I don't know why I let you talk me into it.'

'Because the money's good and you'll be glad to get rid of me for a couple of months.'

There had been an emotional argument the previous day, leaving Toni confused but more determined than ever to have her way. She'd found the job advertised online, standing out like a bonfire from any of the other places wanting staff. The building was gorgeous, the area a honeypot for rich tourists. But Jocelyn kept referring to an event a few years earlier, just after Granddad had died, which involved both Toni's aunts, and left the whole family horribly shaken. 'It's the same hotel,' Jocelyn wailed.

'So what? They won't make the connection, with my surname being different. And look what they're paying! They must be really grand. They'll teach me a whole lot of useful skills.'

'I thought you wanted to be a psychiatrist, not a chef.'

'Psychologist,' she corrected for the hundredth time. 'And cooking's always going to be important. I can have it as a second string.'

Toni was a painfully sensible girl, as Jocelyn regularly remarked. Sporty, popular, hard-working and unnervingly well balanced – a paragon of a daughter that her parents regularly asserted had been left by the fairies in place of their actual child. The other four were like feral creatures by comparison.

They were expected at Broad Campden for tea – an event that carried some significance for the sisters, who did not meet very often. Jocelyn was younger than Thea, but they had been bracketed together as 'the little ones' by an older sister and brother. They had shared one of Thea's house-sits in Frampton Mansell at a time of crisis for Jocelyn, with a resulting embarrassment and near-estrangement born of intimate revelations concerning Jocelyn's marriage.

'That must be it,' said Toni, as they drove slowly through the village. 'That looks like a hearse outside.'

'So it does,' said her mother. 'I wonder what the neighbours think about that.'

'They probably think it makes them special. I would, anyway. See how shiny it is.'

'Old, though. I think they got it pretty cheap.'

Thea came to the door, and led them into the kitchen. Drew's children were at the table with electronic gadgets. The dog was doing her best to attract attention, which Toni gave very readily. Drew himself was elsewhere.

Jocelyn and Toni gave an account of their day, laying out the dilemma for Thea's consideration.

'Haven't you got a bike?' she asked. 'It would take less than an hour to cycle to Lower Slaughter from here. Much less, probably. We'd love to have you to stay over the summer. We've got a spare room.'

'Spare cupboard, more like,' said Stephanie. 'Big enough for a hobbit, just about.'

'It's perfectly big enough,' Thea said. 'There's a full-sized bed in there to prove it.'

'Except it's folded up,' argued Stephanie.

'I *have* got a bike,' said Toni thoughtfully. 'But ten miles seems an awfully long way. I've never been more than about two. I'd be scared.'

They all looked at her with varying degrees of sympathy and scepticism. Jocelyn spoke first. 'I'd be scared to let you,' she admitted.

'Well, it's just an idea,' said Thea. 'Oh – here's Drew.'

The husband and father entered the room with a wary smile. 'So many females!' he said.

'There's me,' Timmy reminded him. 'I'm not female.'

'Thank goodness for that. Hello, people. Good to see you.' He had met his sister-in-law and all her children at his and Thea's wedding. Even with guests limited to immediate family and closest friends, the numbers had swelled to over twenty. Toni had been selected as the nearest thing to a bridesmaid, carrying flowers and watching over her aunt. She had felt conspicuous and did not enjoy it very much.

Between them they explained to Drew about the job and the hotel and the cycling idea. He expressed no opinion on any of it, for which Toni felt grateful. She had already concluded that Drew was a very nice man. The funeral business intrigued her, and the children were no worse than her own numerous siblings. Their lack of a mother made them more interesting, too. A summer spent with this family might turn out to be exactly what she was looking for, combined with the novelty of working long hours in the hotel.

'Okay, then – thanks,' she said, when they'd stopped talking. 'I'll do that. If you're sure?'

'That was quick,' said Jocelyn, with an anxious frown.

'Does that mean you're really going to stay here, in the little room?' said Stephanie.

'Oh, good,' said Thea, a notch less heartily than was called for. Toni caught the tone and shot her a questioning look. If her aunt was going to see her as a nuisance, that could spoil the whole thing.

But it was soon smoothed over, and in a jerky, interrupted fashion, the decision was eventually made. Toni should phone the hotel, accept the job, and practise her cycling. Drew would unfold the spare bed and move the boxes and bags that cluttered the little room.

After a meal together, during which Thea and Jocelyn reminisced across forty years, mother and daughter took their leave. 'You will watch out for her, won't you?' pleaded Jocelyn. 'It seems terribly sudden. She's not eighteen yet.'

'Eighteen is more than old enough to manage something like this,' Thea began, but was quickly silenced.

'Don't start that again,' her sister said. 'We all know your views about mollycoddling.'

'See you next week, then,' said Thea to Toni. 'It'll be an adventure.'

'And we'll love having you here,' said Drew.

It worked out much as expected. The cycling was exhausting on the first day, tiring on the second and almost easy by the third. There were hills and valleys, and the bike lacked many modern refinements to make such terrain easier. The work at the hotel was menial, but there were breaks and diversions enough to render it acceptable. The worst part was cycling back to the Slocombes' after dark. Headlights dazzled her, and her own lights never seemed bright enough to convince drivers that there was a cyclist to be aware of. 'I'm going to be killed, I know I am,' she panted, as she got in at midnight one night. Drew was still up, unusually, because he'd taken a phone call about a death that evening.

'Please don't be,' he begged. 'That would be a tragedy.'

'I saw a very odd thing today,' she went on, too fired up to contemplate going to bed. 'Can I tell you about it?'

'Go on, then. Ten minutes is all I can do before bed, though.'

'There's a patch of wasteland next to the hotel. I mean, it's not full of rubble and junk. Just not used for anything. Lots of weeds and long grass. Anyway, I saw a woman, quite old, wandering through it, this afternoon, with a basket. She picked a few things, one at a time, very carefully – I couldn't see what they were. I decided she must be a witch, making up a brew for a spell.'

'Or a flower arranger?'

'Or a poisoner. Some of those plants must be poisonous.'

'Or gathering seeds for her own garden. Lots of things go to seed in July.'

'She looked like a witch. Long skirt and ankle boots.'

'Pointy black hat?'

Toni laughed. 'No hat. Grey hair, tied back.'

'Winemaking, and that's my last idea,' he said.

'You should have been there. She was *furtive*. She didn't want anybody to see her.'

'Bedtime,' he said. 'What time do you start tomorrow?'

'Eleven. Nice long break in the afternoon, as well. Not many bookings for dinner, so we can chill for a bit longer.'

'Maybe your witch lady will come back and you can ask her what she's doing.'

'No way. I'd be too scared.'

The woman with the basket *did* come back, and Toni saw her again. It was three o'clock and the lunch was all done, everything washed and put away, tables cleared, ready for a fresh set of cutlery, glassware, flowers and menus for the evening. The staff each had an hour of freedom, though not everyone took the same hour. Hotel guests could demand snacks and drinks at any time, and someone had to be on hand to provide it.

Hotel guests, she had discovered, were a special breed of human being. They appeared to acquire a powerful sense of entitlement the moment they walked into the foyer. Complaints poured from them on every imaginable topic. Pillows were too soft, showers too hot, beds too close together, door locks inoperable, windows likewise, plumbing too noisy, soap too small. The list was endless, as well as being the source of hilarity in the staff quarters.

'Sounds just like Fawlty Towers,' said Drew, when she recounted some instances to him. 'People expecting to see herds of wildebeest crossing the savannah in Torquay.'

The reference was lost on Toni, who could not remember ever seeing the programme, but she was pleased to have given Drew something to laugh about. Pleasing Drew had become quite important to her. The way he listened so attentively to everything she said, keeping his eyes on hers the whole time, made her feel warm and special. She found herself conjuring his face at odd times of the day, and thinking what a lovely man he was.

'I might show up one day to have a look for myself,' said Thea. 'I could have afternoon tea and scones.'

'You could,' Toni agreed. 'I could show you around, if it's not too busy.'

'I want to come,' said Drew, boyishly. 'I want to catch that witchy woman.'

'What?' said Thea, so they explained.

'She'll be making exotic salads or soups,' was her first guess. 'With wild garlic, or rosehips or something.'

'I said she was a winemaker,' said Drew. 'Same sort of thing.'

'No.' Toni was emphatic. 'It was much more suspicious than that.'

'Have you seen her again?' asked Drew.

Toni shook her head. 'It was only two days ago. I haven't given up hope that she'll come back and I can get a better look at what she's picking.'

'We can't both go. Someone has to be here when the kids get back from school.' Thea had finally accepted that the routines of school formed the framework of her day, and nothing could take precedence over them. There was still another week to go before the end of term. Toni had been released early from her sixth-form college, much to Timmy's envy. The summer holidays were regarded as a burden and a relief alternately by Thea, who claimed to have forgotten everything about the life of a parent of primary-age kids. 'I think Jessica had a lot of friends she stayed with,' she said vaguely. 'Not to mention the cousins and grandparents. I don't recall her being around very much.'

Drew's children had yet to make any serious friends at the new school, despite having been there for two terms. They had no plans or projects in mind for the holidays, and there was no suggestion of a family week at the seaside. The presence of Toni was celebrated as a welcome break from the usual pattern, even though she was out almost all the time.

It was the next to last day of term when Thea fulfilled her promise and called in for tea at the Lower Slaughter hotel. She pulled rank over Drew, leaving him to receive the children when they got home from school by bus. 'It's *my* niece,' she reminded him.

The hotel was dauntingly luxurious, and she would never normally have thought of entering its portals. She even knew a moment of doubt as to whether they would actually let her in. Was Toni allowed to have non-resident visitors? How much would they charge for a cup of tea? But nobody accosted her, and she was relieved to see a couple in their thirties wearing

very ordinary clothes, coming down the staircase.
What had she expected, she asked herself. Diamond
tiaras and mink coats? People were people, and there
were all sorts of reasons why they might spend two
hundred pounds on a night in a hotel. Honeymoons,
escapes, or just a wish for the experience – for one
perfect night of their lives.

She went through to the lounge without anyone
challenging her, and waited for Toni to appear. The
instructions had been precise: Meet me in the main
lounge, and we'll find a corner somewhere for a chat.

It happened exactly that way. Carrying a tray
containing a pot of tea and two cups, Toni led her
aunt up two flights of stairs to a door onto an open
terrace on the first floor. It had a low wall around
it, and overlooked hills and woodlands to the
north-west, with Upper Slaughter the only visible
settlement. Getting her bearings with difficulty, she
worked out that Notgrove and Naunton were in that
rough direction, but that in general there were miles
of sparsely inhabited landscape, giving the lie to
claims that England was grossly overpopulated, with
no space for any more people or houses.

Tables and chairs were scattered across the space,
all of them unoccupied. 'Nobody much comes out
here,' said Toni. 'It's my special place. Look at the
wonderful view.'

'I am looking,' said Thea. 'It's fantastic.' She had
been worried that memories of her previous stay in

this village would taint the day, but nothing she could see carried any painful associations. It felt like quite a different hotel from the one at the centre of that horrid experience, now fading into the past.

'Oh – she's there! I didn't think she was ever coming back.' Toni pointed to some land perhaps eighty or a hundred yards away. 'Look at her.'

Thea quickly located a woman with a basket on her arm, looking like a Victorian watercolour, except that this was someone of at least seventy and therefore probably insufficiently winsome for an artwork. 'Hush. She'll hear you.'

'I don't think so. And if she does, she won't spot us. People don't look up this high. I sit here and watch them come and go, and they never once notice me.'

'Good place for a sniper,' said Thea.

'Perfect. I wish I'd got a telescope. I could see what it is she's picking, then.'

Thea squinted into the late-afternoon sun. 'Can't see a thing,' she complained. 'She's against the light.'

'Watch for a minute.'

They kept up the scrutiny, tracking the woman's erratic progress across a small triangular patch of ground that lay between two fields. It had overgrown hedges and no visible gateway into it. Thea was reminded of the burial ground that Drew had inherited in Broad Campden. An anomaly of history, somehow dropped off some old deeds and ignored by the Land Registry. The countryside abounded with such slivers of land, despite the high value attached to any little patch of grass these days. They became invisible, except to the plants and small animals who enthusiastically colonised them.

'Doesn't it look suspicious to you?' Toni murmured. 'I think we should see where she goes, and find out what she's doing.'

'There are so many innocent explanations,' Thea demurred. 'But it does seem a bit odd, I agree.'

The woman had moved out of the sunlight to a shadowy stretch of hedge, where they could see her plucking small quantities of some kind of plant. 'Deadly nightshade, I bet you,' said Toni.

'Bit early for blackberries,' said Thea. 'But there could be rosehips.'

'Hemlock.'

'Wood sorrel.'

'Hey – you really know your plants, don't you! Did Uncle Carl teach you?'

'He did. You remember him, of course.'

'I do, absolutely. He took us all on nature rambles, like something out of the Famous Five. Showed us what was edible and what wasn't. I thought I'd forgotten it all, but it's coming back to me now.'

'Did you ever try to dig down for the nut at the end of the wood sorrel root?'

'Once or twice. I don't really believe it's possible.'

'Neither do I. The root's as thin as a hair. You'd have to be a fairy or a leprechaun to manage it.'

Toni laughed. 'Or a witch, maybe. Don't you think she's like a witch?'

'She is a bit. Oh!'

The woman had been stretching up for something in the hedge above her head, and stumbled backwards, almost falling. Her basket flew off her arm, and landed upside down.

'Shh!' adjured Toni.

But the woman had heard Thea's gasp of alarm, and was looking their way.

'Keep still,' whispered the girl. 'She won't see us.'

She was right. The questioning face never raised higher than the ground floor of the hotel, with the blank side wall revealing nothing more interesting than a staff parking area. A car engine told them there was a vehicle coming or going, which would most likely divert the woman's attention. After a few seconds, she returned to the calamity of her spilt gleanings, and knelt to recover them.

'They're obviously very important to her,' said Thea.

She had realised that her own habitual curiosity was reflected in her niece – some genetic quirk had bestowed it on the girl. The resulting sense of fellowship was sweet, and made her smile. 'You're just like me,' she said. 'Nosy about people.'

'I am. I'm *burning* to know what she's up to. None of the theories can be right. She's being so selective in what she picks. It's not enough for jam or wine or soup.'

'It might be if she just wants extra flavour.'

'I *know* it's poison. She's planning to poison somebody.'

'We'll probably never know,' sighed Thea.

'If she comes again, I'm definitely going to follow her.'

'You can't. You'll get the sack.'

Toni wriggled her shoulders in frustrated agreement. 'Oh – I forgot to tell you. From this weekend, there'll be a room here for me, if I want it. I told them I did. Is that okay? It feels a bit ungrateful of me, but it would obviously be much easier if I could live in. I need to move before Saturday. There's a massive wedding that day, and we've all got to work overtime.'

Thea was surprisingly sorry to hear this news. 'Oh, of course it would be better. But we've got used to you now. We'll all miss you.'

'I can come and see you on my days off. And it has been great to really learn how to cycle on the roads. It's a brilliant sense of freedom. You can see why people rave about it.'

'That's good.'

When they turned back to check on the woman, it was to see her in the further angle of the little field, hitching up her skirt before clambering over a lower section of hedge.

'She'll break it down, and let animals through,' said Thea. 'That's no way to behave.'

'Can't see any animals,' Toni reported, standing up and trying to peer into the adjacent field.

'She's through it now. Must have used it before. I can never get over or through hedges, however hard I try.' Then she thought of a hedge in Duntisbourne Abbots that she had got through, and added, 'Hardly ever, anyway.'

'Now we'll never know what she was doing. It'll haunt me for the rest of my life.'

'No it won't. I'm going to go down there and follow her. She's got to have a car close by, if she doesn't live in the village.'

'I assumed she did live here. Why do you think she doesn't?'

'Because if people know her, they're more likely to question what she's doing . . .' Thea paused. 'Except, that's not really true, is it? They'd notice a stranger more quickly, and be more suspicious. Silly me.'

'We're both silly. We're playing a childish game, spying on her and making idiotic guesses about her.'

'You started it,' said Thea with a laugh.

'I know I did. Let her get on with her winemaking or whatever innocent thing it is.'

'I really would like to follow her,' said Thea. 'I've hardly ever done it, and I'm sure it would be fun.'

'You'd have to keep me informed of where you were, on the phone. And I have to be back in the kitchen in about ten more minutes, so that won't work. And she'll be well away before you can get anywhere near her. Once across a couple of fields, she'll be impossible to trace.'

'I suppose so.'

So they left it, and spent the final minutes talking over Toni's transfer to the hotel and whether she should leave her bike in Broad Campden or take it with her.

Thea went home to break the news that the very popular lodger was leaving them. It was hard to know who was most upset amongst Drew and the children. 'She's very good company,' he said. 'Makes me realise what I've missed by not knowing you at that age.'

Thea tried to overlook the very slightly creepy implications this sentiment carried. Husbands did lose their heads over nubile young girls, and it would be folly to assume that hers was an exception. Although he *was*, insisted an inner voice. They'd only just got married, for goodness' sake. So she smiled, and said there did seem to be some similarities between her and Toni. 'She's more like me than Jessica is,' she said.

'We saw the witchy woman,' she added. 'I must admit she was behaving very suspiciously.' And she supplied details.

'Must be pretty athletic to get over a hedge,' said Drew.

'We thought she'd probably made a place, with footholds that didn't show from where we were. And that means she must be local, I suppose. We wondered about that.'

'You are two nosy women,' he teased. 'I think you've corrupted poor young Toni with your insatiable curiosity.'

'I think she was already that way before she even came here. And hotels are a perfect breeding ground for that sort of interest. All those stories that you never hear the end of. People having illicit liaisons, or hiding from their in-laws, or spending money they never ought to have. It must be thrilling.'

'I'm sure it is. Especially for someone planning to study psychology. She can construct all kinds of theories about what makes people do what they do.'

'Including picking berries or seedheads in a neglected field, wearing a long skirt.'

'I'm really sad that she can't run to a hat as well. Even a floppy straw article would complete the picture.'

'No hat.'

'Pity. It would have proved conclusively that she's a ghost. She might still be a ghost, of course. Who wears long skirts these days?'

'Some old ladies do. Tall ones, with long grey hair. It's a look.'

'What did Toni decide to do with the bike?'

'She'll keep it with her at the hotel. Then she can go on exploratory rides when she has some time off. She seems quite smitten by the Cotswolds. I told her to go to Naunton, and Northleach and Winchcombe.'

'And you can meet her at some of them, with Stephanie and Timmy. You'll be wanting to have some outings with them. You'll all go mad if you just stay in the house for six weeks.'

'I thought we could set Stephanie to doing some grave-digging, and Timmy can man the phones.'

'A hundred years ago, that's exactly what we'd do. If they had phones then. Did they?'

'In the big houses, yes. Just about. I'm sure we'll all have a wonderful summer,' she added bravely.

Toni was even more consumed by a need to know the end of every story than Thea had guessed. Despite the many distractions of the job, with the backroom gossip and the never-ending demands and the important upcoming wedding, the Case of the Woman in the Field maintained its place at the top of her priorities. She was perhaps gathering food for pet rabbits – or goats. That was Toni's latest theory. New ideas occurred every day, only adding to the frustration of not knowing which, if any, was true. She couldn't really be poisoning anyone, surely. Poisoning was very out of fashion as a method of murder, with the tox analysis so advanced at the pathology labs.

The morning of the wedding dawned slowly, with low cloud and the threat of rain. Hotel staff scuttled feverishly in all directions, carrying tables, flowers, dishes, luggage. Toni's tiny room was barely accessible past a large pile of chairs that had been moved out of the banqueting hall, to create space for dancing. 'Isn't that a fire hazard?' she asked, having been reading some health and safety literature. Nobody bothered to reply.

It all passed in a whirl. The bride herself was from Burford, but her parents lived in Upper Slaughter and the groom was from Cheltenham. They each had large families and many friends. Toni was promoted to one of the waiting staff, carrying plates endlessly to and from the kitchen, struggling to remember all the rapidly learnt etiquette for handing food to people. There was no time whatever in which to think. The menu was relatively simple: choice between cream of vegetable soup and grilled sardines, then roast duck, and sherry trifle. But there were flamboyant accoutrements, and a few special diets to watch out for, which raised it well out of the ordinary. Seventy-five people sat down to eat.

The wedding service itself had been held in the local church, with an old-fashioned procession to the hotel. The wedding breakfast was at half past two. By half past four, ten guests had been prostrated by the most severe gastro-enteric trouble. Some vomited where they sat, including a boy of ten who had eaten far too much.

Ambulances were called, and one old man looked so close to death that the bride burst into screams at the sight of him. She herself appeared unaffected, but her new husband had disappeared into the Gents many minutes earlier, and failed to return.

Toni could not shake off a sense that she had blundered into the set of a disaster movie. People were panicking, throwing accusations and clutching their stomachs as if they'd been knifed. Paramedics materialised, kneeling beside white-faced victims and asking earnest questions. The moribund old man was carted away on a stretcher, with the bride calling 'Grandad!' forlornly after him.

And where was the groom? Suddenly that was the main question. 'Rupert – where's Rupert?' everyone was wanting to know. A group of male friends went off in search of him, followed by the hotel manager who was almost rigid with anxiety and horror.

Nobody was in control, Toni realised. She concluded that she could do very little good where she was, so went outside to check the situation there. There were two ambulances already and a third was turning into the driveway. More guests were collapsing with every passing minute, some of them evidently unable to control their own bowels. 'Good God, it's like an outbreak of cholera,' said an elderly woman. 'I saw something of the sort in India, back in the fifties.'

The smells and sights were deeply disgusting, and getting worse. In those moments, Toni learnt that whatever vocation she might develop, it was not going to be as a nurse. Nor a doctor. Nor a paramedic. She was repelled by the whole business. She had to get away, and the only place she could think of to go to was her terrace in the sky, far above all this vile commotion.

Once there, she raised her head to the leaden sky and breathed in deeply. The rain had held off, by a whisker, but the air was moist and the light poor.

Then she saw the woman in the field. She was not carrying a basket, or wearing the same long skirt, but it was unmistakably her. She had her hands together under her chin, still posing as if for a Victorian painter, watching the scene outside the hotel, smiling broadly.

The door opened and Toni was joined by one of the junior chefs. He was twenty-four and there was a growing mutual interest between them. 'Hi, Matt,' she said. 'Do you have any idea who that woman is, over there?'

He peered down. 'Oh, that looks like Mrs Tompkins. She's a brilliant cook – makes all sorts of chutneys and pickles and so forth. We buy them from her. She did the soup for the wedding today, actually. I thought you'd have noticed her delivering it this morning. She must have taken days over it.'

'No,' said Toni. 'I didn't see her.'

Matt went on, seeming eager to talk, 'And I know her son. She had him late and he's terribly spoilt. He wanted to marry Samantha, I think.'

'Samantha?'

'The bride. They must be quite miffed that this Rupert bloke got her instead.'

A piercing cry from below interrupted them and they both leant over the parapet to see what the trouble was. They could just see a stretcher being loaded into the newly arrived ambulance. The bride, in her frothy white dress, trotted alongside and then climbed in after it. 'Rupert!' she wailed, over and over again.

'Uh-oh,' said Matt, while Toni turned to look again at the woman in the field.

'Probably not the wisest choice of soup-maker,' she said. 'Not with all that hemlock or toadstools or deadly nightshade that grows over there.'

'Probably not,' said Matt, with an uncontrollable giggle.

Making Arrangements

She knew it wasn't fair to blame Drew. She should have thought of it, at least as much as he should. It was, after all, her problem and not his. They were her painful memories and sudden associations, from a time years before she even met him.

But she felt it, all the same. His careless, hurried words – 'Oh, I'm sure you'll be fine. It's high time you gave it a go. I'm not sure of the details, but there's a woman coming about her husband. He sounds a bit young, but that shouldn't be a problem. Now, I'm really late for Mrs Frangipani at the hospice.'

'She's not called that, you idiot. I thought you were always mega-careful with their names.'

'It's Frantileni. I know perfectly well, but I always think frangipani's such a nice word. Now, it's your last chance to ask me anything. You've got the diary, coffin catalogue, stuff about the paperwork and legal requirements.'

'How young was he?'

'Um . . . don't know. Too young.' He shook his head. 'You'll be fine,' he repeated. 'Just be yourself. Don't overdo the sympathy. Give her time to think of any special details. It was a sudden death, so she won't have been prepared for it.'

The first quivers of apprehension assailed her then. 'Um, Drew—' she began, but he was already almost out of the door.

The woman was due at ten, which was imminent. She was called Linda Padwick. Her husband's body was in the mortuary at Gloucester. 'Some ghastly accident with a horse,' said Drew, who had contacted the Coroner's Officer already.

Horses were a daily feature of Cotswold life, with racing stables, riding schools, stud farms and livery all preoccupying a fair portion of the population. Accidents involving them were common enough to go unremarked, or at least fail to make front-page news. But people seldom actually died at the hooves of a horse. She remembered a bizarre story told by Den Cooper, husband of Drew's partner Maggs, where a young woman was killed when a horse headbutted her. It had led to Den's biggest murder enquiry, eventually, shaking him for a number of reasons. Thea tried to concentrate on this aspect of Mr Padwick's death, rather than lingering on the consequences for his wife.

But it was impossible. As she waited for Linda Padwick to arrive, Thea was thrown back nearly five years to the moment when she herself had been forced to visit an undertaker and arrange the funeral of her own young husband.

The person who dealt with her had been a woman. A woman who was almost shockingly friendly. Thea's clouded, horrified mind had nonetheless retained almost every detail of that hour, ever since. She recalled a foolish final notion that the whole thing was a prolonged dream, where the most terrible events were happening. And then here was this woman coming onstage from a land of good cheer and normality. 'Good morning. My name is Christine Woolley. Please sit down.'

Thea, and her sister Emily (who had won the muted contest as to which sibling should go with her) sat side by side across a desk, in the bland room.

'Cremation, I gather?' said Christine, checking a card in her hand.

The word had conjured appalling images for Thea – Carl's flesh melting in the flames, inside a great gas oven. 'That's right,' she said. She knew Carl would have preferred a burial, and initially that had been her intention, seeing herself perpetually visiting a grave in a charming little churchyard. But Jessica, their daughter, had been adamant that cremation was to be preferred. Damien, Thea's brother, had gently explained the drawbacks of a burial. Damien was profoundly religious, but had no qualms about this means of disposal, and had offered to officiate at Carl's funeral, which had given Thea some hours of conflict. Almost everything anybody said to her created inner conflict. The fact that it was Emily beside her at the undertaker, and not Jessica, was painful. Jess had been nineteen, quite old enough to deal with the questions and decisions. But she claimed to care nothing for the details, having won the argument over cremation.

She heard a car arriving in their rural cul-de-sac, and went to open the door. Her shaking hands felt as if they belonged to someone else. She wasn't going to be able to do it, she thought furiously. She was going to let Drew down, and serve him right. How could he not understand how hard this was going to be?

Linda Padwick was devastatingly young. Mid thirties at the most. At her side was a boy, who looked about ten. Surely there was some mistake? Surely these were quite the wrong people, intending to go elsewhere, not bereaved at all.

But they were. 'Mrs Slocombe?' asked the woman. 'I'm Linda Padwick. This is Alex.'

'Come in.' Thea held the door wide, smiling inanely at the child. 'We're through here.'

She led the way into the room that had been originally intended as a dining room, but which they had transformed into an office. It had its own phone, a filing cabinet and a matching set of upright chairs. There was a table, rather than a desk, and Thea carefully seated herself at a narrow end of it, to avoid facing her customers like a bank manager or head teacher. She remembered the sensation from her own experience, feeling like an applicant for a job or a troublesome student.

Memories were being sparked repeatedly, quite beyond her control. Something in the young boy's face reminded her of that hum of excitement that so shamefully intruded on the shock and misery and horror. To have a sudden premature death in the family made you special. It took you abruptly off the rails that you'd assumed were unalterable. People took notice of you. You were forced to learn how to do things you had never imagined. You had joined a club that was strange and exclusive and frightening.

Seated at right angles to each other, they began the business in hand. 'Thank you for coming to us,' Thea said. 'We do appreciate it.' The presence of the boy was proving to be more inhibiting than she had expected. While having no objections in theory to his being there, his youth and vulnerability brought added reasons to be wary of what she said.

'You will have been contacted by the Coroner's Officer?' she went on. 'So you know it's all right to proceed with making funeral arrangements?'

Linda Padwick's silence finally acquired significance. Three or four minutes had elapsed in which she had said nothing at all. She nodded slightly, her gaze on the table in front of her.

'Mum?' said Alex. 'Are you okay?'

'What?'

'You're not saying anything. You're supposed to say something.' He met Thea's eyes. 'She's in shock, you see,' he explained. 'The doctor gave her some pills that would make her feel better. I think they stopped her talking.' Anxiety flickered across his face. 'Sorry,' he finished.

'That's all right. There's no hurry. We just have to find a day and time that would be good for you, and a few other details.'

'Good for me,' Linda Padwick repeated in a whisper. 'Did you say "good"?'

Uh-oh, thought Thea, resisting an urge to apologise. *Let's not start playing that game.* 'Yes, that's right. I expect there'll be a lot of people coming. We should try to fix a time that will suit most of them. Obviously, you can't satisfy everybody's needs, but on the whole Fridays are usually the best choice.'

It worked very well. 'All right, then. Have you got enough space for all their cars? Where exactly . . . ? I can't see the place where'll he'll be . . .'

'Buried. No, you can't see it from here. It's about a quarter of a mile away. We can walk down there for a look, if you like. When we've finished up here.'

'We joked about it, you know. Natural burials and all that. Everyone in my family has always been cremated.' The new widow winced. 'But that felt so . . .'

This time Thea did not finish the sentence. There was nothing about cremation that made the experience any better or worse, in the long run. In the short run, it was probably easier. Certainly quicker, cleaner and less inescapable. She remembered flickers of resentment against Carl for being such a dedicated ecologist, ideologically committed to burial because it didn't involve fossil fuels. It gave her enormous difficulty when it came to deciding between his wishes and their daughter's. Eventually she took the line she thought was the more sensible. After all, a grave was a burden. Drew himself had discovered this when his wife had died; the resulting hypocrisy had shocked several people. Rather than interring Karen a few yards from his back door, he had used a much more distant cemetery. Now that he was living full-time in the Cotswolds, it hardly mattered, of course.

She gave herself a shake. 'All right, then. Shall we say Friday of next week? Is that too far off for you?'

'What day is it today?' It was a genuine question, and Thea felt no surprise.

'Thursday. We could have it sooner, if you preferred that. Even Monday might be feasible, but most people will expect quite a bit more notice than that. We would bring him here in a day or so, and get everything ready. Have you any particular sort of coffin in mind? We can get woven willow ones, or a kind of cocoon made of felt. There are a lot of alternatives these days.'

'Have you got somewhere cool, then? I don't want him embalmed.'

'We never do embalming. And yes, we've installed a

cool room at the back of the house. You can come and see him any time you like.'

'There's been a post-mortem.' Both women glanced at the boy, and Thea understood that his mother was growing much less confident of the wisdom of including him.

'That's no problem. It doesn't leave any marks.' A lie, of course. It left a grotesque line of black stitches down the length of the torso. But the scalp was replaced carefully and glued down. The face was almost always untouched.

'The horse left marks,' said the widow. 'It kicked a hole in his chest. Broke his sternum and ruptured his lungs.'

'Bloody thing,' said Alex loudly. 'I think it should be shot.'

Thea cocked her head. 'I don't suppose he did it on purpose.'

'She. It's a mare. Dad never liked her.'

'Never mind that,' said his mother. 'She's gone now.' Loss was stark on her face and Thea glimpsed a story that she might never be told. Husband and horse were both gone, and Thea understood enough of the processes involved to suspect that the two might become amalgamated in Linda's emotions.

'She was Mum's favourite,' the boy supplied helpfully. 'Dad was trying to put some salve on a cut when she kicked him. She hated him, you see. And me,' he concluded proudly. 'Men infuriated her.'

'Stop it, Alex. The lady doesn't want to hear all that.'

If only you knew, thought Thea. The image of a jealous horse lashing out at the well-intentioned man was filling her mind. It was so entirely different from the careless driver who had killed Carl that she relished it for that reason alone.

'We'll have a normal coffin,' said Linda Padwick. 'Plain, but solid. I don't think he would have wanted anything newfangled. The felt thing sounds awful.'

Privately, Thea rather agreed with her. She had only seen pictures of them so far, but they carried very little appeal. They were also hugely expensive.

'I've got to fill all this in,' she said, indicating a printed card on the table. 'For the records.' She proceeded to ask full name, age, occupation, address of the deceased. Mentally, she was checking off the remaining tasks, worried that she would forget something crucial. 'Who do you want to officiate?' she asked.

'Sorry?'

'Somebody to take the service . . . I mean ceremony. To keep it together.' She floundered. What were the right words? Drew had told her what to say, and it had flown out of her head. 'We can find you any sort of officiant – humanist, for example.'

'Won't *you* do that? We don't want any prayers or hymns or anything. None of that meant anything to Colin. Do we have to have somebody else? Did you say "officiant"? That's a very odd word.'

'It is, isn't it? Well, no, you don't have to have anybody. Drew can do it. Or a family friend. You can do absolutely what suits you.'

Damien had done it for Carl, in the event. Enough people had insisted on a conventional church service for Thea to go along with it. They had sung two hymns, both of which she found herself soothed by in the event. 'Dear Lord and Father of Mankind' was a gem, by any measure. Words and tune had between them filled her with a few seconds of consolation. She had considered 'Abide with Me' for the solid associations that linked her with earlier times and thousands of other funerals. But after a lot of dithering, she had opted for 'Now the Day is Over' because it was full of the right sort of feeling. She had insisted on all eight verses, focusing intently on the words. She still remembered the lines: *Comfort every sufferer/Watching late in pain;/Those who plan some evil/From their sin restrain.* They made her imagine that Carl was still out there somewhere, helping to prevent bad behaviour, in her if nobody else.

'We'll just gather at the grave, then, and anyone who wants to can say something, and then we'll just . . . bury him.' Linda reached for her son's hand. 'Is that okay, darling?'

The boy shrugged. 'S'pose so.'

He didn't know anything different, Thea realised. It was unfair to ask him. And yet it was probably the right approach, making him feel involved, that nothing was being concealed from him.

'Is he your only one?' she asked Linda.

'No, actually. He's got two little sisters. They're only four.'

'Twins?'

'I'm afraid so.' Linda sighed, and rolled her eyes, and then, as Thea watched, remembered that these old habits might have to be jettisoned. Having twins had made her special for a while, but now she was additionally singled out in the eyes of the world. A young widow with three children. The twinness would fade into relative insignificance.

'Will they be at the funeral?'

'Oh, yes. They'll never understand where their father's gone otherwise, will they? I don't believe in lying to children.'

'No,' said Thea, thinking of Drew's Timmy, and how losing a parent was never going to be all right for anybody under the age of about eighteen. And even then . . . 'Alex, you have some idea what's going to happen, have you?' She asked the question out of concern at the look on his face. She had seen fear, anger and bewilderment. All entirely to be expected, but surely her job was to try to assuage them.

'He's going to be put in the ground. Buried. In a coffin.'

'That's right. And the grave will always be there for you to visit any time you want to.'

'Mmm. Except I can't drive, can I? So how would I get to it?'

Thea waited for the boy's mother to state the obvious. Instead she said, 'You won't want to, though, will you? What would be the point?'

'I might.' Both fell silent, the air between them brittle.

'You know what some people do?' Thea suggested, much too brightly. 'They write a little letter and put it in the coffin. Nobody else would read it, so you can say whatever you like to your dad, and it'll stay there with him for ever. Your sisters could maybe draw pictures for him. Or you could find some photos.' *Help me here*, she silently ordered the woman, with a pleading look.

Linda Padwick gently shook her head from side to side, and her eyes rolled up towards the ceiling for a moment of sheer exasperation. 'All this mumbo-jumbo,' she said. 'What earthly good does it do? I just wish we could have it all finished and done with.'

Her remarks were at least getting lengthier, Thea noticed. And she was showing a lot more vitality than at first. Whether or not this was a good thing remained unclear. There was an implication that Thea was getting it wrong, saying too much, making assumptions. This woman was not here on a social visit. They were never going to be friends. It was a business transaction, and any straying off that path carried all kinds of risk.

Linda's remarks had not gone down at all well with her young son. He looked hurt and embarrassed. 'I might do a letter,' he said uncertainly. 'But I don't know what to say in it.'

'Oh, Alex,' moaned his mother. 'There isn't anything *to* say, is there? Just that you'll always remember him, I suppose. You're old enough now not to forget him. Not like the girls. You know what he was like, what he thought about things. We'll all have to get used to getting on without him. That's all there is to it.'

'The girls won't forget him. I won't let them.'

'Good. That's good. We'll be okay, sweetie.' She reached over and put an arm round his shoulders. He tolerated the embrace like any boy of his age: not quite old enough to push it away, not quite young enough to see it as his due. Thea could not decide how damaging it would be for the boy to be so abruptly deprived of his father.

Linda was fully engaged with the child, forgetting where she was and why. 'At least we know he didn't do it on purpose. Leave us, I mean. Not like some fathers we can think of – right? He didn't mean to go. It was a horrible accident, and there's nobody to blame for it.'

'Jocasta's to blame,' he corrected her. 'She did it.'

'Yes, but she didn't know what she was doing. It was all instinct. He must have touched a sore place and she just kicked out automatically. He was just in the wrong place at the wrong time.' She raised her eyes to meet Thea's. 'He was squatting down, you see, right beside her leg. At least, that's what we think. We didn't find him for a while, but there was a camera that caught most of it. The stables have got CCTV. Well – they all have it these days. I haven't been able to watch it yet, but my dad had a look and says it's all there, pretty clear. He bled internally. It was too late when someone went to look for him.'

It was a compelling story, and Thea was suitably compelled. Nothing whatever like her own Carl's fate, then. He had died instantly, like a lightning flash, in which he could not possibly have known what was happening. This Colin Padwick had lain there in pain and fear and solitude until he died. Had the horse turned around to see what she'd done? Had she nuzzled worriedly at him, or stamped on him again in triumph? What degree of loathing had she really felt for him? Was it nothing more than an anthropomorphic theory?

'How awful,' she said weakly.

Linda made a grimace of agreement, still holding the boy. 'Oh, well. Is there anything else we need to do here?'

It felt as if they'd barely started. Surely there had to be a whole lot more to be arranged. It had taken her and Emily at least an hour to go through everything with the undertaker when Carl had died. This woman had arrived barely twenty minutes ago. 'We still haven't established the exact time,' she said.

'Oh, probably afternoon. Say three o'clock? That should give people time enough to get here. There are some cousins in Lincolnshire, and an old friend in Suffolk. They've all got busy lives like us.'

Thea looked again at her card, with most of the boxes already filled in. The Padwicks lived near Stanton, she noticed. She remembered Stanton from the Christmas before last. It had struck her then as a horsy sort of place. Riding stables and all that sort of thing. Accidents must be a regular part of that way of life, surely. Falls and kicks and bites – big volatile animals with far too little brain-to-strength ratio. Thea had never greatly liked horses, and certainly never trusted them. It was only a matter of time before a great hoof came through her car windscreen, she believed. The little roads were full of the damn things.

'Yes, that sounds fine,' she said, writing the time down in the appropriate slot. 'We'll meet at the graveside, then, shall we? We'll leave from here with the coffin – you can follow if you want to, of course. Make a procession of it.'

'Can't we use Sultan?' Alex asked, his head raised in alarm. 'You said we could bring him.'

Thea waited, pen poised.

'Oh, darling. That would be such a business. I don't know how it would work.'

'Well, *ask* then,' he urged her, sounding very adult.

Linda sighed. 'Sultan is – was – Colin's horse. He's a great big hack. Quite an ugly thing, really. Alex thought he might be able to pull the coffin on a cart, but he's never done that. It wouldn't work at all. Sorry, lovey, but I don't think he can come.'

Thea tried to visualise some sort of role for the horse. She recalled images of funerals with horse-drawn hearses, black plumes and glass sides to the vehicle. As far as she knew, there had never been any such provision made by Drew for any of his customers. 'Well,' she said. 'We could think about it.'

'We could make a *travois*,' said Alex. 'He wouldn't mind that.'

Both women stared at him.

'A what?' said Linda.

'It's a thing the native Americans used. We've been doing it at school. They're easy to make. We could put Dad on it, and Sultan could pull it.'

'Never heard of such a thing,' said Linda. 'What makes you think the horse would tolerate it?'

'He would,' insisted the boy. 'He'd hardly even notice it.'

'What are they made of?' asked Thea.

'Poles. In a triangle shape. Then you weave rope, or string, dried reeds – whatever – across to make a sort of bed. They used them for old people, or somebody who couldn't walk. You can easily find it online, if you look.'

'Alex, this is silly,' said Linda firmly. 'What would people think, if we dragged your father down the street on a thing like that?'

'What does that matter?' Alex spoke Thea's own thoughts.

'Oh, it doesn't really. But honestly, darling, I don't think it's realistic at all.'

'I have to admit . . .' Thea began apologetically. 'I'm not saying it's impossible, from our point of view. But we would have to talk to my husband.'

A sense of losing control made her waver. She was letting Drew down, letting *herself* down. As for poor young Alex, she felt a complete traitor in her failure to support his idea.

'No, no, I'm sorry,' said the widow firmly. 'Alex, I know I said it would be nice to include Sultan somehow, but not like this. We'll all go back to the stables afterwards and get him something special.'

'Then you'll send him away, like Jocasta,' the boy accused. 'I *know* you will.'

'I promise you I won't.'

Thea knew she had been rescued, but felt no gratitude. This was descending into a bottomless hole of personal feelings that had no place in Drew's office. 'Um . . .' she said. 'Maybe we should walk down to the field now. It'll take ten minutes or so.'

'All right,' said Linda quickly. 'Good idea. Do I have to sign anything?'

Thea scanned her documents worriedly. 'No, I don't think so. I'll write you a card with everything we've decided, if you hang on a minute.'

Alex eyed her scornfully. 'If you put it all on the

computer as we go, you could just print it out right away,' he told her.

'I suppose I could. But we're not sure that's the way we want to do things. It seems a bit too official, don't you think?'

'I don't know,' he said with a frown. 'It should be official, shouldn't it?'

The undertaker who had arranged Carl's funeral had referred repeatedly to a computer screen at her elbow. Databases of available slots at the crematorium, ministers of religion, status of the body, and other arcane material had made the process seem painfully impersonal. There was a system and Carl had been slotted into it, regardless of who he had been and what he might have wanted. Only when Emily had put up a hand and taken them onto a different path had things changed. 'Our brother will officiate,' she had said. 'And we will need more than the usual twenty minutes that you're offering.' After that, they had gained a better quality of attention.

'Oh, hang on,' Thea remembered. 'I have to give you a written statement of costs.' She pulled out another printed form and started writing. Drew had taken her over this part of the job with great care, more confident since having a lengthy session with an accountant, three months earlier. The key, he explained, was to ensure that every outgoing was included and then to add a clear three hundred pounds on top. 'That's our only reliable income,' he told her. 'In a lean week, with only one funeral, that's what we'll have to live on. But if we get three or four, we'll be rich.'

'Hardly,' Thea had said, but she was amenable to the general principle. One funeral a week did not seem unduly optimistic, and indeed, in the first five weeks of opening they had notched up eighteen burials.

'That's the publicity,' said Drew. 'It won't keep on like that.'

But Drew had found additional work in the area, officiating at cremations and giving talks to affluent Women's Institutes. One had paid him two hundred and fifty pounds for an hour's talk, including questions.

She started to explain her workings to Linda, who waved it all away. 'Oh, that doesn't matter,' she said. 'He had very good life insurance.'

There was no answer to that, so Thea pressed on. 'There's nothing hidden behind vague phrases like "administration costs" or "overheads",' she said. 'What you see is what you get.'

'Great,' said Linda Padwick. 'If that's how you want to do it.'

It was a long list, but Thea had all the figures to hand, and the total came to barely half that of a conventional funeral. 'We don't charge for the plot itself,' she explained. 'Because it doesn't cost us anything.'

'What about mowing the grass? Maintaining the hedges?'

'Oh, Andrew does that. His salary is included in the costings.'

'Andrew's your husband?'

'No, our employee.'

Linda leant forward, her interest snagged. 'But how can you know what proportion of his salary to charge me? That can't possibly work, surely?'

'Er . . .' said Thea, who had asked the same question herself not long ago, and failed to fully understand the answer. 'We have to make a guess as to how many funerals we'll do in a year and then divide it.'

'A guess. I see.'

'It's standard business practice.'

'Maybe it is. Well, let's hope it's a good guess, then. And I hope you've included all the extra bits of tax and insurance – stuff like that.'

'Are you an accountant?' Thea suddenly asked.

'Not exactly. But I did part of the course, before I had the kids.'

'Well, this is it, all done now.' She handed the sheet over, and Linda took it.

'Too cheap,' she said firmly. 'People will think they're getting a substandard service if that's all they're spending.'

Carl's funeral had cost almost four thousand pounds, despite having no additional cars or a fancy coffin. She had wondered ever since just where so much money could have gone. At the time, it felt like paying for capable hands, reassurance that all the protocols had been satisfied, leaving nothing for her to worry about.

'Well, they're not,' she said. 'We like to think of ourselves as an ethical business, only charging for services actually provided.'

'You won't last long like that. I don't mean it unkindly, but I think you're missing some tricks. I wanted to spend more. It sounds ridiculous, I know, but it's as if I owe it to Colin to pay out a lot of money. It's the last thing I can do for him. There he was, trying to make my horse feel better, *my* horse who we all knew hated him – and what does she do? Goes and kills him, ungrateful beast. How am I ever going to get around that? I'm not, of course. But I want the funeral to be the best I can make it, and for that, rightly or wrongly, I need to spend a lot of money.'

Thea looked at Alex, sitting restlessly in the chair that was too big for him. 'We'd better go,' she said. 'You'll have lots to do.'

'None of it seems very important. But Alex wants to go into school this afternoon for some reason. We'll have a bit of lunch and then I'll take him.'

Thea led the way along the street of Broad Campden, trying not to feel self-conscious. The villagers had mostly accepted the arrival of an undertaker in their midst without much complaint. But the occasions where a cortège, however modest, had crawled past their homes towards the burial field had not met with universal approval. Two or three people had made a point that they were not Wootton Bassett and had no wish to become known for funerals and death, however tasteful and ecological they might be.

'They'll get used to it,' said Drew. 'The Staverton people did. And we'll bring them some business. The pub's likely to do well out of us.'

'That woman's watching us,' said Alex, nodding towards a window. There was a face staring out of a ground-floor room, the brow furrowed. 'Do you know her?'

'Not at all,' said Thea. 'I thought that house was always empty during the week.'

'Maybe she's a burglar, then,' said the boy. 'Although she'd be daft to show her face, if she was.'

'Stop it,' said his mother.

The field was down the small road leading to Blockley. Very little traffic used it, most of the time. At the insistence of the council, about a fifth of the field had been roped off as a parking area, leaving four acres available for burials. 'That's more than enough,' said Drew bravely. 'But it means we'll have to have them in proper rows, which is a shame.' At the Staverton burial ground, there were few straight lines, the graves scattered around at odd angles. The ground rose in gentle mounds there, and Maggs had created winding pathways. By contrast, the new one was much more regimented.

'There are nineteen graves here so far,' she told her customers, pointing to a corner where the first row had been situated. A few young saplings had been planted as markers, but essentially it just looked like a flat, square field.

'How many will it hold altogether?' asked Linda.

'Well, in theory, about four thousand, but we don't want to put them too close together. Quite a lot, anyway.'

'That's incredible! You'll never find that many people wanting a place like this.'

Thea gave her a startled look. 'What's wrong with it?'

The woman reached for her son's hand. 'Alex, I don't think he'd like this, would he? It's . . . I don't know. Just not *right*.'

The boy said nothing. Thea hurried to defend her livelihood. 'It's still very new. When there are lots of trees and rocks and paths, it'll be really nice. It's totally quiet and peaceful. We'll be putting some seats in, as well. And maybe a building over there, if we can get permission.'

'What kind of building? A chapel, you mean?'

'Oh no. More like a pavilion, with a list of all the graves, and somewhere to sit if it's raining.'

'But you might not get permission?'

'It'll take a while,' Thea admitted. 'But I think we'll get it eventually.'

'I don't like it. I'm sorry. I know it's terrible of me. But it's just so . . . bleak. Colin liked people, and noise and *things*. He'd want to be more in the middle of everything.'

Thea felt close to screaming. Obviously she had done something wrong. What had the stupid woman expected?

'Well . . .' she said helplessly.

'Listen. I'll pay you for the wasted time. I am really sorry. You must think me such a fool. But I *can* change my mind, can't I? And you *have* helped me a lot. When I came to you this morning, I was just a mess. I hardly knew what I was doing. You got me thinking and talking more than I've done for days. You've woken me up.' She laughed grimly. 'And now you probably wish you hadn't.'

There were many things that Thea wanted to say, ranging from a furious tirade about wasted time to a much more mellow acknowledgement that she too had woken up to a few things during the course of their conversation. She managed a stiff smile and a shrug. 'Of course you can change your mind,' she said. 'Nothing's irrevocable.'

'A cremation would be,' said Linda. 'At least I'm sure about that. I'm not having him cremated.'

'Can we use Sultan, then, after all?' asked Alex.

'Maybe,' said his mother. She looked down at him, bringing her face squarely to his. 'Maybe you know better than I do what we ought to do.'

'No, I don't. But I think he'd like a horse to be there. So he can forgive Jocasta for what she did. Sort of. I mean . . .' he tailed off. 'It wasn't really her fault,' he added.

'Nor yours,' said Thea boldly. 'It was just an awful accident.'

'Sometimes accidents feel like crimes, though, don't they?' Linda blinked away the sudden tears. 'As if somebody somewhere did a wicked thing.'

'Believe me, it's quite different,' Thea insisted, as much for her own reassurance as Linda's.

'It isn't, though. He's just as dead either way.'

They walked back, saying very little. Mother and son got into their car and drove off, with Thea watching them. She felt drained of energy, unhappy and obscurely ashamed.

'I'm not doing that again,' she told Drew when he came home. 'Sorry, but that's definite.'

'But *why*?' He was still trying to get to grips with the loss of a funeral that would have been good publicity for the business.

'Lots of reasons. I don't know whether I can explain, but it was more than I could manage. You never thought, did you, that it might bring Carl back? He was almost there in the room with us. At least – that wouldn't have been so bad. But it was as if I was arranging *his* funeral all over again.'

'Oh.'

'And it would be like that every time. Like *Groundhog Day*, over and over, time after time.'

'I don't think it would,' he argued mildly.

'And when she said the field was *bleak*, that was

like a punch in the mouth. I saw it through her eyes, for a few minutes. I don't know if I can shake that image. I'd be scared that every family would suddenly change their minds, like she did.'

He went pale. 'Thea . . . what are you saying? We're in this together, aren't we? I can't run the business without you.'

'You could. Andrew could do a lot more. But no, I'm not abandoning you. At least, I might be a bit. I want to get a job. Oh – and I think you ought to charge people more for the funerals. And get back to the council about that building we want.'

'A job?' he repeated. 'What sort of job? Are you telling me you're going to be out all day, every day? What about the children? Answering the phone? How would that ever work?'

'Don't panic.' She put a hand on his arm. 'I don't mean right away. Most likely it'll be next year sometime. Just don't ever ask me to arrange another funeral, okay. Everything else is up for discussion.'

He pushed her hand away. 'And don't you think that every time I do it, that Karen isn't there in the room with me as well? The Karen I betrayed by burying her somewhere else – not where she wanted and expected to be? I have to work through that guilt every single time.'

Guilt – the old enemy. Even when there was nobody to blame, just as Linda Padwick had said, it felt as if somebody somewhere had done a wicked deed.

She hoped young Alex had been granted his wish, and that Sultan would find a role to play at his master's funeral. You really couldn't blame a horse, whatever dreadful thing it had done.

When Harry Richmond
Sold His Cottage

It came as quite a nasty surprise to Harry to discover the great gulf between deciding to move house and actually accomplishing it. A multitude of people had to be confronted, their numbers burgeoning as time went on. His house – he preferred to think of it as a cottage – was unarguably desirable. As he understood things, almost everyone wanted a Cotswold cottage built from local stone in 1903. Garden. Views. Easy access to Cirencester and the motorway. But the phrase *in need of modernisation* was apparently a deterrent to buyers, despite everything in the building being perfectly functional.

So his shock was profound when after a whole month only two sets of people had shown even a glimmer of interest in buying it. The estate agent was an impatient young man festooned with gadgetry, who chewed his lower lip and repeatedly warned about the slackness of the market just now. The endlessly vaunted shortage of housing bore no relation to the desirability or otherwise of a three-bedroomed cottage in an area largely populated with the affluent and the retired. A young family could not afford it, and the rest might find it too isolated. 'It's a minority taste,' said the young man rudely.

He was plainly puzzled as to Harry's reason for wanting the sale in the first place. But Harry of course could not tell him. He could hardly even bear to rehearse to himself the details of the incident that was driving him out of the home he had loved. He turned his thoughts away from the blood that now tainted it. All he knew was the guilt that followed him night and day, from which the only possible escape was to go and live somewhere else.

But what if he couldn't sell it? A month had already been far too long to wait. If there had been any choice, he would have gone to stay with a friend or relation. He would have rented a room in a small hotel, or taken a caravan to the Peak District. Instead he was forced to stay there, the guilt eating away at him. Surely, he demanded of himself many times, a normal person would have got over it by now. Instead it intensified day by day. Every item on the radio seemed to remind him. He would be caught unawares by a casual word and be wrenched back into his unhappy thoughts. It deprived him of sleep and gnawed at his self-respect.

One of the potential buyers was a young wife sent by her busy City financier husband to choose them a handy hideaway for weekends. She had three children under five, left in London with the nanny. Harry found himself feeling sorry for her when she came alone for a second viewing. 'I'm sure to get it wrong,' she said worriedly.

Harry's habitually sympathetic manner quickly had the story pouring out – how they had so much money since Scott's latest bonus that the only sensible thing to do with it was to buy another property. Somewhere safe and civilised for the children. 'He says we should get a dog as well,' she sighed. 'He thinks an Irish setter would be nice. I have no idea what I would do with an Irish setter.'

Harry entertained a vision of a large dog digging up his garden and shuddered. 'It would be a pity to keep such a big animal in London,' he said. 'I think they like to run free, miles every day.' Privately he thought his cottage deserved better than occasional visits from an urban family who would have little idea how to make it feel loved, with or without an Irish setter.

'I know,' she said wretchedly. 'But Scott thinks because I don't go out to work I have all day to exercise a dog and teach a two-year-old his alphabet and keep in touch with all his relatives. And just for good measure, I'm to refurbish a country cottage in the latest style.' She looked again at the narrow utilitarian staircase and the dado running around the dining room and sighed.

'*Three* children, did you say? You might want a bigger garden, in that case.'

She smiled. 'It sounds as though you're trying to talk me out of it. Why are you moving, anyway? I think I'm supposed to ask you that.'

He had prepared an answer in advance. 'My sister tells me the time has come to reduce my horizons. That's the phrase she used.'

'Are you going to live with her, then? Where is she?'

He flinched at the very idea. 'Oh, no. That would never work. I expect I'll get a flat.'

'With no garden? Wouldn't you miss it terribly?' She had already detected his fondness for the well-stocked flower beds and borders and natural area at the bottom, despite his efforts to be casual about it. At least she had ignored the padlocked shed, to his relief.

'The rheumatism won't get any better,' he said with a sigh.

'Well, I should tell you I've got two more properties to consider. I've been to all of you twice now and it doesn't get any easier.'

He had no answer to this, but simply looked at her. She was early thirties, fair in her colouring, and nicely spoken. The sort of off-the-shelf wife you would expect a City financier to choose. Biddable, presentable, fertile. She would fit quite readily into Cotswold society, with the coffee mornings and book groups and fundraising dinners. Harry flinched again at the way the world had gone when he wasn't looking. He still had friends who worked the land, planted trees and fashioned stone walls. He actually had no intention of moving into a flat. His plans were both vaguer and more ambitious than that. He was going to atone for what he had done – somehow or other, that was his goal.

'Just go with your heart,' he told her, hoping he didn't sound fatuous. 'Which one can you imagine yourself in most clearly?'

She shook her head. 'I don't know. The thing is, they all have to be more or less gutted and remodelled. Scott wants a place where he can get some peace away from the kids. So that means four bedrooms, ideally. But they *cost* so much. Even with his bonus, it's a huge amount to spend. I think you're right, actually. This one isn't quite big enough for what we want.'

At least she didn't say *need*, he thought grimly.

The other prospective buyer was altogether different. A woman by the name of Mrs Langrish (he never learnt her first name) in her late fifties, with an eye to retirement with a husband named Edmund. Edmund featured in almost every sentence, until Harry felt he knew him intimately. Edmund had a troublesome knee. The replacement joint had never properly worked, and they were going to have to do it all again. Edmund had a very ancient mother who seemed set to live to a hundred and ten. 'People *do* these days, you know,' said the woman crossly. Edmund had a daughter by a brief early marriage who was always nagging him for money. 'Just what right she thinks she has, at her age, I can't imagine.' Edmund belonged to a very active historical society which centred around the events of the Crimean War. He went to obscure places like Cappadocia and the Black Sea with a group, leaving his wife to hold the fort on her own. Their younger son, Alistair, had taken his time in leaving home, but now he'd finally gone, his parents wanted to start again on their own. Harry had a sense of an escape to a hideaway where Alistair would never find them.

'I think it's a bit near the main road,' she demurred. 'If we have a cat, it might get killed.'

'Perhaps,' said Harry judiciously. A cat was as unappealing a prospect as an Irish setter had been, bringing horrible images of the slaughter of small rodents and birds. Harry had possessed a cat himself until recently, but it had been a lazy, domesticated creature, antisocial and unadventurous.

Mrs Langrish was gracious enough to apologise for her reservations about the cottage. She hated to hurt his feelings, he could see. He could not disclose to her his much more complicated reactions to the dawning realisation that she was not going to buy the place. He really did have to leave it, and yet he cringed from the changes to the poor old cottage that would result. It served him right, he repeatedly told himself. He should never have done what he did.

*   *   *

He went to see his sister Muriel in Bisley, not to confess his crime, but to apprise her of his decision to move. It was a visit he had postponed too long, only increasing his dread with every passing day.

'Move?' she shrilled. 'What in the world for? You're not dying, are you?' She gave him a close inspection, to see whether this might be the case.

He was tempted to invent a terminal condition, which would serve a useful purpose for the moment. But the implications were far too complicated for it ever to work. 'No, I don't think so,' he sighed. In his mid seventies, he supposed that he was more or less dying from natural causes. But it might take another twenty years.

'So what in the world are you thinking? Have you gone mad?'

Again it was tempting to answer in the affirmative. Indeed, he thought it might even be true. His deed and the subsequent reaction to it would certainly seem bizarre to many people. 'A bit, perhaps,' he said.

'What's it worth, then? Do you need the money? Have you been gambling? Or is there an expensive floozie you've been hiding from everyone?' She jittered around him, firing questions and hardly waiting for answers. Muriel had always been a nervous, restless creature, and the ageing process had yet to effect any changes.

'Stop it,' he said. 'I was thinking it might fetch close to four hundred thousand, but it seems I have been unduly optimistic. Thus far, nobody has come close to mentioning a figure, because nobody seems to want the place. But I am determined to move, you know.'

'But *why*?' she almost screamed. 'What about your precious garden? And all that *stuff*?'

He no longer took the same delight in the garden as he had for much of his adult life. But he could not explain that to Muriel. 'The pub gets noisy,' he said weakly. 'Especially at weekends, when it's full of children.'

'Rubbish,' she dismissed. 'You like the sound of children.'

'Not so much these days,' he told her. 'And I have to start disposing of much of the clutter. It'll be very refreshing. I want a new start somewhere else.'

'But *where*? You're not leaving the Cotswolds, are you?' They both looked out onto the little street that was the centre of Bisley. Colourful, quiet, serene – it was obviously the best place in the world to live. 'You don't want to move in here with me, do you?' The thought plainly caused her acute horror. 'That would never work.'

'No, no,' he said. 'I was thinking perhaps a little town, like Tewkesbury or Bromsgrove.'

'Tewkesbury? *Bromsgrove*?' This time it was a real scream. 'Have you ever even been there?'

'Once or twice. They both have a good deal to commend them for somebody of my age. Groups, outings, interesting shops. I think either one would be most congenial. And then there's Droitwich or Kidderminster. All with good buses and attractive countryside close by.'

'Blimey,' said Muriel weakly. 'You really have gone mad.'

He went home feeling lonely, guilty and misunderstood. Who could he ever confide in? Not one person. He drove past a dozen idyllic stone houses, many built a century or more before his, but some a lot more recent. They were all beautiful. He had always taken pleasure simply from the appearance of the many-hued stone, from deep mustard to a particular yellowy grey that spoke of age. He had loved the gardens, and created one of his own that took a well-earned place in the picture. Many of these houses were only occupied at weekends or during school holidays. His might well become just such a one, if Scott-the-financier got his way.

Once home, he walked around his rooms, assessing the contents. Books, china, pictures, rugs – but no flowers. Until recently he had always maintained a fresh vase of flowers on the table in front of the window. Not any more. On one level he blamed the flowers for what had happened.

He could – he must – leave here without a backward glance. He had spent twenty happy years amongst people he had felt companionable towards, and who showed every sign of reciprocating. They accepted him without question, welcoming him into their own homes, confident of his good character and decency. The village of Duntisbourne Abbots was just across the main road from his cottage, close enough to walk to, but not so close that he felt observed or judged by the inhabitants. There were even one or two working farms in the area, where he had been known to go and buy eggs. He knew a farm where the daughter kept a small free-range flock in the traditional fashion. It was a relaxed way of life, on the whole. The double murder that had taken place so shockingly just a mile from his home, when he first met Thea Osborne, was well into the past now. The storm had abated and recriminations reduced to a trickle.

But he was undeniably solitary, for all that. His son was gone, living his own life and completely detached from his parent. He sent emails three or four times a year, and a Christmas card, all very friendly. He and Harry met rarely on neutral territory for strained lunches in country pubs, and reminded each other that they were father and son and that surely had to matter. But they quickly ran out of anything to talk about. Paul had married his beloved, a theatre designer called Bobby, and they lived a contented life in Hornsey – a place that had no real character for Harry. He had trouble even finding it on a map.

I am a poor lonely old man, he mumbled to himself, knowing as he said it that he was being disgracefully pathetic and self-pitying. He had his sister, and a very adequate set of good friends. He had his wits –

although recent events gave rise to some doubt on that subject.

And he still had the number for Thea Osborne's mobile.

Thea had arrived as if dropped from the sky, a few years previously; a young widow still suffering the acute effects of her sudden bereavement. The two of them, almost thirty years apart in age, had formed an instant bond. He had acted as protector, facilitator, confidant and liaison between her and the local people. He had observed her vulnerable state and been tempted to capitalise on it. He could have extended his role of protector, taking her into his arms and keeping the horrid world at bay. But he didn't, and she stepped back, standing on her own two feet and visibly healing. The fact of a murdered man on the property she was responsible for gave her backbone and a sense of perspective. Harry was glad for her, at the same time as he was sorry when she left. He heard later that she had jumped into a relationship with a police detective only a few months after the Duntisbourne Abbots business. *Could have been me*, he said wistfully, while knowing he was far too old for her.

But it would do no harm now to call her. Assuming her number hadn't changed, of course. There had been some talk about her movements over the past few years, with shocking events following her from one house-sit to another. Snowshill, Winchcombe, and the village of Daglingworth, only a little way south of where he lived – they and other places had all seen Thea involved in investigating violent crime. He had been aware that she was becoming a figure of some renown, encountering trouble on a regular basis. She was, it seemed, increasingly expert at getting to the heart of things. The local newspapers had begun to label her as 'The House-Sitter Sleuth' and such fatuous epithets as that. And then he had noticed a piece headed 'From Sleuthing to Undertaking', which told of Thea's recent marriage to a man named Slocombe, and their opening of a burial ground near Broad Campden. An unusual event, by any standards, but all the more so for the fact that these were so-called 'green burials' with much less of the ritual and fripperies that went with a standard funeral.

Harry had been intrigued. And very slightly repelled. What was that lovely woman doing getting herself into such work? She ought to concern herself more with the living, free of death and all its trappings.

He wanted to call her. He had wanted to for the past three years. But he could never think of a pretext that could justify so doing. Nor could he now – except a threadbare idea of asking her if she knew anybody who might like to buy his cottage. He wanted to tell her he was moving, just in case she decided to pay a sudden visit. It would be a shame if she found new people in the house. He hated to think that this might happen.

So he did it. With a shaking hand he pressed the buttons, feeling himself grow hot with anxiety as he listened to the odd burring that replaced the usual ringing tones of a proper phone. He disliked mobile phones on principle. Was it not obvious that the things ought never to have been invented?

It dawned on him that there was a clear danger to what he was doing. Thea Osborne – or Slocombe as she must be now – was gifted with an almost uncanny ability to sniff out wrongdoing. Did he perhaps hope that she would do the same with him, exposing his transgression and thus providing some sort of absolution?

She answered with a slightly wary 'Hello?' Her phone, of course, had failed to inform her of who was calling. He was a 'caller unknown' and that itself was unnerving, he supposed. Even Thea, who was so fearless, might be bracing herself for an unwelcome shock.

'Thea? You might not remember me. Harry Richmond, in Duntisbourne Abbots. It's three years ago and more now, I suppose . . .'

'Harry!' The tone was unreservedly warm. 'Of course I remember you. How nice that you've called me. I'm living in the Cotswolds permanently now, you know.'

'So I understand. I was wondering . . . the thing is . . . would you like to come over one day, for tea or something?'

'That would be lovely. How are you anyway? It does seem an awfully long time.'

'I'm older,' he said, with a strangled little laugh.

'And wiser?' she said teasingly. She sounded free of care, settled, confident. She sounded older and very much wiser herself.

'Definitely not wiser. I'm a foolish, fond old man these days. I've put the cottage up for sale. It's a month ago now, at least. Nobody wants to buy it.' Again the painful laugh, which carried very little humour.

'That sounds bad,' she said.

'Bad that I'm selling it, or bad that nobody wants it?'

'Both.'

This time his laugh was more like the real thing. It *was* funny. An unfamiliar sense of delight flashed through him. Had he been a fool to let this woman go? Wasn't she something deeply precious, to be treasured and kept and enjoyed, regardless of what people might think? 'When can you come?' he asked.

'Tomorrow?'

It was like a wonderful gift. 'Perfect,' he said. 'Come at three, and I'll have cake. Can you remember how to find me?'

'I think so. Head for that pub, and you're just past it.'

'Exactly. Will you bring the dog? I have fond memories of the dog.'

'What about your dog-phobic cat?'

'Gone. She'd be very welcome.' The dog had been an integral part of Thea, he recalled. A soft, patient spaniel that made few demands and offered a unique companionship that Harry could scarcely comprehend.

'She's enjoying her new life here. Drew's got two children and they take her for walks across the fields. Actually, three isn't a very good time. I have to be here when they get home from school. There are still a few more days of term, before they finish for the summer. Drew has to go and see someone about a funeral. Would the morning be any good for you?'

'Of course. Coffee instead of tea. Biscuits instead of cake. Ten-thirty?'

'That should be fine. And why not have cake? Such rules are made to be broken.'

He laughed, marvelling at how much better he felt.

But another phone call ten minutes later ruined his mood. It was the estate agent calling to tell him that Mr and Mrs Armstrong-Beavish wanted to come and look at the house again that evening.

'Really?' said Harry. 'I thought they'd decided against it. You do mean the City trader bloke and his nice little wife, I suppose? It that really their name? Armstrong-Beavish?' His contempt was startling even to himself.

'I believe we informed you of their name before the first visit,' said the young man stiffly.

'I expect you did,' said Harry, feeling defeated.

The couple arrived at seven that evening. The sun was just disappearing, leaving the garden in shadow and making all the rooms seem gloomy. Harry did none of the recommended tricks involving grilled coffee beans or lavender-scented sachets. The kitchen was its usual self, an unwashed saucepan in the sink and a cobweb over the window. Harry was tidy, but not obsessively so.

'I thought you'd decided against it,' he said to the wife, who had greeted him like a close friend.

'Scott wanted to see for himself,' she said, with a minimal roll of her eyes.

Scott was fortyish, with elegant black hair and a twitchy, darting glance. He resembled an actor given a part he felt unequal to, after striving desperately to attain it. He avoided Harry's eye and stared impertinently into the corners of the hallway. 'Could I see the garden?' he asked. 'I understand there's a shed. Does it have a secure lock?'

'Not really. Just a padlock,' said Harry. 'Why – what are you planning to keep in it?'

'Tools. You realise we shan't be here during the week. The place will be vulnerable. It's very close to a main road, after all.'

Harry made no attempt at a smile. He was visualising security cameras, keypads, bars on the windows. What sort of relaxing country retreat would that be for his wife and children? Or even for himself, come to that. 'I would have thought that the road worked in your favour, in that respect. Any intruders would be seen by people driving past.'

'Complete myth,' snapped Scott. 'Nobody would bother to stop, would they? And it's convenient for criminals to make an escape.'

'I see,' said Harry, trying not to catch the eye of the wife. He was also trying not to feel sorry for her. She'd married the man, after all, presumably not at knifepoint. 'Well, let's have a look at the shed, then.' He very much did not want to visit the shed, but if it was unavoidable, the sooner it was over with the better.

Scott and his wife followed close on his heels, politely admiring the borders full of colour. Harry grew dahlias, gladioli, lupins, carnations. He liked tall things, and packed them in closely together. There was garden both front and back, and everywhere there were flamboyant blooms at almost every season of the year. It never felt like work to him, the snipping and feeding, weeding and transplanting. The rewards far outweighed the effort, sometimes to the point of making him feel mildly guilty. Admiration was generally misplaced, he felt. Six weeks ago he had decided to clear an overgrown area at the far end of the garden, preparatory to making new beds for yet more colourful flowers. Crocosmia, perhaps, with some alliums to keep it interesting in the early summer.

That wasn't going to happen now.

Scott peered through the window of the shed when Harry failed to offer to unlock it for him. 'Hmm,' he said. 'Looks to be a good size. Is that one of those brushcutter things? I always fancied one of those.'

'I got it for the bits the mower can't cope with,' said Harry. 'I could leave it for you, if you like. I won't need it again.'

'Looks good as new,' said Scott, suddenly showing a much more human aspect. 'I'd pay you the proper price for it.'

'As you like,' shrugged Harry.

In the house again, the couple exchanged a few words, showing no inclination to exclude Harry from their deliberations.

'I think this will be ideal,' said Scott. 'I don't know why you were dithering.'

'I thought it might be a bit small. And the road . . .' defended the wife. 'We'll be able to hear the traffic.'

'We'll replace the windows, of course.' He looked around the sitting room. 'And it might be an idea to move the staircase. That way we could make another room upstairs.'

Move the staircase? Harry almost screamed aloud. How could such a thing even be possible? He made a choked, snorting sound, which attracted two very different responses. The wife expressed silent sympathy, while Scott just smiled. 'It's not as hard as you might think,' he said. 'If it opened into that second bedroom, we could turn the existing landing into a room – do you see? It takes a certain sort of imagination, I suppose,' he finished immodestly.

'I see,' said Harry weakly. He didn't see at all. Where would the bottom of the staircase be, he wondered. How very odd the hallway would look without it. He closed his eyes against the images of devastation. It wouldn't be his problem, he told himself. He'd have a nice town house somewhere, easy to maintain and close to the shops. It was all his own fault. He had brought it on himself. This was his punishment and he must take it like a man.

'Well, I think you've got a sale,' said Scott heartily, determined not to recognise the pain before his eyes. People made their own destiny, in his opinion. Harry had put the house on the market, after all. Why should he be sorry when the logical result took place? It was the same with his wife. She'd been more than happy to marry him and have all those babies. It was exactly what she'd said she wanted. Why did she sometimes seem so gloomy about it these days? It was past his comprehension.

Harry took a deep breath, fighting the sudden vertigo that gripped him. Was it really happening? Would he pocket the hundreds of thousands of meaningless pounds and walk off into the sunset to enjoy his final years in futile comfort? It made him angry to think of it. Angry? He paused, listening to himself. Where was the guilt that had impelled the move?

Ah – there it was, sitting like a malevolent spider in his middle. It hadn't gone away, after all. He was in its thrall, and there was no escape.

'Oh!' he said. 'Thanks.'

Scott laughed. 'Don't you want to know what I'm offering? I'm knocking twenty grand off your asking price, given that there's so much work to be done on it. That's generous,' he added, pushing his face forward to emphasise the point. 'You'd be very lucky to get that much from anyone else.'

'I expect I would. Thank you,' he repeated. 'What happens now?'

'I'll phone the agent tomorrow. We'd be looking at completion by Michaelmas.'

Michaelmas? When was that? Harry had a dim memory of his father referring to the date as one by which rent must be paid and accounts balanced. It was never mentioned these days. Then he remembered the daisies of the same name, which flowered in the autumn. 'That's September, isn't it?' he said.

'Twenty-ninth. That gives us over two months. Should be time enough, wouldn't you say? No chain, as I understand it.'

'That sounds an awfully long time,' said Harry worriedly. Another two months in the cottage struck him as unbearably long. 'Couldn't you make it quicker?'

Scott sucked his lower lip for a moment. 'Sooner might be awkward. Cash-wise, I mean. I'd lose by it, you see.'

Once again, Harry did not see at all. The man was a banker or stockbroker or fund manager or something equally incomprehensible. His instincts were going to be to maximise investments and juggle interest rates and play all kinds of unwholesome games with numbers. And good luck to him, Harry thought, with a glance at the wife, whose eyes had grown round with something that definitely wasn't excitement.

'Well, perhaps I could move out before that,' he said.

Scott tilted his head like a disappointed schoolmaster. 'Really? Before you get the money? That would be very rash. What if I change my mind? Nothing's sure, you know, until the contracts are signed. My advice to you would be—'

'Come on, Scott. Let him do what he wants.' The voice was startlingly firm. The wife, the dithery, unhappy little wife, had spoken. 'You won't change your mind, will you? Let's just shake hands on it, and get home.' She glanced at her watch. 'I want to see how Laurie's cold is. I know he had a temperature when we left.'

'All right, then,' said the husband affably. 'Mission accomplished. We'll soon have this place licked into shape. I always wanted a pad in the Cotswolds. Well done, kid. You did well to find it for us.'

Harry watched them go, his heart sagging unhappily in his chest. It was all his own fault, he reminded himself.

Thea was on the doorstep just before ten-thirty next morning, minus her spaniel. She was eyeing the For

Sale sign by the gate when Harry opened the door.
'Funny how they always make you feel sad, isn't it?'
she said. 'I suppose nobody really enjoys change.'

That gave him pause. He had never regarded himself
as a person resistant to change. There was nothing
virtuous or admirable in such an attitude. And Thea
herself had just undergone a very large change in her
life. 'I'm not sure that's the problem,' he said slowly.

'So what is?' she asked directly.

He looked at her, matching the reality with the
memory of a woman not seen for three years. She was
small and slim and beautiful as he remembered her.
The style of her haircut had changed, and something
about her clothes struck him as different. Hadn't she
been ever so slightly *scruffy* before? Now she was neat
and clean, although the garments did not look new.
He gave this a moment's thought, concluding that it
had been the disarray and personal neglect of grief in
that earlier encounter, in which hair was not cared for
and shoes were not brushed. She was recovered, then,
insofar as a person ever truly recovers.

'You look wonderful,' he told her.

'Thanks. Are we going in? Or shall we sit out in the
garden? I do love your garden.'

'The kitchen,' he decreed, trying to ignore the stab
of regret at the mention of his garden. 'Coffee in the
kitchen.'

'Okay.' She was giving him the same close inspection
that he had given her. He turned away, trusting her to

follow him down the hallway and into the room at the back.

'The new people are going to move the staircase,' he said, almost too softly for her to hear him. 'Can you believe it?'

'What? That's ludicrous,' she said. 'I never heard of such a thing.'

'I suppose anything's possible,' he said.

'I need you to explain the whole business. We've got a lot of catching up to do. Where are you moving to? What about your sister?' She laughed. 'I'll never forget your sister.'

'Nobody does.'

'Well?'

He postponed his replies until the coffee was poured and a fruity farmhouse cake was sliced and proffered. He was mentally rehearsing his opening lines, unable to judge what to explain and what to leave out. Inside him somewhere a juddering panic was building. What had he been thinking of, to invite this lovely inquisitive woman into his tainted home? Didn't he know that she would extract the truth from him? Had confession been his intention all along?

'Are you ill?' she asked with devastating directness. 'Is that it?'

'Oh no. There's nothing the matter with me. Not physically, anyway.'

'So what? You'll have to tell me, you know. Isn't that why you phoned me?'

'I'm not sure. I was just asking myself the same thing.'

'Come on, Harry. It can't be anything too terrible.' Then she caught herself, with a quick little shake of her head. 'That's a stupid thing to say,' she reproached herself. 'Of course we both know that things can be absolutely terrible. They come out of the clear blue sky at us, don't they. Just when we're minding our own business.'

He had no advance warning of his reaction. The flood of tears was at first bewildering. He couldn't think when he had last cried. It felt as if it hadn't happened for about fifty years. The heat and damp and impossibility of control were overwhelming. He could hear the small explosions emerging from inside his face and marvelled that he could make such sounds.

Thea laid a gentle hand on his arm and waited.

'I wasn't minding my own business, though,' he said thickly, after a few minutes. 'I was going where I should not have gone. And I killed. I did a wicked, horrible thing, and it won't leave me alone. I can't stay here any longer. I can't get it out of my mind while I live here.'

'Who did you kill?' She looked out of the window at the garden, as if knowing the answer. And yet, she couldn't know – not the horror of it, the blood and screams and bone-deep guilt and sorrow.

'You might not understand,' he whispered. 'I don't

think anyone could understand. It was just one small unimportant life. One of countless that die every day. You'll think I've gone insane.'

'An animal,' she realised.

'An animal,' he agreed. 'Whose deaths we seldom even mark as of any meaning. I never marked them myself. I have witnessed hundreds of little deaths, been responsible for some of them, eaten their flesh and worn their skins. And then, as you say – from a clear blue sky, it all changed. It was like having a blindfold torn off.'

'Because you did it yourself, without intending to. What was it?'

He blinked away the last of the tears, the emotion too deep for weeping. 'I was using my new brushcutting machine on a patch of nettles and brambles at the end of the garden. I wasn't doing it carefully. Just charging at it like a brainless old bull. I couldn't really see what was in front of me, with the flying debris and dust. I didn't even hear the scream at first. It was the blood that alerted me. It sprayed all over the machine.' He felt the contents of his stomach heaving upwards, his throat burning with disgust and shame.

'You killed a hedgehog,' she finished for him. 'Any other creature would run away, but the poor thing just rolled into a ball and hoped for the best.'

'Just as they do in the road,' he nodded.

'I'm guessing it didn't die right away.'

'Two legs were sliced off, and a great gash down its

side,' he said thickly. 'I picked it up, but the prickles hurt my hands, so I dropped it again. Its little face – have you ever looked closely at their faces? They're desperately sweet. And I dropped it because it pricked me. It died, but not right away. I did nothing to assuage its suffering. I see that pathetic wounded thing every time I close my eyes.'

'And you think by moving away that's going to change?'

'It will be better,' he said with certainty.

'I hope so.' She looked dubious. 'Though it might take more than that.'

He gave her a look. 'You're going to suggest I open a hedgehog sanctuary – atone in some way. I thought of it. But it's too big a matter for that. I have come to abhor the whole human race, you see. There's a bottomless pit of cruelty and exploitation and unimaginable guilt. I could so easily have left that wild area to its own devices. I should have known there were creatures living in there, whose well-being I ought to have cared about. Do you know – if I could be granted one wish, it would be to reduce the intelligence of human beings to about one per cent of what it is. The world would be so much better if we could manage that.'

'The world is what it is,' she said. 'That sounds trite, but it's true.'

'And I intend to tread upon it as lightly as I can. I shall find a little house in a row in a town, eat no meat and perhaps find my way to some kind of acceptance.

I shall have plenty of money, at least. Perhaps I'll find some constructive use for it.' He gave a wan smile. 'The new people might have a dog. Man's accomplice in subduing and tormenting other species.'

She sighed. 'I wish you luck, Harry. I fear you're going to need it.'

Little Boy Lost

Stephanie was ten and a half, fond of Studio Ghibli films, drawing and Thea's dog Hepzibah. She tried to like Pokémon stuff for Timmy's sake, but that was more than she could manage. The best thing about her dad marrying Thea was that the dog lived with them now. She was there in the kitchen every morning, curled in her basket, waiting for someone to come and talk to her. Stephanie was always first down, to enjoy a private cuddle and a little walk in the garden before anybody else got up. She had always wanted a dog of her own from when she was about three, but Dad always said they didn't have time to look after it properly, with her mum so ill, and the job so unpredictable.

The move to the new house had been exciting, at first, although Timmy didn't think so. He had wet the bed every night for the first month, and cried a lot. The people at the new school had called him a wimp and a freak, because his dad was an undertaker. Then at last the summer holiday had started and everything got a lot better, right from the very first day.

It was now the fifth day, and the strange laziness of not finding school clothes, arguing about the packed lunches, scrambling into the car, was still a novelty. Thea was painting the house, quite slowly, letting Stephanie and Timmy help, even though you could see she didn't want to. There was wallpaper all the way up the stairs, which she said had to be pulled off, so they did that mostly. 'I like wallpaper,' said Stephanie, rather to her own surprise. 'Can I have some in my room?'

'Surely not,' said Thea. 'Nobody has wallpaper any more. It's expensive.'

She was always saying things were expensive, even though they were nowhere near as poor as they had been before. Dad was busy with the burials, and people kept asking him to give talks, and Thea had people living in her other house, who paid her.

'I like it,' Stephanie insisted. 'Dad'll let me have some, you see.' She tried not to do that too much, but the fact remained that Dad was her parent, and Thea was not. He obviously had the final word on things.

The summer holidays were a problem for Thea, as anyone could see. She couldn't just go off anywhere she liked, because of the kids. They didn't have anybody else they could go to, unless somebody took them all the way down to Somerset, where they could stay with Maggs. Timmy often asked if they could do that. He missed Maggs a lot. He wanted to play with her baby, and tell her what was happening in his Pokémon comics. Thea would only listen to about one minute of Pokémon talk before she just stopped taking any notice. It was very rude.

But the Maggs idea was never taken seriously. 'Where would you sleep?' Thea always said.

'On the sofa, or the floor,' Stephanie replied impatiently. 'It's summer. We could have a tent outside.' She had once slept in a tent when her friend Donna asked her to go on a holiday to Dartmoor with her and her mum. It had been wonderful.

Dad had laughed. 'In Maggs's tiny garden? Where would you pitch a tent?'

'It's not tiny,' said Timmy. 'She's got blackcurrants and potatoes growing in it.'

'And no space for anything else,' said Dad.

All this frustrating stuff cluttered her mind now, as she watched Hepzie go round the garden. The one here wasn't nearly as big as the Somerset one, although the house inside had more rooms. Everything was different. There were big cupboards, like little rooms, here. The windows wouldn't open unless a strong person heaved them upwards, using curved metal handles. Stephanie really didn't like the windows. Two of the stairs creaked, even when a small person like Timmy trod on them. The telephone was in a square little hall at the foot of the stairs, and when it rang, it made an echo all round the house. When you went outside, you couldn't tell what time of day it was by the passing traffic. At North Staverton, there were busy times every morning and afternoon. In the road here, nothing ever went past, because it didn't go anywhere. It just stopped at a field, which was a stupid thing for a road to do.

'Morning!' came Thea's voice from the back door. 'Looks like another nice day.'

Stephanie lifted her face to the sky, only now noticing how blue it was. 'Yeah,' she said.

'What did we say we might do?'

This was surely a trick question, the sort of baby talk that adults often went in for. Checking to see if the kids had been listening properly, was how it felt. 'Can't remember,' she said.

'Neither can I,' said Thea with a laugh. 'We'll have to think all over again.'

'Dad's got a funeral at twelve. We should polish the vehicle.' The children never called it a hearse, although Stephanie knew this was the proper word for it. She and Timmy were expert at buffing the chrome to a gleaming finish and washing off any streaks of mud. The vehicle was big and expensive and very special. In North Staverton, they hadn't needed anything like it, because the burial field was right beside the house and people carried the coffins. Now it was nearly half a mile to the field, and that was too far.

'He won't need us to be here. In fact, he probably

hopes we'll go out somewhere, and leave him and Andrew to get on with it.'

'So where can we go?' Stephanie sighed softly. Outings with Thea were mostly okay, but sometimes she made them walk too far, or started telling them boring history about Cotswoldy things. Sheep, or canals, or ruined monasteries. It was hardly ever interesting. The best ones were when they went to a town and did shopping and had lunch somewhere like KFC. Thea and Dad both thought KFC was awful, but a bit less so than McDonalds, for some reason. Neither of them would let Hepzie in, though, so if she was with them, they mostly went to pubs and sat in the garden.

'That's what we have to decide,' said Thea. 'So far, the plan seems to be that you and Tim polish the hearse for a bit, and then we get out of here well before the funeral. Like eleven o'clock. It's nearly nine now, so that gives us loads of time.'

Then Dad and Timmy came down together, and Hepzie gave the little boy an exuberant greeting, which was lavishly appreciated. Stephanie watched with her customary mixed feelings. Everything about her brother was tinged with a sadness that would never go away. Even when they were playing something wild, shrieking and laughing and getting out of breath, it was never completely happy. Quite often she thought it must be her fault somehow. She had stolen too much of Dad's love by being the first to be born. She could read Dad's mind and Timmy couldn't. And people usually liked her more. People such as teachers and other children. Sometimes it made her wish Timmy would just disappear, so everything would be less complicated.

She could see that her stepmother was making a real effort to be nice. She was always looking for interesting places to visit that weren't going to be crowded and expensive. ('Stepmother' was a word she had only recently begun to apply to Dad's new wife, as a result of a conversation with two girls at school who explained the whole thing to her, in airy tones of patronage.)

'Mickleton Tunnel might be worth a look,' said Thea now. 'Timmy – you like trains, don't you?'

The boy looked up at her. 'Are we going somewhere on a train?'

'No, no. I don't think they run there any more. But the tunnel's still there. It took five years to build and there was a big fight. A riot, in fact. It must all have been very exciting. Isambard Kingdom Brunel did it himself, and he's the most famous engineer of that time. There are quite a lot of disused railway tunnels around here, actually. I've even been inside one of them.'

Timmy made no attempt to respond. 'Mm,' was all he said.

But Thea was not daunted – which Stephanie did admire in her. 'Listen, Tim – this is where we live now.

We ought to find out as much as we can about the area, don't you think?'

He shrugged. 'When was the fight in the tunnel, then?'

'Quite a long time ago. But the point is, people still talk about it, and try to understand exactly what happened, and why.'

Stephanie felt obliged to intervene. 'Is there anything to *do* there?' she asked. 'Can we go *in* the tunnel? Or the other one, that you've been in?'

'No,' Thea admitted. 'And you wouldn't want to, really. It's cold and wet and dark and scary.'

'Like a grave,' said Stephanie, feeling rather pleased with herself.

'Horribly like a grave, except you can at least breathe, and people can hear when you shout.'

Stephanie gave her brother a little nudge. Being buried alive was one of their favourite games. They used the small space underneath the bunk beds as an approximation. They regularly asked Drew whether it had ever *ever* happened. And he always stoutly denied that there was any chance at all that it could. But Stephanie had caught a look between Dad and Thea that made her doubt his assurances.

They had played the game for as long as she could remember. It might even have begun before Mummy died. So when she had to be buried, the game became horribly real, and Stephanie had upsetting dreams that made her cry. She had begged Dad not to put Mummy in the Peaceful Repose field, and by a wonderful miracle, he had listened to her and done what she asked.

Except now it didn't matter, because they didn't live there any more anyway.

'Can we go to a town?' asked Timmy. 'I want to buy things.'

'What things?' asked Thea.

'Don't know, really.'

'We will know when we see it,' said Stephanie impatiently.

'Well, we could try Moreton, I suppose. I could get some light bulbs. And then maybe you'd like a garden centre, if we can find one. They've got all sorts of things in the big ones. Toys, books, kitchen stuff. How about that?'

The children gave a cautious endorsement of this plan. Garden centres were okay. 'Can we take Hepzie?' Stephanie added.

'Probably not. Only in the outside part, I expect. I could have a look at the roses. Your father did say we should have some in pots to show people, in case they want to plant one on a grave.'

Stephanie laughed at this, imagining a rose bush growing out of the middle of a dead person, its roots twining around the insides and the backbone. Sometimes, they didn't use a proper coffin, but just wrapped the body up in hessian or woven sticks. She thought she might draw a picture of it when she had some spare time.

'What's funny?' asked Thea, and got no answer.

* * *

So they went to a garden centre somewhere near a place Thea said was called Stanton, which she had stayed in not very long ago, and it was huge, and Thea let them wander around it on their own, while she looked at roses outside with Hepzie. Stephanie became fascinated with a collection of garden gnomes, each one with a different expression and a different implement for gardening. They were lined up on a shelf, and she pretended they were alive, whispering to each other, and then jumping down to play in the night when all the people had gone.

When she looked round, there was no sign of Timmy, but she wasn't worried. He couldn't come to any harm. Even if he went outside or into the car park, he was old enough not to get run over. He had probably gone to the loo, she decided. If so, he'd be away quite a while. He took absolutely ages to wash his hands and dry them.

So she wandered into another area of the enormous shop and found a pile of rugs, which she carefully looked at, one by one. She wanted a rug for her bedroom. The new house had enough rooms for her and Timmy to get one each. He had the bunk beds, sleeping in the bottom one, and she had a new bed all of her own. Thea kept asking if they had any friends who'd like to come for a sleepover, but there was no chance of that. All Stephanie's friends were left behind in Somerset, and they never even emailed her, even though Dad had organised her own personal email address on his computer. He was so behind, he didn't understand that nobody sent emails any more.

The rugs were lovely, and she pulled out a red and purple one she especially liked. Then she heard some noise from the front, where the tills were, and decided to see what was happening.

'Take that dog out!' somebody was shouting. 'No dogs in the store.'

'So how do you expect me to pay for these plants?' Thea's voice rang out clear and bossy. She was only small, but people always had to take her seriously. Stephanie felt a mixture of admiration and embarrassment, and hurried to the spot.

'I'll take her out,' she said. 'And can I have a new rug for my room? They're over there. I want the red one. It's on top of the pile.'

Thea handed over the dog lead, and said, 'How much is it?'

'Eleven ninety-nine. It's not very big.'

'I'll go and have a look. Where's Tim?'

'Somewhere around. He might have gone to the loo.'

'When did you last see him?'

'I don't know. I was looking at the gnomes, and he must have gone off then. He's here somewhere.'

'Take that *dog* out,' said a woman.

'Actually, Marion, we don't ban dogs in here,' said a man who was trotting towards them looking rather anxious. 'It's a matter of discretion. Big bouncy ones

can be a problem, but I think we can allow this one.'
He smiled at Thea.

'Thank you,' she said. 'Now, can I leave these roses
here, while I go and find my little boy?'

'And look at the rug,' Stephanie reminded her. She
wanted to say *He's not your little boy*, but decided to
save it for another time.

'Of course,' said the man.

'You haven't seen him, have you? A boy on his
own?'

'How old is he?'

'Almost nine.'

'What's he wearing?'

'Oh, I don't know. Jeans. Trainers. The usual
things.'

'Nine,' repeated the man thoughtfully. 'That's old
enough to find his way around. Did he go back to
your car, perhaps?'

Thea gave Stephanie a questioning look. 'Did you
fall out with him?' she asked.

'No! Not at all. I don't know where he is. Come
and see the rug.'

'Shut *up* about the bloody rug. We've lost your
brother. Give me the dog. I'll go and see if he's gone to
the car.' She grabbed the lead and charged off, leaving
Stephanie and the shop man to follow if they chose.
Stephanie felt a great fury building inside her from the
injustice of the sudden change of manner. Next thing,
Thea would be blaming *her* for Timmy going off. And

all the time, he was sure to be in the loo. That was where he always was. He liked to see different toilets, and play with the squirty soap thing.

'He'll be in the loo,' she said loudly.

'All right. We'll go and see, then.'

The man was really quite nice and sensible, she decided, as she followed him through a large expanse of the shop. They passed her rug on the way, which made her feel cross again.

'I'll pop in and see if he's there,' said the man. 'And if he's in any sort of trouble, I'll call you, okay?'

Stephanie privately thought that the system where men and women went into different toilets was stupid. It didn't happen like that at home, and it only made everything complicated and embarrassing. Timmy had used the Ladies until quite recently, because he said it smelt nicer. Stephanie remembered Dad taking her to the Gents when she was younger. 'What sort of trouble?' she asked in puzzlement.

But the man had gone. She waited almost no time at all before he came back again. 'Nope. Nobody in there,' he reported. There was a line between his eyes and his mouth had gone tight. 'Now what?' he asked, although she didn't think he was really expecting her to answer. 'We'd best go and find your mother,' he decided.

'She's not our mother,' said Stephanie. 'She's only just got married to my father. My mother's dead.' She always felt a small stab of satisfaction when she said that. It had such a dramatic effect on people, and made her feel special. It made Mum feel close, so she could almost hear her laughing at the very idea that she had actually died.

'Ah. I see. Well, she's in charge of you, in any case. Come on.' He lifted an arm towards her, and she understood that he was intending to take her hand. Then he changed his mind and let it fall again. 'Sorry,' he muttered. 'My little girl is only five, so I have to hold her hand most of the time.'

She was glad he had his own child. It gave him added substance in her eyes.

'I'd go crazy if she ever went missing,' he added. 'It's every parent's nightmare.' His voice had gone funny, and she noticed his hands were in tight fists.

'Timmy's okay,' she said. 'He's just here somewhere.'

'Yes, but *where*?' he demanded, sounding a bit like Thea, only even more worried.

Stephanie was feeling rather a failure, now that Timmy was not where she'd said he'd be. She looked all round the great expanse of the shop, trying to get a hint of his whereabouts. It was so big and so full of things like furniture and lawnmowers and tubs full of bulbs, that it seemed impossible to guess where one small boy might be. 'I expect I can find him,' she said, with an exaggerated confidence.

'I can't let *you* go off on your own as well,' he protested. 'Then we might have *two* missing children.'

'I promise not to leave the shop,' she said.

The man's worried frown had deepened. When Thea came in again, making a sort of storm around herself, so that everyone knew she was there, he hurried towards her. Stephanie moved inconspicuously towards the far back of the store, because she had had an idea.

There were several small tents erected in a pretend campsite, with various chairs and portable stoves and sleeping bags scattered around.

'Tim?' she whispered, at the entrance to a domed orange tent. 'Are you in there?'

'Here,' came a breathy reply, from a triangular blue neighbour. 'In here. Come in quick.'

He was sitting at the back of the tent, looking scared. 'Sit down,' he ordered her. 'Don't let them see you.'

'Who?' Her first thought was that he was playing a game with some imaginary Pokémon monsters, and would get into extreme trouble with Thea as a result.

'There's a man and a woman outside. The man was in the Gents. He was on his phone and he said he was going to do the job right away. He didn't know I heard him. I followed him, and he went out to the place where they've got stone statues of rabbits and Greek people. He picked up a rabbit and hit another man on the head with it. He's out there now. He's probably dead. The woman was keeping watch, and I think she might have seen me, so I ran away and hid in here.'

Stephanie pushed her face right up to his, and put

her hands on his shoulders. 'Is all that really true?' she demanded.

'True as true as true,' he assured her. 'I saw a *murder*. And now they'll murder me if they can.'

'Are you sure they saw you?'

He hesitated and then shook his head. 'I think they didn't, really. I hid in here just in case.'

'Thea thinks you've been abducted.'

'They always think that.'

The children had both been treated to harangues at school about stranger danger and people who wanted to hurt children and cross boundaries and generally do very nasty things. It provided good material for games afterwards, and made for great excitement in those rare moments when there was no supervising adult in sight, but nobody really had much idea of what it all meant in actual physical terms. Strangers were some peculiar breed that were not at all like the boring, inattentive, busy people who filled the streets and shops and cinemas. Strangers lurked behind hedges or jumped out of cars and grabbed you just when you were minding your own business.

So Timmy's killer must be one of these, or something very close to it. 'We can just tell the man and take him to look at the body, and everything'll be all right,' she said. 'The murderer will have gone by now, anyway. You're perfectly safe.'

'I was *very* scared,' he said.

'You were clever to hide in here without anybody seeing.'

'I ran all round in a big circle, and nobody took any notice of me. There's hardly anybody in here anyway. But grown-ups can't run – did you know that? I mean, they *can*, but if they do, they look stupid, and other people notice them and wonder what's going on. I thought the woman might follow me, so I pretended to go outside again, so she would have lost me because I was clever,' he concluded.

'Come on. We'll have to tell Thea all about it. She knows about murder.'

'Maybe Dad can do his funeral.'

'That would be great,' said Stephanie, still quite a long way from believing that a man really was lying dead amongst the garden statues.

They crawled out of the tent, almost into the arms of Thea and a man they hadn't seen before. Both their faces were angry, but also astonished. That sort of look that says *I don't believe you could do something so awful*. At least it stopped them from shouting or even talking. Stephanie seized her chance.

'Tim was very cleverly hiding from a man who wanted to hurt him,' she explained. 'It was a stranger, who has done something terrible.'

'Oh, shut up,' said Thea. 'We're going home. No nice lunch for you two. I've had more than enough for one day.'

'That's not fair,' Stephanie shouted. 'You're not

listening.' She turned to Timmy. 'You tell them.'

The boy cringed and Stephanie's heart lurched. He was so obviously frightened. 'I want Daddy,' he whimpered. The only person in the world he could still rely on, his sister realised. And even Dad had gone and married this uncomprehending woman who wasn't capable of keeping them safe.

'It's what Stephanie said,' he choked out. 'There was a man, and I was hiding from him. And a lady, as well. The man hit someone outside.'

'At least go and have a look,' insisted Stephanie. 'Then you'll see if he was making it up or not.'

Thea paused. 'I never said he was making anything up. But I do think we've caused enough trouble for these people, don't you? They've got the entire staff out looking for you.'

'No, no,' soothed the woman from the tills, who had just joined them. She seemed to have had a complete change of heart since shouting at Thea about the dog. 'The manager asked me to come and tell you everything's under control now. He says it's nothing we can't handle. All in a day's work.' She smiled and lifted her shoulders, looking from face to face.

The new man who'd turned up with Thea seemed to disagree. 'The lad's got a story to tell,' he said. Stephanie had noticed the way he watched Timmy's face from the moment he crawled out of the tent. 'We should maybe listen to him.' The words sounded friendly, but the voice did not.

Timmy cringed against his sister and said nothing.

The man was big, with very short hair and straight black eyebrows. Thea, standing beside him, looked about half his size. 'Don't worry about that,' she said. 'The main thing is, we've found him. Now, let me just pay for those roses and we'll be out of your way.'

Stephanie burnt her eyes into Thea's face, saying nothing out loud, but making the point just the same. 'Oh, all right. Show me that rug, and we'll see if it'll go in your room. I did say I'd get you some things for it, didn't I?'

The grudging tone went a long way towards spoiling the pleasure, but didn't entirely ruin it. The rug looked even more gorgeous on second viewing. Thea had Timmy's hand tightly in hers, which was absolutely not necessary, but he looked as if he was almost glad about it. He kept glancing back over his shoulder, and then out through the big windows to the rows and rows of plants in pots outside, and the fruit trees, containers and distant statues. Stephanie whispered to him, 'We'll tell Dad all about it when we get back, and he'll make sure it's put right. Okay?'

Timmy nodded, half-reassured.

The rug was paid for, and the three of them went back to the car, each carrying a rose in a pot. Thea opened the boot and set the plants upright, carefully packing them with whatever bits and pieces she could find, to stop them from falling over. Hepzie was jumping at the window in a delighted greeting. 'Steady on,' said Thea. 'We've only been gone twenty minutes. If that.'

Stephanie had difficulty with the passage of hours and minutes. Dad had spent a number of patient sessions trying to explain how to tell the time from a clock or watch, but she still hadn't altogether grasped it. Thea had wondered aloud how she could be so dim about it, when the whole business was simplicity itself. That had hurt her feelings, and made it even more difficult to concentrate. How long was twenty minutes, she wondered. Long enough for Timmy to go to the loo, hear a man talking on the phone, follow the man, witness his attack on someone, hide in the tent, get found by his sister, and try to explain to Thea what had happened? It seemed a lot for so few minutes. It seemed impossibly much, in fact. And that meant Timmy had made most of it up. Maybe he'd just gone to the loo, then decided to test out the tent.

Then she remembered that Thea hadn't put the dog in the car until after Timmy was lost. So maybe there had been *another* twenty minutes before that, in which Thea had chosen her roses and Stephanie had moved from the gnomes to the rugs.

She sighed. Thea was hassling them to get in and strap themselves into the back seat. Timmy had a booster seat, but she was tall enough to do without. She was four feet ten, which was only three inches less than Thea.

'I don't think it's fair to stop us having a pub lunch,'

she said bravely. 'We haven't done anything bad. *You're* the bad one, for not listening to Timmy, when he tried to tell you something really important.'

Thea started the engine, but didn't drive. She seemed to be taking deep breaths, and when Stephanie caught sight of her in the rear-view mirror, she could see that her eyes were shut. 'I know,' she said. 'I should never have left the two of you on your own in the first place. I didn't think it would hurt. I thought – what can happen in a garden centre, of all places? And here you are, quite all right, except for the fuss and bother of Timmy hiding in a tent. That *was* quite bad, you know. And that story can't possibly be true. Think about it. How would anybody ever get away with attacking someone in broad daylight, in a place like this?'

'He did, though,' said Timmy, suddenly loud. 'I *saw* him. It was just over there, the other side of that fence.'

The fence was only a few feet in front of them. Timmy had always been adept at spatial connections. He always knew which window went with which room, in any house he visited. He remembered the way streets went, in a new town, and could retrace his steps effortlessly. And he was an observant child. Even Thea had to acknowledge that.

'Well, let's try to forget all about it now,' said Thea, absently stroking the top of her spaniel's head. 'It's lunchtime. I suppose we could go to a pub somewhere, if you're good. One with a garden that Hepzie can go

in. I can't actually think of one at the moment.' Again
she closed her eyes. 'I know – there's one just up the
road in Stanton. It'd be nice to go there again. It's got
lovely views.'

She put the car in gear and began to reverse out
of the parking space. 'Can I open a window?' asked
Stephanie. 'It's hot in here.'

'Wait a minute.' Thea turned the car, and then
pressed buttons that opened both rear windows an
inch or so. The car park was sparsely occupied, but
two newcomers were driving in, forcing them to wait
where they were for a moment.

'Listen!' said Timmy. 'Somebody's shouting.'

Stephanie twisted around, trying to both see and
hear what might be happening. Nothing looked
unusual.

'They've found the man,' said Timmy with uncanny
certainty. 'Wait. Thea – wait.' His tone was so urgent
that Thea automatically obeyed him. Still keeping
an eye on her in the mirror, Stephanie could see
uncertainty on her face. 'It was true, what I told you,'
Timmy pressed on. 'True as true as true.'

The shouting had stopped, but things did seem
to be happening. The short-haired man came to the
entrance of the store, with a phone to his ear. He
looked sharply from left to right, then straight ahead,
like a robot. Stephanie giggled.

'What's funny?' asked Thea, also rather sharp.

'That man.'

'He's their security chap. Catches shoplifters and finds lost children. He's called Dave. He talked to me when we were searching for Timmy. He does the heavy lifting as well. They employ lots of people, you know.'

'So what?' said Stephanie.

'So I'm starting to think—' But she got no further, because Dave had spotted them and was flapping a hand at them like a demented traffic cop. 'Oh, damn it. He wants us to wait. Why didn't we leave when we had the chance? All that faffing about, and now look.'

'They've found the man,' repeated Timmy. 'And now they're calling the police, and I can tell them who did it.'

'That must be right,' said Stephanie. She gave her brother the warmest possible smile. 'We should have believed you.'

'Didn't *you* believe me?' He looked at her all wounded and reproachful.

'Not *completely*,' she confessed.

'It's probably something to do with my credit card,' said Thea.

But it wasn't. Dave came trotting up to the car, his gaze firmly on Timmy. 'You said you saw it,' he began breathlessly. 'You *saw* what happened. Our machinery man, Eddie, is lying out there with the statues, just as you said he was. I thought I should go and have a look, just in case – and there he was.' Amazement seemed to be clouding his mind. 'So you'll need to tell the police about it. Tell them who did it.'

'He's only a child. They can't use him as a witness,' Thea protested.

'Oh yes, they can.'

Timmy was halfway over the front passenger seat, trying to explain to Thea that he was quite able to provide helpful testimony and catch the murderer, his knee digging painfully into Stephanie's thigh. Hepzie was trying to lick him, under the mistaken impression that the excitement had something to do with her.

'Stop it, both of you,' said Thea. 'Let me get the car out of the way, and we'll see what they want.'

Dave led them all back into the shop, except for the dog. There was a group of customers standing by the tills, muttering to each other. 'Come through to the back,' Dave urged them. 'We can wait in the office.'

Stephanie found herself with no part to play other than as an observer. She observed Timmy as he focused on the face of the nice manager who had helped her search for him. 'That's him!' he cried, pointing a wavering finger. 'That's the killer!'

He had to be wrong, Stephanie thought. Thea went further, and told him not to be ridiculous. But the man simply slumped onto a chair and put his head in his hands.

'He had it coming,' he mumbled through his fingers. 'That Eddie – he had it coming.'

Then the police finally turned up, first going outside to check the body and establish that the man really was dead. None of that was visible or audible from the office. Nothing happened for what seemed like ages, and Stephanie was hungry and worried about Hepzie in the hot car. Then a woman who obviously knew Thea came in, and asked a lot of questions, some of them addressed to Timmy and some to Dave, and then they took the manager away.

'We can go now,' said Thea. 'At last.'

'But he's a *nice* man,' Stephanie burst out. 'He can't be the murderer.' She had pieced together only part of the story, and was left with this glaring anomaly.

'He is a nice man,' Thea agreed. 'And he killed a very nasty one.'

On the way out, Timmy gave a muted yelp, and pointed to the cafeteria, where a woman was clearing tables. 'That's the lady,' he said. 'The one who I thought might have seen me.'

'Never mind that now,' said Thea firmly. 'I think the police will do whatever they need to, where she's concerned.'

Stephanie had caught references to somebody called Angela with a daughter called Ruby, who Eddie had done something bad to. Eddie did bad things to little girls, that much she had understood. And the manager had a little girl of his own. He was only being a good father, then. Perhaps the police would give him credit for that.

Later, when they tried to explain everything to Dad, he pulled her to him, with a shaky hand. 'What a world!'

he said. 'Where even a garden centre isn't safe.'

Thea put an arm around Timmy, and kissed his cheek. 'My hero!' she said. 'I hereby solemnly promise to listen to every single thing you say – always.'

'Even the Pokémon?' Stephanie challenged.

'Even the Pokémon,' said Thea.

Stephanie and Dad burst out laughing.

'Good luck with that,' said Drew.

The Stone Man

The church was at first glance not especially impressive. A church was a church was a church, thought Maggs dispassionately. It had only been suggested as a meeting place because it was easy to find. And easy to park close by in the main street running through the little town of Winchcombe.

Meredith was kicking her heels repetitively against the bar of her buggy, shouting in time to the kicks. She also leant forward and back every now and then, like a child on a swing, urging more progress, faster momentum.

'Have a heart, kiddo,' said Maggs. 'I'm going as fast as I can.'

The child twisted round to glare at her mother. The one-year-old face was a comical mixture of its two parents, an intriguing illustration of genetics at work. Very dark hair framed a high brow and lean cheeks. Brown eyes, set deep and close together, and a wide mouth gave every expression a healthy dose of character.

'She's no beauty,' Maggs had announced, a week or so after giving birth. 'The top of her face is Den and the bottom is me. She's a shunt.'

'Pardon?' Drew had said. He was holding the baby at the time, blowing out his cheeks and crooning like any besotted grandmother. Drew Slocombe had always been fond of babies.

'You know – when criminals weld two different cars together to make one they can sell. Merry's just the same – it's hilarious.'

As she grew, Meredith became more and more distinctive. 'We'd certainly know her in a crowd,' said Den.

Maggs was propelling the buggy along the narrow pavement of Winchcombe's high street, only a little way from the church. She had agreed to meet two friends there, and possibly Thea, if she wasn't too busy. Thea Osborne who was now Thea Slocombe. A summer day out had been proposed with a picnic lunch planned in the grounds of Sudeley Castle. The friends both had babies of much the same age as Meredith, which comprised the whole reason for the three-way relationship. They had met in the antenatal class and bonded in the way women do under such circumstances. A bonding that extended to several other new parents, in fact. There had been three reunions of the full group during the year, where infants had been compared obsessively. Maggs had come away with a shaky suspicion that her child was neither genius nor beauty. This picnic in Winchcombe was with the two women who had seemed to be the most uncritical. They both felt sufficiently unsure of themselves, with fractious offspring and absent husbands, for Maggs to feel less threatened by competition. Parenthood had never greatly appealed to her and the experiment had not been a wholesale success. By great good fortune, Meredith seemed to understand and accept this with equanimity.

Maggs had mixed feelings about the Cotswolds since Drew and Thea had moved there, leaving her in charge of the burial ground in Somerset. The existence of Meredith was more than enough reason for her to resent the change of circumstance. 'How am I supposed to run it on my own, with a one-year-old child?' she had demanded.

'You'll manage,' said Drew. 'I did it when Stephanie was a baby and Karen went back to work.'

'Yes, but . . .' grumbled Maggs. The truth was that the workload was quite within her competency, especially with Den such a dedicated father. He and Drew were both very much keener on small infants than she was herself.

The church, on closer inspection, was a surprise. There were quirky embellishments in the form of gargoyles and castle-style battlements all along the top of the wall facing her. Looking up further, she glimpsed a golden bird on top of the tower. When she tried to point all this out to her child, there was little response. 'Oh, you,' she said.

But then Meredith surprised her, pointing upwards and piping 'Man!' quite beyond any mistake.

It was the fifth word the child had uttered in her life, after 'Oops!', 'nahnah', 'Dadda' and 'okay'.

'Still not bothering with me, then,' Maggs complained, trying to see whether there really was a man on the church roof. It took a minute to realise that the child was indicating one of the gargoyles over the main door. 'Not much wrong with your eyesight, anyway,' she said. 'He is rather splendid, I admit.' The stone figure was wearing a hat and apparently struggling to free himself from the building. Strictly speaking, he wasn't a gargoyle at all, she reminded herself, because he served no function as a water spout, which she believed to be the strict definition. He was something stranger and more unsettling. It was easy to accept the idea that he'd once been a real man, trapped by some magic as a punishment for folly or wickedness. He did look a bit of a fool, she decided. Then a shadow fell across his face, or something of the sort, and he seemed for all the world to be moving.

Meredith squealed. 'Man!' she repeated.

'Right,' said Maggs. 'Let's have a look to see if there are any more of them.' She pushed the buggy over a patch of short grass, to where another grotesque was trying to escape from the stone on the corner of the building. This one had a wide grinning mouth, and was possibly female. Meredith was craning round to look back at her original favourite, rather to Maggs's irritation. 'There are lots of them, look,' she tried. There was a massive arched window round the corner, with figures above it.

But she had no chance to go and inspect them. 'Hiya!' came a voice from the church porch. 'Over here.'

It was Olivia with her little boy Simon. Olivia who had moved to Stroud, in the south of the Cotswolds, and wanted to stay in touch. Olivia who was thirty-eight and an insurance assessor. She had dark-brown hair and very big hands. Her husband, John, was over forty with a previous wife and family. He had attended one class, full of complacency and world-weariness. Maggs and Den had both felt desperate urges to hit him. As far as Maggs could ascertain, he had suddenly increased his working hours when his new son was born, leaving Olivia to handle the whole business pretty much on her own. It had once or twice occurred to Maggs that her own situation, with Den so very attentive and involved, might come over as complacency to her less fortunate sisters. She had given in to the urge to play down the fact that things were going quite significantly well as far as Meredith was concerned. Instead she talked about the uncertainties of their income, and the sense of desertion that came with Drew's move to Broad Campden.

Now Maggs waved and went to join her friend. 'Have

you seen Annie?' she asked. Annie was thirty-one, fair in colouring and generally positive in her approach to life.

'We're having four,' she had announced to the class with a laugh. 'Preferably within five years. Like a litter of puppies.' Maggs had warmed to her immediately, while at the same time envying the affluence that made such a prospect viable.

'Nope,' said Olivia, in answer to the question. 'We've been inside for a look and she's not there.'

'We'd better wait a bit, then. How's things, anyway?'

Olivia rolled her eyes, which had shadows beneath them. 'I've forgotten what a night's sleep is like, for a start. And he won't *eat*.' There followed a predictable catalogue of complaints about the trials of life with a small child, ending with, 'I gather Annie's Bethany's perfect,' with the hint of a sneer. Maggs was reminded yet again that a new mother was expected to find life intolerable and to moan loudly about it at every opportunity. The facts as she saw them, however, were not like that at all. A baby was far more robust and forgiving than she had ever imagined, despite close contact with both Drew's children from infancy having taught her much about human resilience, both in adults and children. Meredith was perfectly reasonable in her demands and slept well enough provided her days had been sufficiently active and stimulating. The general fuss and self-pity that Maggs witnessed amongst new parents sometimes made her wonder if she came from some quite different species.

Olivia was waiting for a suitable response, she belatedly realised. 'Last I heard from Annie, Bethany was suffering pretty badly with her teeth.' She looked at Simon, who was deeply asleep. 'Looks as if the fresh air has tired him out already,' she noted. 'It'll probably make him hungry as well. Have you tried spicing his food up a bit? Meredith loves curry and anything with onion in it.'

The woman's large brown eyes grew even larger. 'Curry?' she repeated, as if Maggs had said *arsenic*. 'But that does such ghastly things to the nappies.'

Maggs shrugged. She had hoped for more adult conversation, while knowing that this was a forlorn wish. Olivia was working three days a week, and Annie shared a nanny with another family, so both mothers were pursuing their chosen professions. From what Maggs could glean, that meant that both sets of parents virtually never saw each other. Her own work as alternative undertaker, arranging burials in a field for eco-minded customers, was very seldom mentioned. After the nervous and mildly scandalised giggles that had emerged from the class when she first disclosed the deplorable fact, she and they had opted to avoid any further direct reference to it.

'Well, it's half past eleven already,' she said impatiently. 'Merry's going to want some lunch soon. Have you seen all these fabulous carvings?' She pointed at the stone man, whose eye she had felt on her for the past ten minutes. Meredith had been burbling nonsense to herself, also staring up at the figure from time to time. A feeling born of medieval superstition was taking hold of them both, Maggs thought fancifully. 'I'm sure he's watching us.'

'Who? What?' Olivia looked startled. 'Where?'

'The gargoyle. There's a few of them, but the one just up there has a much more lively look than the others, don't you think? I could have sworn he moved just now.'

'You're mad. It's just a carving. Probably meant to ward off evil spirits. Isn't that always what they were for?'

'Probably.' Maggs was finding it difficult to drag her gaze away. High up on the wall like that, he would see all kinds of behaviours and secrets that those on the ground were too distracted to notice. 'I think there's something special about him. There must be a story somewhere.'

'I thought so when I first saw him,' came a new voice. 'You expect him to burst free at any moment, don't you?'

'Thea!' Maggs embraced her employer's wife with genuine gladness. 'It's ages since I saw you. How's everything? Where's Hepzie? We're waiting for Annie. You'll like her. This is Olivia. And Simon.' Simon was slumped uncomfortably in his buggy, head lopsided and drool on his chin. Thea barely glanced at him.

'Hello,' she said to Olivia. 'And hello to *you*, little Meredith. What a big girl you are now.'

'She's just said a new word,' Maggs announced with pride.

'Wow! She's a prodigy.'

'I didn't hear it,' said Olivia, with a hint of sulk.

'It was before you got here. She said "man" and pointed at the chap up there. Where's Hepzie?' Maggs asked again. She had a great fondness for Thea's cocker spaniel.

'I left her with Drew and the kids. They wanted to take her on a walk over the fields. I thought she might be a bit of a handful, with all this lot.' She looked from buggy to buggy, and then asked, 'So where's this other person? I've got all sorts of goodies here for our picnic.' She indicated a bulging bag, which had the neck of a wine bottle protruding from the top. 'Including some Cava. It'll be horribly warm if we don't bustle.' Then she smiled. 'Isn't Winchcombe *gorgeous*? Like another age. I forgot how amazing it is.' She waved at the street of small characterful houses leading away from the town centre. 'They're all different, you know. There's a kind of madness to it.'

'We should give up on Annie and just go,' said Olivia. 'She can phone to find out where we are.'

'Hard to stick to precise times with a small child,' said Thea, as if she knew what she was talking about. It was well over twenty years since she'd had to worry about such things.

'What was that?' Maggs had heard a sound that penetrated all else. Traffic was passing, people were talking, but through it all she caught a small whimper – which did not come from either child close by.

Both Thea and Olivia looked at her blankly. 'What was what?' said Thea.

'I heard a baby cry. Just a quick bleat. Over there.' Maggs pointed to the side wall of the church and the yew trees facing it.

'It must have been a cat,' said Olivia. 'There's nobody there.'

'I'll just pop round and see,' said Maggs. 'Cats don't make that sort of noise, especially in the middle of the day. They're virtually nocturnal, you know.'

'Leave Meredith here, then,' said Thea. She laughed. 'Wouldn't it be funny if you found an abandoned baby in the church porch? That would please him up there. Just like old times, it'd be.' She waved at the stone man. 'He must have seen a whole lot of that kind of thing. Wonder what he thinks about the twenty-first century. Must be boring by comparison.'

But nobody was listening to her. Maggs had gone round the wall into the church grounds and Olivia was intent on trying to straighten her little boy.

'Hey! Come here!' Maggs was suddenly shouting at them. 'Call the police. Quick!'

'What?' Thea began to push Meredith's buggy through the church gate. Then, seeing that Olivia hadn't moved, she abandoned her charge and went on alone. 'Watch her, will you,' she called back at the other woman, who turned to her and nodded. She looked almost frozen with bewilderment.

Maggs was at the corner of the church wall beyond the big window, staring down at something out of sight at the back of the building. The very familiarity of her stance told Thea that this was terribly bad news. As she approached, she could hear the whimper that had alerted Maggs. It definitely wasn't a cat, but a lamb might make such a sound. But what would a lamb be doing in a churchyard? Before the question was formed, she was standing at Maggs's shoulder, seeing for herself exactly what was there.

A child was sitting in a buggy, pushed right against the church wall. Inches away lay a human form, crumpled and still. The side of the face was misshapen. Fair hair formed an untidy halo around the head. The light summer clothes were not disarrayed – cut-off blue trousers and a cream-coloured shirt suggested a carefree day in the sunshine, something far too flippant and optimistic for death to stand a chance of prevailing. But death had prevailed anyway. 'It's Annie,' said Maggs. 'And Bethany.'

'She's dead,' said Thea.

Maggs squatted down and laid a gentle hand on the bare neck. 'Still warm,' she said. 'But no sign of a pulse. It must have happened only a little while ago – maybe while I was right here with Merry.' Her eyes widened. 'Where's Merry?' she demanded.

'Just over there. Olivia's with her. She might be phoning the police, like you said.'

'We should go and see. And take Bethany with us. She can't stay here.'

'No.'

Maggs gripped the buggy's handle, only to realise that it was impossible to move it without touching the child's dead mother. 'Help me lift her,' she ordered Thea. 'I can't get her away otherwise.'

As they carefully extracted the pushchair and its occupant and set it down a few feet away, the little girl repeated the soft cry that had first alerted Maggs. It was definitely like the bleat of a lamb, Thea insisted to herself. A self-effacing little sound, almost apologetic. 'Poor little thing,' she groaned. 'What a dreadful thing to happen.' She looked up. 'Do you think a stone fell off the roof or something?'

'Can't see anything,' said Maggs, in a steely tone.

'What then?'

'Somebody bashed her, Thea. Isn't it obvious?'

'What with?'

'I don't know. There's plenty of stuff lying about.'

'I can only see stones. Why couldn't one of them have fallen on her? Why can't it be an accident?'

'Because she'd have had to be lying down with the side of her head facing up. Nobody does that. Or standing with her head bent down to her shoulder.' Maggs enacted the posture, making her point quite vividly. 'It wasn't an accident.'

Thea was visibly resisting the inevitable conclusion, one hand on the buggy, rocking it slightly. Maggs led the way back to the church gate. Olivia was standing passively outside it, Meredith and Simon sitting side by side in their buggies. Simon had woken up and was reaching towards Meredith, his face full of keen interest. He was a nice-looking child, Maggs thought idly, but little Bethany far outshone both the others when it came to looks. New-grown blonde hair framed a winsome little face. Big blue eyes and a ready smile made her everybody's darling. A poor, motherless little darling now, which was a tragedy beyond imagining.

'Did you call the police?' she asked Olivia.

'Pardon? Oh – no. I didn't know what I should say to them. What's the matter? Where's Annie? That's Bethany, isn't it?' She eyed the child with something like distaste.

Maggs spoke slowly and loudly, in the belief that this was the only way to get through to the woman. 'She's been attacked. She's lying round there dead.'

Olivia's eyes went oddly opaque and tiny. They seemed to draw into her head like a snail's. 'No,' she whispered. 'I don't believe it.'

'Well, it's true,' said Thea. 'Let me make the call. You two should see to the little girl. Phone her father or somebody. She's the important one now.'

Maggs forced a smile at little Bethany, who was a lot smaller than her own chunky daughter. 'Poor old you,' she crooned. 'We'd better get somebody to come and take you home, eh?' Bethany wriggled her shoulders coquettishly and ducked her chin. 'Where's your bag, then?' Every mother carried a large bag filled with spare nappies, wipes, food, drink, clothes, toys and assorted objects deemed essential for a day out with a small child. Bethany's was slung over the bag of her three-wheeled pushchair. 'No wonder it was so heavy,' Maggs muttered, as she removed it. 'Let's see if there's some nibbles in here.'

She unpacked a plastic box, which proved to contain a veritable feast. Only then did she remember they had scheduled a picnic, which explained the hard-boiled eggs, muesli bars, cold sausages and quite a lot of fruit.

'She can't eat that here,' Olivia protested. 'Simon's going to want some if you start feeding her now. She doesn't look hungry, anyway.'

Maggs ignored her and calmly broke a muesli bar into thirds, issuing a piece to each infant. 'It's for distraction,' she said shortly.

Thea had walked a few yards away, speaking urgently into the phone. 'Yes,' she repeated loudly. 'You'll find us easily. Three women with three small children. Outside the church in Winchcombe.' She threw Maggs a glance of appeal, to which there was no possible response other than a friendly smile.

'Have you ever had to do this?' she asked Olivia, for no clear reason. 'Dial 999, I mean.'

'Me? Absolutely not. The whole thing's terrifying. I

just want to get away and let the police do whatever it is they do. I'm hopeless with anything like this.'

'There isn't anything like this,' Maggs corrected her shortly. 'This is just about as bad as it gets. Lucky the kids are too young to understand.' She looked at Bethany, nibbling quietly on her wholesome snack. 'Poor little thing. What monster would do such a thing to an innocent child?' Her insides were congealing, her hands beginning to shake, and she wondered at her own reaction. Then she remembered Karen Slocombe, Drew's first wife, who had died and left two small children to get along as best they might. The association was suddenly unbearable and she felt her face crumple. 'And what did Annie ever do to deserve this?' she sniffed.

'I still can't believe she was killed on purpose. How long do you think they'll be?' Olivia was jittering from foot to foot. 'Can't we get further away?' She glared angrily at Maggs. 'Why did you have to go snooping round there anyway? We could be practically at the picnic place by now.'

Maggs worked as an undertaker; she knew the strange effects that death could have on people. She had seen apparent heartlessness before. But this was personal and altogether unacceptable. 'And leave this little sweetheart beside her dead mother? Don't you think it's lucky I heard her when I did?'

'Oh – I suppose so. I don't know what I'm saying. It's all such a *shock*.'

Thea came back to join them. 'They'll be here in a few minutes,' she said. 'One of us ought to stay with her, really. It's the decent thing to do.' She looked Olivia squarely in the face. 'You were her friend,' she hinted.

'Me? I'm not going. What about Simon?'

Meredith prevented any response by kicking her feet violently against the buggy and breaking out in a tuneless babble that was plainly preparatory to expressing displeasure.

'She wants to get out,' said Maggs.

'She's not walking yet, is she?' asked Thea. 'You can't let her crawl around here on the pavement.'

'She could have a bit of freedom amongst the gravestones,' said Maggs. 'She's used to gravestones, after all, even if ours are a bit different.'

'No, she can't. Besides, they're mostly around the back. There's nothing much on this side.' The mood was turning dark, the horror of Annie's death throwing a grim pall over everything. But at the same time, the children must not be upset, if it could be avoided. 'What about phoning her husband?' Thea reminded Olivia. 'You must have the number.'

'Why must I? All I've got is Annie's mobile number. Her phone'll be in her bag, presumably, with all her numbers in it.' She shook her head as if there was nothing more to be done.

But Thea was not to be dismissed. 'This bag?' she asked, raising the one that Maggs had removed from

Bethany's pushchair. 'We can look for it, then. Her husband's number is sure to be in it. What's his name?'

'Mike,' said Maggs. 'They're Mike and Annie Henderson. But are you sure we should? Isn't it better to wait for the police?'

Thea was rummaging in the bag. 'I can't see it, anyway. She must have a handbag somewhere. Still with her, probably.'

The appearance of a police car put an end to the matter. Two uniformed officers, one male and one female, stood alertly before them, waiting for enlightenment. For Thea there was a numbing familiarity to the whole procedure, but for Maggs it was new and traumatising. Despite the fact that her husband had been a policeman for some years, she had experienced little direct contact with the force. Her ageing parents had lived most of their lives in Plymouth, reasonably law-abiding, but in no way relishing any attentions from the powers of justice. The general attitude had been that they were a necessary evil, liable to get things wrong and pursue ill-chosen avenues when it came to enforcement. Maggs was a natural rebel, thinking for herself and disdaining many of the smaller social rules when it suited her.

But this was a violent death and the police were an inevitable component. They had to be given facts, carefully and patiently, once they had inspected the body and called for all the different individuals necessary for the investigation of a murder. The presence of three little children evidently discomposed them. The female officer almost wept when she understood who Bethany was.

Quite why it was Maggs who supplied the essential information, rather than the capable Thea or the more closely connected Olivia, remained obscure. 'Her name is Annie Henderson. She lives in Somerset. She has a husband called Mike. I last saw her six weeks ago, or thereabouts.' She turned to Olivia every few seconds for confirmation of everything she said. Finally, she burst out, 'Really, Olivia knew her much better than I did. They kept in closer touch.'

So finally the police questioned Olivia, who said there was nothing more to add.

'What exactly were the arrangements?' asked the female officer. 'Time you were to meet, and what you intended to do? When did you last see your friend?' She frowned. 'How late was she, before you found her?'

'Um . . .' said Olivia, looking at her watch. 'We were meant to meet here at about eleven. Both Annie and Maggs had to drive about fifty miles, so we weren't sure if they'd arrive exactly on time. We were going to have a picnic in the park, and let the children have a bit of freedom.'

The policewoman looked to Thea. 'And you? How are you connected?'

Thea hesitated, struck by the assumption that she could not be the mother of any of the babies. She was forty-five. The assumption was, strictly speaking, wrong.

'I've known Maggs a long time,' she said. 'And Meredith's my god-daughter – sort of.' There was to be no formal christening, but Thea had accepted the role of 'special aunt', which would in earlier times have been formalised by the church.

They all knew that the questions were barely relevant. These junior uniformed officers were not authorised to engage in any sort of real investigation. All they had to do was complete a few initial basic details, the prime one being the identity of the deceased. Unless there was one even prior to that: was the victim actually irrevocably dead? For that a police doctor must attend – and that person was expected at any moment.

Olivia was the first to point out that she for one could not think of any reason to hang around. 'The children will be getting hungry,' she said impatiently, ignoring the residual traces of food in the infant fingers. Then she glanced at the knot of inquisitive passers-by, hovering on the pavement opposite the church. 'And it's not really good for them to be here, is it?'

Nobody contradicted her, but neither did they agree. 'Where's Mrs Henderson's car? She did drive here, presumably?'

The three women gave equally blank looks. 'No idea,' said Maggs. 'Most likely along the street somewhere. There was plenty of space when I got here. Where are you parked?' she asked Olivia and Thea.

Thea waved towards the town centre. 'Just down there,' she said.

'Me too,' added Olivia.

Very little time had passed since the police officers had arrived, Maggs realised. There was still a sense of controlled panic, holding the line until reinforcements showed up. Hypotheses, sidetracking into a search for a weapon or questions as to relationships all had to wait for more senior investigators. There was no way the positioning of cars could be relevant.

'We can't just go,' she said, looking at Thea. 'Can we?'

'Not really,' said Thea. 'They'll soon be here. It might be somebody I know,' she finished hopefully. 'Like Gladwin.'

'You know DS Gladwin?' asked the female constable.

'Oh yes,' Thea told her. 'And DI Higgins.' She could have added more names, but refrained. As soon as anyone from CID arrived, her intimate connections with the local police force would become apparent. Winchcombe itself had been the scene of two brutal murders not so long ago. Thea had found both the bodies. The sudden appearance of a third made her both angry and weary.

Maggs noticed Olivia throwing strange looks at Thea. Confusion was plain on her face, as well as a sort of apprehension. There had not been time for proper introductions, she remembered, so Olivia knew almost nothing of Thea's background. The house-sitter who moved from one Cotswold village to another, encountering bad behaviour on an epic scale almost everywhere she went. The new wife of alternative undertaker, Drew Slocombe, who was attracting considerable attention since setting up a new burial ground near Broad Campden. Olivia knew only that Thea and Maggs had been friends for some time, having somehow been connected through their husbands. Maggs had been deliberately vague, hoping to elaborate properly over the picnic.

'I think we should go,' said Olivia again. Her small son was grizzling and showing clear signs of needing to escape from the straps that imprisoned him. Not for the first time, Maggs grieved over the way little children spent such a lot of their time tied into some contraption or other, ostensibly for their own safety.

But then two more cars drove right up to where they were standing, oblivious of any normal parking rules. Five people emerged and were quickly standing along the pavement, asking questions and pulling on protective clothing, in one or two cases. Maggs, Olivia and Thea were ushered to one side and asked to wait. Activity and bustle ensued, with police tape barring entry to the church, a horrified vicar suddenly appearing for good measure. Maggs looked to Thea for some sort of explanation based on her experience, but she just shrugged. 'Not Gladwin or Higgins,' she sighed. 'Nobody I know at all. Pity.'

A young man in plain clothes came up to them. 'Mrs Cooper?' he asked. Maggs raised a hand. 'Good. Would you be kind enough to come with me, please?'

'Why me?' she muttered, but went willingly enough. She felt a small lurch of pride at being the one singled out. They must think her the most competent and responsible of the three, she concluded.

Annie's body still lay exposed to the sky. A man in a suit knelt beside her. More men were stringing tape in a wide arc from church wall to shrubs at the edge of the grassed area. 'Do you recognise this?' the original policewoman asked her, holding a handbag aloft.

'Actually, I do,' said Maggs slowly. 'That's Annie's bag. I remember it from the classes. We all admired it.'

It was a very distinctive item, made of soft purple leather and very expensive. A present from Mike, on first learning she was pregnant. She had made a great display of it, more than once. Seeing it now, surviving its proud owner, gave her a piercing pain. What would happen to it? What significance could it ever have, along with all Annie's other possessions? Bethany might inherit it eventually, perhaps. But would she want it? If she was told that it had lain beside her dead mother, containing her personal things, would she not be repelled by it? Perhaps Mike would sell it or thrust it at Annie's mother for disposal. For the first time – which given her occupation had to be rather shameful –

Maggs considered the fate of a dead person's belongings. Just so much clutter, in most cases, their meaning gone along with the person who had valued and loved them.

And then a distinctive sound was heard from inside the bag. Automatically, the policewoman reached in and removed the phone, which had indicated the receipt of a text. She looked at its screen and then showed it to Maggs, whose mind began to work as fast as a microprocessor.

JOHN, it said.

'Do you know who that is?' the officer asked her.

'Um . . . I don't think so. Might be anybody. Listen – are we done here? I need to get back to my little girl.'

'Well . . .' The woman looked around for someone to consult. 'Can Mrs Cooper go now?' she asked.

'Go where?' replied a man in jeans, who was probably a fairly senior detective.

'Just back to the street, with the others,' said Maggs.

'No problem,' he nodded.

'So, actually, could we go and have some lunch as well?' she pressed on. 'We were heading for the park. Would that be okay?'

'Leave your contact details, then. We'll want to interview you this afternoon. All of you.'

She smiled co-operatively, and went back to the others. 'They want our mobile numbers,' she told them. 'Then we can get down to the park, and try to eat something.' She looked directly at Olivia. 'I feel too sick, quite honestly. Sick as a . . . whatever it is.'

'Dog,' said Thea. 'Dogs are often sick. What happened back there? You've gone a bit green. Surely not at the sight of a body?'

'Let's get going. I need to think,' was all Maggs would say.

The male constable was hovering, and they gave him their numbers, reminding him of their surnames. Then Maggs led the way back towards the main square of Winchcombe, before turning right down a characterful little street that ended up at the gates of Sudeley Park. Thea paused for a wistful glance down over some allotments. 'I stayed there, a year or two ago,' she said. 'You remember, Maggs.'

'Yes. I came here to confront you about Drew.'

'No, you didn't confront me. You gave me a very sweet apology for being nasty to me.'

They exchanged fond smiles. They did, after all, have a substantial history behind them. From some obscure emotional connection, Maggs leant down and kissed the top of Meredith's head. 'It was a while ago now,' she said.

They found a spot under a huge tree, spreading a cloth on the sparse grass and laying out a modest array of picnic food. Then Maggs looked at Olivia, with a mixture of pity and disgust.

'There's a message from John on Annie's phone,' she said. 'They'll have read it by now. I give them about half an hour to work out what that means. Perhaps you should call somebody to come and take charge of Simon. You won't want to take him with you where you're going, will you?'

Olivia went rigid. 'I didn't kill her,' she said, forcing the words through a tight jaw. 'I admit I was there. We were both early, because I wanted to have it out with her, before you arrived – to tell her she was ruining the lives of two little children, as well as mine and Mike's. But she just laughed and said everyone had a right to happiness, and the kids were too young to notice anything. Besides, she said, their fathers were hardly ever at home anyway.'

Maggs closed her eyes against the rage that swept through her. 'You hit her so hard it killed her. How could that have been unintentional?'

'I didn't hit her. It was that stone man.'

'What the hell do you mean?'

'A piece of stone fell off the roof and landed on her head. She was on the ground, because I'd pushed her over. I was trying to make her go away, before you got here. No way could I sit through a picnic with her, the little bitch. But I didn't kill her. If you told the police we arrived together and never saw Annie, that'd be an alibi for me.'

Maggs could hardly speak, but she choked out, 'I think you're lying. I'm certain you hit her and killed her.'

'But nobody can prove it, if I did.'

Thea made an instinctive move to cuddle Bethany,

as she struggled to understand what had been said. 'Oh, they'll prove it all right,' she said. 'And what'll happen to this little thing now? Not to mention your own little boy.'

Olivia looked at the child, then at the other two, her Simon and Maggs's Meredith. Finally she stared hard at Maggs. 'That's up to you, isn't it?' she said.

For two seconds, Maggs considered these words. If she did supply a false alibi, she would have to live with the consequences for ever. She could never tell Den about it. The police would question her inconsistent testimony.

'Sorry,' she said.

The Blockley Discovery

Blockley retained a special place in Thea's affections. Larger than most of the settlements she had found herself in, it had a more obvious sense of community and a more substantial population of permanent residents. When she and Hepzibah went back there on a misty November day, she felt surrounded by ghostly memories. Tragic things had happened there, as well as some amusing ones. The woods into which one end of the main street simply disappeared were dripping with moisture as well as shedding their colourful leaves. Underfoot it was slippery with them. Beyond the woods were innocent-looking fields that concealed a lost village, abandoned centuries ago and very nearly forgotten altogether. '"Though worlds of wanwood leafmeal lie,"' she muttered to herself. Over the past few weeks she had set herself the task of learning a new poem every few days and the current one was 'Spring and Fall' by Gerard Manley

Hopkins. The effort was considerable, making her fear for her long-term mental capacity, but she hoped the discipline would prove useful in delaying the decline. Drew had laughed at her. 'Poor old lady,' he said. 'Forty-six next birthday and already half demented.'

Drew himself was not quite forty, and this rankled more than it should.

'Let's go and have a look up there,' she said to the dog, who was running loose as usual. The easiest track through the woods began close to the end of the street, and they had automatically followed it, but then veered up a smaller pathway, leading steeply towards open fields. Other alternatives required a muddy scramble up through the trees and over a low stone wall. It all came back to her as she walked. Had Hepzie remembered it as well? She supposed not. The spaniel had been to very many places over the past three years or so.

They were getting tired, having walked all the way from Broad Campden – a distance of at least three miles. It had been a sudden impulse, born of feelings of restlessness and anxiety. Drew had been snappy over breakfast, culminating in a flash of sarcasm that had wounded her, even as she knew she deserved it. She'd been whining about having nothing to do and no money to go anywhere, when he said, 'No problem. Just go and dig two new graves for me, then. That should keep you occupied.' Being small and not especially good with a spade, she had rightly interpreted this as ill-tempered. Drew had more than enough to do that week, with two funerals, a talk and a trip down to Somerset to see Maggs all in his diary. His wife was left with a minuscule amount of paperwork and a couple of phone calls. She was obviously going to be bored, and it seemed quite acceptable for her to say so.

'Go for a walk, then,' he suggested, when she scorned the grave-digging remark.

'All right. I will. Come on, Heps.' And without another word, she had grabbed coat and boots and set out southwards with no clear destination in mind.

It was going to be a long slog home again, she realised now. First there would have to be a good rest in a pub, both for herself and the dog. Hepzie wasn't accustomed to route marches across fields and through woods, especially since they'd moved to the Cotswolds permanently. And certainly anything more than a mile or two was asking rather a lot. On the other hand, it was all good fun, with the cool breeze bringing so many interesting smells.

There was a decidedly interesting smell wafting Hepzie's way, as they climbed through the Blockley trees towards the sweeping fields that lay between them and the main road. She lifted her muzzle and had a good long sniff.

'If that's fox poo you're smelling, don't even think

about it,' said Thea. 'I warn you – you won't be allowed back in the house if you've rolled in it.'

They were soon in the field, where there was no hint of fox, sheep or cow. A few rabbits slipped out of sight, and birds swirled overhead, enjoying the wind, which was suddenly much stronger.

'Let's not go far,' said Thea, with a look at her watch. 'We might find somewhere to have coffee before long. Though they probably won't let you in,' she sighed.

The dog took no notice, but kept up her quest for the source of the scent she could still detect. She zigzagged ahead, nose to the ground, veering off towards a line of trees, which had perhaps once been a hedge. They had been left to attain some height, forming a windbreak, and offering a degree of shelter for any creature hoping to avoid heavy rain or snow. Thea followed, still hoping there were no fox droppings to be found. The stink that a single small dog could carry around for days after rolling in it was appalling. The European version of a skunk, Thea supposed. The only recourse was to give the dog a thorough bath, and nobody enjoyed that in the least.

She could see a small mound a few feet away from the line of trees. There were sticks on top of it, and lusher grass than elsewhere in the field grew around it. Hepzie was pawing at one edge of it. Thea went for a look, her mind still on baths and the long walk home.

'What is it?' she asked. 'I don't want to stay here for long. It's too windy.'

The spaniel pushed her muzzle into a hole she had made and began to tug something. As Thea bent down to pull the dog away, she caught sight of an incongruous piece of material. Thicker than a garment would be, unless it was a heavy winter coat, it had a straight edge and appeared to be a singularly unpleasant shade of green. 'What on earth is that?' she said again.

Hepzie continued to pull at an object from underneath the fabric, until she suddenly shot backwards with something dark and dirty in her mouth. She dropped it and sat down, panting. A very nasty smell was coming from somewhere close by.

'Somebody's buried a dead sheep here,' said Thea. 'Covered it with old carpet and a few sticks, and it's just sunk into the ground. They're not supposed to do that.'

The object was probably a decomposed ovine head or hip bone or something, and she was in no hurry to inspect it. But the dog was showing a renewed interest, and that could not be permitted. Thea kicked the find gently. 'It's a shoe,' she realised. 'A mouldy old shoe.'

Sheep did not wear shoes. It dawned on her that if you could successfully hide a dead sheep in this way, you could hide any sort of dead body. Unwelcome thoughts pushed their way to the surface. It was becoming increasingly clear that this was no sheep. It was a clever concealment of a dead human person.

There hadn't been any detectable smell, until Hepzie disturbed it and let the stink of rotting flesh escape. 'Trust you,' she accused the dog. 'This is exactly what we don't need.'

She felt tired just thinking about the next hours and days. Questions, emotions, explanations. She had her phone in her pocket and she supposed she could call authorities and direct them to the spot. Except, when she put her hands into first one pocket and then another, she realised she had brought a different coat, and not transferred anything from the previous day's jacket. Nor had she brought her bag. All she'd done was grab her purse from the hall table, attach a lead to Hepzie and set out, desperate to get away and give herself something to do.

Now there was too much to do, and not in a good way. When the thought intruded itself, she did not immediately push it away. *You could just turn round and forget the whole thing.* She could drag her dog back into the middle of Blockley, find coffee somewhere and walk home, steadfastly ignoring what the damn dog had unearthed.

Except of course she could not possibly do such a thing. As a house-sitter she just might have managed it – running away from a week or two's stay in someone else's house, burying the knowledge even more deeply than the dead person had been buried. But as the wife of a respectable funeral director, she absolutely could not. Drew, so decent and stalwart, would be appalled if he ever found out. He would never feel the same about her again. There would be a loss of trust, a loss of respect, that would eat away at their marriage until it fell apart. Even the fact of her hesitation would give Drew a few bad nights – if she ever admitted it to him.

She would not admit it, because it was only a moment's madness. She would have to find a phone, which might not be easy. She would be regarded as eccentric, at best, by anyone realising she was walking in woodlands without the ability to communicate with the wider world. Except there were still parts of the Cotswolds poorly provided with signals, so it was not sensible to depend on a phone, anyway. Batteries died, as well.

She walked briskly back down to the woods, stumbling over the small stones on the track that took her into the street lined by handsome houses. As she went, she rehearsed what she would say about her find. Except, there was almost nothing *to* say. A dead person, under a piece of old carpet, with grass growing over it, and some randomly placed sticks to make it look natural. A shoe that had somehow worked its way out, to be found by a passing spaniel. How many people went walking up there, at every season of the year? How many dogs? Why, then, did it have to be *her* dog and *her* accursed curiosity that uncovered the body?

She had to walk all the way to the big hotel before

she found any chance of a phone. She went into the bar with Hepzie on the lead, and abruptly demanded to use their phone. 'I need to speak to the police,' she said.

It was far from being the first time she had done this – there had been Hampnett and Snowshill, Lower Slaughter and Duntisbourne Abbots, and others, where she had been called upon to dial 999. Each time was different. Levels of efficiency and good sense at the other end varied greatly. Directions, explanations, the spelling of names and the strength of emotion were different every time. Here in Blockley – again – she felt more jaded and uncaring than she ever had before. The body was without a gender or a face or any human aspects. It was stinking and abandoned and not so very important to her. Perhaps a homeless man had somehow crawled under the old carpet beneath the trees and simply died there of natural causes.

'We don't allow dogs in the bar,' said a tall young woman.

Thea looked at her. 'Weren't you here two years ago?' Was it two – or three – since she'd spent time in a house just a short way along the street? 'Don't I remember you?'

'Only been here a few months, actually. You'll have to take the dog out.'

'No, I won't. I have to call the police. That's unless you want to do it instead. Tell them there's a dead body in the field above the woods. Been there quite a while from the smell of it.'

'What? You're joking, aren't you?'

'I wish I was. But not many people would find it funny, would they?'

'Why haven't you got a phone of your own?'

'I left it at home, which is three miles away. I went for a walk, with my dog. She found it, really.' She threw Hepzie a venomous look. 'It's all her fault.'

The woman gave up. 'Come on, then. Get it over with. But don't let them come here. It's got nothing to do with us.'

The phone call went averagely well. She was shown into a small office and left alone with her dog, for which she was grateful. She supposed the woman was spreading the news of her discovery to the rest of the staff, leading to a lot of questions and hypotheses and annoyances. Although she remembered that on her previous Blockley experience the locals showed a remarkable lack of concern, as if murder were simply too far off their radar to be taken seriously.

She was informed that it would be half an hour at least before anyone could be with her. It would be appreciated if she could stand somewhere visible, and lead the officers to the spot. Was she certain the person was actually dead?

'Definitely,' she said, trying to recall whether she had been asked this on previous occasions. In any case there had to be a police doctor to certify that life was extinct. The first responder on the phone mostly sent an ambulance for good measure. Sometimes it was used to convey the body to the mortuary, although more usually that was a task for a local undertaker, once authorised by the coroner. Thea did not believe that Drew would appreciate the work this time, even if he were to be asked. As an 'alternative' practitioner, he was not fully integrated into the system. Other funeral directors competed for the work, because the one who did the transporting nearly always ended up handling the funeral as well.

She had twenty minutes to kill, then. 'Can I have coffee here?' she asked the wary-looking barwoman.

'Only if you take the dog outside.'

This was a straw too far. Admittedly the spaniel had muddy feet, but the damage was already done. She was in all other respects a perfectly inoffensive animal, small and well behaved. 'That's so ridiculous,' she protested. 'What possible harm can she do? And don't you think this is a special situation? There's a dead person, a quarter of a mile away. Don't you *care*?'

'Some people are allergic.'

The sound Thea made was very like *Pshaw!* Allergies were self-indulgent and attention-seeking as far as she was concerned. Drew had attempted to persuade her otherwise, using his experience as a nurse for evidence, but she remained unconvinced. 'I know they *think* it's real,' she had agreed, reluctantly.

'And that makes it really real,' he told her. 'It's very

unfair to dismiss something that has its roots in the mind. In fact, it's pretty stupid, as well.'

This recent conversation had startled her. She had forgotten that living with somebody could be frightening at times. They crossed lines, understood more than was comfortable, and told you about yourself. You were always under scrutiny, and even a loving scrutiny like Drew's could be disconcerting. And yet he never let it turn bitter. She had been about to flash back with some criticism of his character, when he'd grinned and put his arm round her. 'Not to say that *you're* stupid, of course.'

'You did say that,' she muttered. 'Don't pretend you didn't.'

'Okay. Maybe I did. But only because I hoped it would make you think a bit. Sorry.'

The trouble was, he was always right. Drew Slocombe never seemed to suffer from the temptations to be bad that others did. She had never caught him in a lie, never seen him cut corners or overcharge a bereaved family. He never seemed in any moral doubt, and that made him a hard person to live up to.

'My little girl's allergic to animals, actually,' said the woman at the bar, very stiff and reproachful.

'Oh, God. Never mind, then. Come on, Heps.' It was obviously a day for walking off with her faithful friend on her lead, head held high and heart seething with complicated rage.

Outside it had turned grey, with a penetrating

wind suddenly blowing down from the higher levels. Blockley was deserted, with nowhere to sit and take refreshment with the dog at her side. There had been a tea shop on a corner, but at some point it had disappeared. There was another pub some distance away, which might well admit Hepzie, but might equally well be closed, or resistant to animals. There wasn't time to investigate, anyway.

The lack of a phone was suddenly a much bigger problem. She wanted to call Drew and tell him what had happened. She wanted to reassure herself that he was still interested, still available. She wanted to be told that he still loved her. *Don't be such a child*, she censured herself. They were *married*, for heaven's sake. There were always going to be rocky times, when life got in their way and everything felt sour. Yes – but not everybody went out and found a dead body in the middle of just such a time.

She crossed the road, for no good reason, finding herself face-to-face with one of the wooden doors covered with notices that she had observed on her first visit to Blockley. Clubs, meetings, items for sale – it had been an indication that here, unlike in much of the Cotswolds, people lived and congregated and pursued their interests. As a way of passing the time, she read them all carefully. Perhaps there'd be one about a missing person, leading effortlessly to the identification of the body in the field. There wasn't, of course. They were mostly Christmas bazaars, carol concerts and an art show. They put her in mind of Stanton, where she had been for the days before Christmas, a year or two ago.

And they made her think about the poor dead person she had found, in a makeshift grave, unmarked and abandoned. There were reasons why every burial had to be carefully recorded in perpetuity. Every life had a significance; a fact that had been evident from the earliest moments of human society. The point, as Drew had observed more than once, was that we would all be dead one day, and didn't we want our descendants to know where our final resting place was? We wanted to be taken seriously and recorded in the annals. In spite of her unusually close involvement with death, Thea had never looked at it quite like this before. Now she could see that there was something terrible about just leaving a dead person to rot anonymously, not even properly buried.

She wondered about the lack of reaction amongst the people at the hotel. Surely they must know by this time that something was happening. She tried to imagine herself in their place, and grasped, in a vague way, how it might be for them. A form of paralysis might well take over, in which any utterance or action could turn out to be wrong. In the unlikely but possible event that one of the staff had actually killed and concealed the person in the field, there would be the added effect of disabling fear and guilt. Once the body was given a name and back story, then the gossip and supposition would begin. And that might well be a long way in the future.

She drifted back towards the woods, the spaniel pulling gently, as if to question the snail's pace. 'You should be worn out by this time,' Thea said. 'We've been walking for ages.'

Apparently this was not the case. The dog showed every sign of eager energy, the closer they went to her fabulous find. Was it still there? Could she have another go at digging it out? Could she *please* savour that enchanting smell again? Such thoughts – if a dog could be said to have thoughts – were plainly being expressed. 'You're disgusting,' Thea told her. 'All dogs are disgusting. I don't know why we bother with you.' On the whole, Hepzie had been reasonably inoffensive throughout her life, but the occasional deposit on the living room floor of a stinking dead thing, plainly in the final stages of decomposition, showed that she had the same horrible instincts as all her fellow canines.

A police car found her with little difficulty. Two men followed her up the track and into the field. The wind had increased, bringing with it a few squally sheets of rain, just as they walked out into the open from under the trees. For the first time all month, it finally felt well and truly like November. Leaves were flying off the birches and willows that edged the field, and Thea wished she'd brought a coat with a hood.

'It's over there,' she pointed. 'The dog found it.' Hepzie was pulling harder on the lead, but Thea couldn't see the mound, or smell the rotting flesh.

'Lead the way,' invited one of the young policemen. He had ruddy cheeks and bright eyes. His colleague was taller and darker, hinting at North African heritage perhaps. Thea liked the look of him, wishing she could engage him in conversation.

She led the way, with heavy feet. The manifestation of another body was dispiriting. She felt haunted and somehow culpable. Almost cursed, with her repeated encounters with crime and violence. For the most part she had explained it to herself by the very fact of house-sitting. When people went away, the pattern changed, neighbours took advantage, grievances emerged. And a bored house-sitter was a dangerous thing. She had probed and questioned outrageously at times, discovering secrets and connections that had been unexamined for years.

This time, she had been an innocent walker, nothing further from her mind than the dead. At least, not the abandoned dead, to be found by her harmless dog. 'I was just out for a walk,' she said aloud to the policemen. They could not, of course, understand the sense of victimisation she was increasingly experiencing. It wasn't fair. She had not been inquisitive or intrusive.

'Mmhmm,' said the man. 'Is it much further?'

'No, not at all. Just here somewhere.' For a crazy moment she thought the whole thing might have been a dream, a hallucination, a figment of a fevered imagination. They ought to be able to see the shoe by now, at least. Then she saw a figure standing under the trees, only thirty yards away, watching their approach. 'Who's that?' she said.

'You might well ask,' said the taller policeman. 'Good morning, sir,' he added, raising his voice a little.

'What's all this?' demanded the man. 'What're you after, then?'

His accent was one that was rarely heard any more, specific to North Gloucestershire, more Bristol than Birmingham, but not very similar to either. He was wearing colourless clothing, grubby but not torn. Thea guessed that he was an employee of a much smarter and richer landowner.

'We had a report of . . . something suspicious up here,' said the ruddy-faced constable. Thea sympathised. What was he supposed to say? To what extent did they trust the word of a woman walking her dog, even if she was the notorious Thea Osborne (now Slocombe) who routinely found dead people? There had been no suggestion that these officers knew who she was, in any case.

'Suspicious?' repeated the man. 'What does that mean?'

'We have to search this area. This is it, right?' he turned enquiringly to Thea.

'More or less.' She scanned the ground. The sticks seemed to have gone and there was definitely no sign of a shoe. She stared accusingly at the nameless man. If he had been interfering with her find, why was he still there? Wouldn't the sensible thing have been to make tracks as fast as he could, and trust that Thea's dog would lose its sense of smell? 'You've moved it around,' she charged him. 'Haven't you?'

'Moved what? Dunno what you mean.'

Hepzie came to the rescue, nosing at and then lifting a clump of grass that proved to have been uprooted and placed over the edge of the old green carpet. She squeaked excitedly as the glorious scent of decomposition wafted free. 'There!' said Thea. 'That's it.'

'Oy! You can't go digging around like that,' said the countryman, half-heartedly.

'Too late,' said Thea. 'There it is, look. Under there.'

There was very little to see. The bright-eyed officer bent down, and gingerly gripped the carpet, lifting it an inch or two. 'What *is* this?' he wondered.

'No need to do that,' said the local man, with a grimace, half resignation, half irritation. 'I can tell you what's in there.'

The policeman paused, nose wrinkled at the smell. His colleague cleared his throat. 'Can't just take your word for it,' he said. 'Not now it's gone this far.' He flapped a hand at the other, urging him to carry on with what he was doing.

Obediently, the officer lifted the carpet another inch. Thea leant forward, seized by a strong sense of responsibility. This was all her doing, and the indications were already telling her that she might have done better to walk away, saying nothing. 'Oh, my God,' groaned the officer. 'That's a bone.'

'Don't disturb it any more, Bobby,' said his mate. 'It's a crime scene.'

'Don't be so bloody stupid,' snapped the watching man. 'Them's sheep bones, you fools.'

'Sheep?' The policemen blinked as if the man had said *dragons*. 'Did you say sheep?'

'But there was a shoe,' Thea protested. 'That's what made me call the police. There was a man's *shoe*.' She stared all around, hoping to find the vital piece of evidence.

'That were mine,' explained the man, with a rueful grin. 'Had a hole in the sole, plus it got muck all over it. Thought I may as well chuck it in with the ewes.'

'How many sheep?' asked the tall policeman.

'Two, that's all.'

'You are required by law to have them incinerated,' the other officer told him. 'As I suppose you know quite well.'

'Just doing as I'd been told,' mumbled the man. 'Don't you go trying to get me into trouble. It's the boss you want to talk to, lazy sod. Can't be arsed to get the tractor and link box down here to gather 'em up. Said they'd never get found up here, if they was covered well enough.' He gave Hepzie a poisonous glance. 'He's right, as well. Not a sniff from foxes or any other thing, till this'n came along. Saw it from two fields away and knew the game was up.'

'What're we going to do, then?' asked Constable Bobby. 'They'll be waiting for a report.' He tapped his belt, where a phone was dangling. 'Lady reported a dead body. It'll be flashing high alert all over the patch by now.'

'We have to check,' said the darker man. 'Can't just take his word for it.'

'Oughta call the boss, then. Should be a warrant thingy, seems to me,' insisted the civilian.

'Where is he, then? Who is he, your boss?'

'Big landowner. Graham Whitebush, his name is. Gone off to the Riviera for the winter. Does it every year. Leaves us with the work.'

'Are you his estate manager then?' asked Thea dubiously.

The man laughed scornfully. 'Me? Just the dogsbody, that's me. Manager's a bloke called Williams.'

'Can we call Mr Whitebush, then? And what's *your* name?' The question came several minutes later than it should have done, which they all realised at the same moment.

'Thought you'd never ask. It's Dave Carter. I can give you my address, if you like.'

Bobby walked around the gentle mound, bending to pick at it here and there. 'Done a good job,' he observed. 'Can't see the edges.' He looked at his partner. 'Stav? What should we do?'

The countryman was still talking. 'Took no time at all. Worst bit was carting the old mat up here. Daft, really. Might as well 'ave done it properly, seemed to me. It's not such a big job, calling the knacker.'

'What did they die of?' Thea asked suddenly. 'The sheep, I mean.'

'Told you – they just lay down and died. The winter was too much for them. Deficiency of some sort, most likely. They were big old girls, I can tell you that.'

'Not foot and mouth, then?' said Stav. What a relief, Thea thought, to have a name for *him* as well.

Dave Carter blanched, and almost crossed himself. 'Don't even think it,' he hissed. 'Besides, that doesn't kill 'em as a rule.'

Hepzie was plainly bored and frustrated. Kept away from the succulent corpses, she sat sulkily at her mistress's feet. 'Can we get on with it?' Thea asked rudely. 'I'm getting very wet.' The slight drizzle had begun to penetrate more than one layer of clothes.

'Whitebush?' Bobby's shoulders and spine suddenly straightened. 'Isn't that the name of the woman who went missing, earlier in the year?'

'What?' said Stav and Thea together.

Dave Carter took longer to react, and then slowly stepped backwards, until stopped by a tree. 'Oh, no,' he said. 'No, no, no. I put them here myself. Two old ewes, like I told you. Like the boss instructed. Mrs Whitebush went to the Philippines to save the orphans. She'd never liked it here. Complained the whole time. She's not *missing*. She just ran off.'

'Not according to her sister and daughter,' said Bobby. 'I spoke to the daughter. She was certain her mother was dead. Told quite a tale about the terrible time she was having with the husband.'

'Hysteria,' muttered Dave stubbornly.

But all four pairs of eyes were on the mound.

Bobby reached for his phone.

Ladies Who Lunch

Moreton-in-Marsh suffered perpetually from a ghostly *the*, missing from its name. Few people felt comfortable leaving it out, even while knowing it was right to do so. Some regarded it as a point of historical pride, an ancient usage that they might not manage to explain, but which was self-evidently significant.

Thea Slocombe sat at a small table in the pedestrianised area of the town and thought about it, in an idle sort of way. It was late September, sunny and mild. She was lunching in solitary splendour, having spent much of the morning running errands for Drew. She was officially a partner in his business, fully participating in the work of Peaceful Repose in various roles. One of these was to visit the dying and discuss with them the sort of funeral they desired. Most were in a hospice, but some were in their own homes and others in residential institutions. To date, she had interviewed seven such brave souls, her respect for them increasing exponentially. It took courage and a rather British sort of realism to confront the paradoxes that any funeral contained. The same questions repeatedly arose: who is a funeral really for? What is its central function? How can a life be most effectively concluded? The closer she came to such topics, the greater her understanding was of her husband the undertaker. He had spent much of his adult life at the heart of these enormous issues. It had made him a far more serious person than any she had ever met. The most prominent question this gave rise to was – did she really want to be quite so serious herself?

Hence the musing over the name of the little town. Was it even in a marsh anyway? Must have been, she guessed. It was on a junction of two prominent roads and still boasted a busy market once a week. It was unapologetically Cotswold in appearance, society and situation. Thea had once been something of a historian, and still found the past a source of fascination.

The cafe she was patronising offered quirky fare in the form of various baps, wraps and salads designed primarily for weight-conscious women with a healthy budget. She ordered a salad composed of exotic leaves, cheese and smoked meat that cost considerably more than she felt comfortable with. The Slocombe family were perpetually short of cash, with the funerals not only sporadic but low-cost. Profits were slender and attempts at 'diversification' limited. Drew acted as non-religious officiant at cremations, for which the fee was modest. He gave talks to groups and provided a prepayment scheme for funerals. Money trickled in, but they were depending alarmingly heavily on the proceeds from renting out Thea's house in Witney. 'It won't be nearly enough for us to live on,' she said, at least once a week.

Drew always replied, 'It won't have to be. The funerals are doing well, at least for now.'

True to the stereotype, there were a few nicely heeled women scattered around the shiny aluminium outdoor tables. Two of them, sitting at the same table, were tapping screens on little gadgets, which Thea supposed no longer qualified for the name of 'mobile'. They were multifunction computers, with Internet and apps. Not very convivial, she thought. Were they competing to be seen as important businesswomen or surrounded by adoring friends? Did they detest each other, therefore opting for any excuse to avoid conversation?

The cafe was popular, with all the outdoor tables occupied. Thea's was in the middle, which made her feel conspicuous. Eating alone was not a favourite activity with her, just as she disliked going into a pub by herself. She wished she had a book with her, or at least a newspaper. The food was slow in arriving, and all she could do was stare into space and let her thoughts run wild. There was some sort of movement at the table behind hers, the chair scraping on the ground and the soft *flump* of a bag tumbling over.

Then a strange hoarse barking rang out from the same direction, and she looked around for whatever great hound might be giving voice. There was no sign of a dog. Instead she saw a woman, who was also alone at her table, put down her fork and bend down to rummage in the bag that was sprawled untidily at her feet. She lifted it onto her lap, and produced a mobile phone. There had been no repetition of the barking.

At that point Thea realised how nosy she was being and turned back. She concentrated determinedly on a fingernail that was minimally ragged. Perhaps she had a file somewhere, and she carefully and vainly went through her own bag item by item, trying not to listen to the voice behind her, which had begun a one-sided conversation. The barking had been an especially ridiculous ringtone, then, and the woman was now speaking to someone not present. She used normal volume, with no trace of self-consciousness. How quickly it had become ubiquitous to talk to an invisible person while surrounded by three-dimensional living, breathing, listening others. It often seemed to Thea that she must be very peculiar to even notice it any more.

The positioning of the tables meant that the woman was slightly behind Thea's left shoulder. She could not look at her without being obvious. But something about the husky voice was familiar, making it impossible to resist taking another peek. The arrival of her salad gave her a useful cover for turning round, on the pretext of creating space for the waitress.

The second look revealed a thoroughly familiar woman of around sixty, middle height, substantial weight and regal manner. Her first name, Thea remembered effortlessly, was Thyrza. The surname, however, eluded her. More facts came to mind: the woman lived in Cranham and had given Thea some very direct comments about her life and character. *Thea*'s life and character, not her own. The barbs had rankled for months, and still had the power to cause discomfort.

She looked away quickly, hoping recognition had not been mutual. Thyrza must have been sitting there unnoticed, when Thea arrived. Her meal was more than half consumed. There was every chance that she had known who it was who had come to sit at the next table. But now their eyes had met, and surely, inescapably, the link must have been made. And yet, possibly not. That was another thing about people conducting conversations on their mobiles. You never knew how much of the actual world around them they were seeing or hearing. You wondered whether they'd duck if a stone was thrown at them, or whether they'd notice if their little child was wailing for attention. Mostly, Thea thought not. In her experience, wailing children were comprehensively ignored by mobile-addicted mothers.

'Good Lord,' the woman was saying – almost

shouting now. 'Use your initiative, why don't you? Nobody has to take that sort of thing any more. Tell him you won't stand for it. Tell him you'll leave if he does it again.'

Sounded like an abused wife lacking the energy to fight back, Thea concluded, suddenly reminded of her own sister Jocelyn, who had once been struck by her husband, before he was frightened into getting help and thereby saving the marriage. Thinking about Jocelyn diluted the loud half-conversation at the adjacent table, but it was impossible to avoid completely. Even the moments of silence, when the invisible person at the other end of the line must be speaking, gave space for all sorts of guesswork. More hypotheses came to mind – a bullied teenager, perhaps, or a disgruntled employee. Clues were in short supply – no name, no revealing epithets such as 'dear' or 'darling' to hint at the relationship.

Thyrza was not afraid to be heard. She never had been, Thea recalled, along with other memories. Her brief time in Cranham would have been unrelievedly unhappy, partly thanks to this woman, if it hadn't been for a surprise visit from Drew, whose sweet attentions had made everything else tolerable. Thyrza remained as a symbol of that time, with her accusations and painful insights.

'Well, you know what my advice is,' the voice continued. 'I don't know why you bother telling me about it if you're not going to listen to sense. What am I supposed to say? You poor thing, it must be awful.' She laughed. 'That's not going to happen, is it? Either you lie down and make the best of it, or you stand up and take control. Simple choice, to my way of thinking. You might think it's complicated, but it really isn't.'

A pause, in which Thea forced herself yet again to focus on her salad and try to plan her afternoon. Then, 'Well, that would be going too far. You would never get away with it . . . No, you wouldn't. The very fact that you're talking to me about it proves that.' The voice was considerably lower, and still dropping. Thea actually leant back an inch or two, the better to catch what was being said. 'You'd be the first person they'd look at, you idiot. And more than that – believe me when I say it isn't what you really want. Haven't you read Dostoyevsky?'

Had *anyone* read Dostoyevsky, Thea wondered with a grimace of sympathy for the wretched listener. Who evidently had not, because Thyrza went on, 'Well, you'd learn a lot if you did. We are all haunted and pursued by our own actions, believe me. They leave very deep wounds.' There followed a kind of clucking that hinted at impatience mixed with a growing alarm. 'Stop it, do you hear me? Stop that now. Get a hold of yourself.'

It was impossibly tantalising. There were surely many more interpretations than the obvious one, which nonetheless persisted. Perhaps they were rehearsing for a play, but who did that on the telephone? Might they even be discussing the disposal of a delinquent puppy? No, no. You didn't threaten to leave a puppy. But it just could be the threat of undergoing an abortion. That would just possibly fit, although again the leaving part was awkward. It would, though, be appropriately distressing, without actually breaking any laws. Thyrza might well be of the opinion that it was a major transgression, doomed to cause everlasting guilt. This effort to find an explanation was like a game of Tetris, making the shapes sit neatly together, twisting and turning them until they did.

Picking at the remnant of her lamb's lettuce, Thea persuaded herself that this was indeed the alarming act that was being contemplated. Getting away with it referred to the father of the foetus discovering the truth. Or maybe it was a puppy, after all. The husband loved and indulged it, thus making life intolerable for the complaining wife. She was going to kill it, somehow. And of course this was a very big step to take. You were not meant to bash any animal on the head and toss it into a pond, as she imagined the unknown person to be planning. That might well be a crime, both morally and actually. Although – had Thyrza used the word 'crime'? Thea thought not. It was all more subtle than that. And yet, it really did sound serious.

She was distracted from her theorising by fresh remarks, which did indeed continue to behave like

Tetris blocks, filling the picture more and more.

'Well, use your head, there's a good girl. There's a world of difference between standing up for yourself, and doing something you'll regret for ever. Go and have a coffee and get some perspective back. You know you can phone me any time.'

A silence followed, in which Thea drained her elderflower pressé and kept her face averted. Now she had the gender of the listener established, her concerns grew more solid. Surely it could not possibly be as it sounded, because that would mean there was a woman on the brink of murdering her abusive husband, regardless of what her sensible friend was telling her. She had a peripheral awareness of somebody close by paying more than usual attention to events going on beside her table. Thea raised her head and met the gaze of an elderly lady with sharp brown eyes and the hint of a smile. *An ally*, Thea thought, without understanding why she might need such a person.

It then became apparent that her attempts at hiding her face had been in vain. 'Don't I know you?' came the first woman's voice, barely a foot from her ear.

Thea turned slowly, unsure whether to be offended that she was not better remembered, or relieved.

The woman went on, 'I can't quite remember . . . oh, yes! How stupid of me.'

'We only met once or twice,' said Thea.

'More than that, surely. Still doing the house-sitting,

are you?' There was a nasty twist to her mouth as she said it, conveying scorn and distaste.

'Actually, no, not any more. The last one was a while ago now, in Chedworth.' She tried to sound casual, matter-of-fact, but it wasn't convincing in her own ears. Chedworth had not ended any more happily than most of her other commissions.

'So what brings you to Moreton? If I might ask.' Again the snide undertone, the implication that Thea was due some sort of chastisement. She remembered Thyrza's indignation at Thea's habit of asking such questions of people she hardly knew, and wondered if this was a deliberate payback.

'Nothing in particular. I was in the area, feeling hungry, and I found a parking spot right outside, so I decided to stop for lunch.'

'Hmm.'

'I've finished, anyway. I'd better be going.'

'Not going to ask me why *I'm* here, then? After all, it's quite a way from Cranham. And as you know, that's where I live.'

'None of my business,' said Thea lightly. She was tempted to say something about the careless ease with which people used phones in public, heedless of who was listening. She wanted to hit back at Thyrza's earlier imputations of intrusion and impertinence, with an accusation of rudeness. She could see the old lady, two tables away, making no attempt to conceal her interest in the scene. *Loosen up*, she told herself.

This is how things are now. Stop being so reactionary.
If old ladies were happy with the ways of the modern
world, why couldn't she be as well?

'So true,' said Thyrza, watching her face. 'But
minding your own business never was your strong
point, was it?'

She was having a politely vicious fight in a quiet
little Cotswold cafe for no reason at all. It was almost
a rerun of a similar fight they'd had in Cranham. Was
it unfinished business for Thyrza? Had she, Thea, done
something unforgivable that warranted this attack?
Perhaps she had – she did remember a feeling of shame at
the extreme curiosity she had shown, the rude questions
she had asked, the burning need to make people admit
to what they had done. Looking back, she could hardly
remember what had happened, and how all the people
were linked together. An old man had died, and for a
short time nobody had seemed unduly upset. Perhaps
when they eventually did become distressed, they
concluded that it was all Thea Osborne's fault.

And then she thought of the phone call and much
became clear. This subtle attack was a deliberate
distraction from the strange conversation she had
heard. She was not meant to pursue it; not meant
to ask, 'Who were you speaking to, and what is she
planning to do?'

Instead she said, 'That's a very odd ringtone you
have on your phone. It's not your son's dog, is it? I
remember he had a poodle.'

Thyrza grimaced. 'It's idiotic, isn't it? Philippe gave me his old phone, which had that thing on it. I have no idea how to change it.'

Suddenly the woman was human again. Thea laughed in spite of herself.

Thyrza went on, 'Don't you feel we're completely dominated by all this technology? They know so much about you, where you are, who you're talking to. And yet, it's so useful. How did we ever manage without it?'

'It's nice to see you again,' Thea ventured, not at all sincerely. She hadn't liked the woman when she'd met her before, and very little had happened in the past ten minutes to alter that. 'It seems a long time ago. How is everybody now?'

'We survived. Most of us, anyhow.'

It was impossible to directly raise the subject of the phone call. Who, what, why? Was somebody really planning to commit murder? The answers, if there were any, would hardly be true. 'I suppose there must be lasting damage,' she said woodenly.

'Indeed.' Thyrza picked up her phone and dropped it back into her bag. 'Well, I suppose I should get moving. Things to do, people to see.' It was a clumsy quote, followed by a faint smile. 'As they say,' she added. 'I don't expect I'll see you again.'

'You might,' said Thea. 'I live here now. Well – not *here*, but in Broad Campden. It's not far away.'

'Oh?'

She knew, thought Thea in a flash. The syllable

had been uttered in quite the wrong tone, with no surprise in it, no sense of accepting fresh information and tucking it away. Again she recalled the exchange in Cranham, where it became evident that Thyrza had a comprehensive knowledge of Thea's movements, reputation and character. Now she knew that the Slocombe family had opened for business in Broad Campden. Of course she did. It had been front-page news in the area. They had gone overboard on advertising and publicity. So, some kind of game was being played, here in Moreton. Something malicious and threatening was going on. Had the call from the unhappy wife been part of it, or an annoying interruption? Thyrza hadn't sounded annoyed. She had, if anything, revelled in the opportunity to give loud advice. Too loud, Thea now suspected.

'Who were you speaking to just now?' she asked, throwing manners to the wind. 'You obviously want me to ask about it.'

'Obviously?' The woman tilted her head, conveying an air of complacent superior knowledge. 'I haven't the least intention of answering such a question. Goodbye, Mrs Osborne. Sorry – that's changed, hasn't it? I'm afraid I didn't catch your new name.'

'Slocombe.'

'Oh, yes. Well, I'm sure I'll see you again.' There was a look on her face that seemed to be saying something more, along the lines of *I am determined that we will meet again.*

'I'm easy to find, anyway,' said Thea. 'Broad Campden. There's usually a hearse outside the house.'

It was all fizzling out, anyway. The waitress had come back to remove her plate and suggest a pudding. Thyrza's table had been cleared and the bill was awaiting her attention. Time was going by and Thea had somewhere to be. Nobody was killing anybody. It was all smoke and mirrors and a pathetic attempt at a practical joke, obviously aimed at Thea herself. Even the old lady had started to read a paperback, and seemed no longer to be interested.

She left Moreton feeling puzzled and slightly victimised. Thyrza did not like her, and yet she really did seem to want to see her again. The phone conversation might have been conducted loudly and publicly, but it had not been initiated by her, which gave it authenticity. Something sinister was definitely going on.

When she got home she poured it all out to Drew, who was duly attentive and intrigued and mildly annoyed on her behalf. He made her repeat as much of the conversation as she could recall.

'I can't see any innocent explanation,' he concluded.

They puzzled away at it for the rest of the day and into the evening, in between producing a family meal and listening to Stephanie and Timmy reporting the events of their day at school. The change of schools had been a trial for them both in different ways. Timmy was susceptible to teasing on the grounds of being the son of an undertaker. Stephanie had developed a precocious class consciousness and was scathing about the offspring of film directors and horse trainers who shared the classroom with her. It was a thriving school with wondrous results, making it attractive to Cotswolds-dwellers who might otherwise have paid for private education. The children wore expensive clothes and signed up for adventurous excursions that Drew found it impossible to afford. Rather than experiencing this inequality as an embarrassment, Stephanie had chosen to see it as an illustration of cultural dysfunction, flaunting her poverty with pride. 'They'd have no idea how to survive in a holocaust,' she said.

Drew and Thea smiled at her fondly, and agreed with every word.

'She knew who you were, right from the start,' Drew picked up the Thyrza discussion over the washing-up. 'So she would know you'd react to what she was saying on the phone. What did she expect you to do about it, I wonder?'

'Nothing, surely? What on earth *could* I do?'

'She might have been trying to alert you to something that's going on. I mean – are you certain she really dislikes you? I didn't pick that up at the time.'

'You weren't really there. The whole family found me extremely annoying.'

'But they respected you at the end. They must have done. They'll have followed your movements since then, with Stanton and Snowshill and all the rest, and read about us settling here. They probably see you as a solution to all sorts of problems.'

'I don't see how,' she said.

'You're not seeing much, are you?' he reproached her. 'I don't think you're even trying.'

'I'm too furious. She was pretty nasty. You should have seen the look on her face. Although she was quite friendly at times, as well. It was all very confusing.'

'Hmm,' said Drew, and shook dishwater from his hands. 'I haven't finished thinking about it, all the same.'

The children went to bed and the TV was switched on, and still Drew was on the case. 'It seems such a coincidence that you were both there at the same time.'

'She couldn't have known I was going to come and sit at the next table. Even if she'd been following me before that – and I can't believe she was – that couldn't have been planned.'

'Okay. So she thought quickly when she realised it was you. Maybe she did somehow initiate the phone call, with a signal you missed. After all, she was there first, and you didn't notice her for a while. Let's say she needed you for something. That's my best guess. She dragged you in, knowing you'd be intrigued. There's a connection with crime, you being famously nosy, all the stuff that happened in Cranham. She wants you to do something.'

'Like call the police and tell them some nameless female is planning to kill a man?'

'Exactly. She knows they'd listen to you, when they'd just laugh at anybody else.'

'They'd laugh at me as well. Even if they did listen, there's nothing to go on.'

'Let me think a bit more,' he said, and was quiet until bedtime.

In bed, he summarised his thinking. 'What if the police did take you seriously, and went to Thyrza and asked to examine her phone? The number she was talking to would probably be in there. You can give them the time, more or less exactly.'

'And where would that get them? Why not just ask her outright who she was talking to and what it was all about?'

He tutted. 'Far too simple. They have to have hard evidence.'

'Of what?'

'At the very least, that she was getting at you personally. You could accuse her of harassment.'

'Don't be silly.'

'You're right,' he apologised. 'I got carried away. But it's a nice little puzzle, just the same.'

Next day, Thea paid more than usual attention to the local radio station, half expecting to hear a report of a murdered man and missing wife, suspected of the killing. But there was nothing of the sort. She went over and over the conversation obsessively, trying to find any thread of logical elucidation that she and Drew might have missed. She tried to tell herself that such conversations were overheard every day and nobody worried about them. Then she decided that the whole thing was probably unreal anyhow, and that Thyrza might have been talking to herself, loudly attracting attention for some insane purpose that would be for ever obscure. Drew's idea of getting the police to examine the phone gained in appeal, while at the same time being clearly impossible. Even so, the image of Detective Inspector Jeremy Higgins hovered at the edge of her mind's eye. He was a patient man, benign and approachable. He trusted Thea's judgement, most of the time, despite a few unfortunate exceptions in Stanton.

If she called him, he probably would at least listen.

But then she had a visitor. A small white car pulled up outside the house, catching Thea's eye through the living-room window, where she was standing at the ironing board, dealing with an overdue pile of school shirts. Ironing the clothes of Drew's children was a task she had failed to anticipate when she married him. He had readily assumed that he would do it himself, but Thea had, with absolute sincerity, assured him that it was something she would enjoy. Women, she had noticed, fell into two groups when it came to ironing. They either loved or loathed it. She was in the former group, savouring the hot smell and crisp results. Stephanie and Timmy were the proud wearers of the best-ironed shirts in the school.

Somebody wanting to arrange a funeral, she supposed, although it was almost unheard of for such a person to turn up unannounced. Perhaps they just wanted to make preliminary enquiries, which she could handle quite easily, after the few months of training she'd received.

But then she recognised the elderly woman emerging from the car.

Thea was at the door first, holding it open, her eyes wide with curiosity. 'How did you find me?' she asked. 'You never even heard my name.'

'Mrs Hastings sent me. That is, she told me your name and where you live, and I took it from there.'

Hastings! Aha! 'Why?' she said, completely at a loss.

'You caught her making that phone call yesterday. That wasn't supposed to happen.' The old lady smiled. 'Let's start again, shall we? My name is Doreen. I live in Moreton. I first met Mrs Hastings six months ago, through my daughter.'

'Wait a minute. Come in and have coffee or something. It's so nice of you to take the trouble to come and explain. I've been going mad trying to make sense of it all.'

'It's not nice of me at all.' Suddenly the visitor's expression was much less friendly. 'It's purely self-interest, I assure you.'

'Oh?'

'I need you to be a witness, when I contact the police.'

Thea sat down at the untidy kitchen table, where she had gone to make coffee. Doreen had followed her, and was standing in the doorway. 'So there *is* a murder being planned,' said Thea.

'That's what I'm still trying to discover.'

'Wait,' begged Thea. 'I'm completely lost.'

'I really wish I didn't have to tell you. Can I sit down?'

Thea waved at a chair, and half-heartedly pushed some papers and magazines aside. 'Of course,' she said.

'Make the coffee, love, and I'll see if I can explain. Mrs Hastings has behaved very badly, I can tell you.'

'She never did like me much, but I always thought she was decent enough.'

Two mugs of instant coffee were produced, plus a tin of rather dull biscuits.

'Is that so?' said Doreen.

'Didn't she tell you? She must have said something when she told you who I was.'

The woman flushed. 'Well, I fibbed about that,' she admitted. 'It wasn't her who gave me your name – I heard enough in Moreton for me to track you down. Alternative undertakers are fairly thin on the ground. You've got a strong Internet profile, too. You and your dog. There are pictures of her on a number of websites.'

'Heaven help us.' The local press had included Hepzie in some of their reports, including photographs.

'So, *please* explain. I'm dying to know what it was all about.'

'She robbed me,' came the stark reply. 'She stole from me when I invited her into my home.'

'Gosh!'

'You might well say "Gosh". She'd been sent by my daughter because we thought she might have some assistance to offer me. As it turned out, all she did was to steal from me.'

'I don't remember what she does for a living. I'm not sure I ever knew.'

'Among other things, she's a valuer for an auction house.'

'Is she? I didn't know that.'

'Well, the thing is, I was hoping you could arrange to meet her again, somewhere public, just for a chat. She did sound as if she'd welcome the chance, after all.'

'She did,' Thea agreed. 'Although I have no idea why.' She frowned. 'There are two completely different things going on here, it seems to me. That girl on the phone, and your grievance against her for robbing you. Is there any connection?'

'I think there might be. Let me explain.'

Thea listened in rapt fascination.

With Doreen's help, Thea made an arrangement to meet Thyrza again, in Chipping Camden. It was a lot further from Cranham than Moreton was, but the woman made no objection. The day was dry, and they sat outside in the garden of the Eight Bells. 'Expensive,' groaned Drew, when she told him. But it turned out not to be as bad as feared. The building itself was as lovely as any other ancient Cotswold hostelry. Thea knew she would never tire of them.

Doreen was sitting inside, close to a window that looked out on the garden. 'How come she didn't recognise you in Moreton?' Thea suddenly wondered.

'She's only seen me once, and I made a few changes,' was the reply. It was increasingly clear that there was more to this woman than first appeared.

Thryza was prompt and lunch was ordered. She settled comfortably on the outdoor wooden seat, bag on her lap. Thea tried to broach the subject of the overheard conversation in Moreton. 'I haven't been able to get it out of my mind,' she said. 'I absolutely have to know what happened next. Was it as drastic as it sounded?'

The woman smiled broadly. 'I *knew* it would hook you,' she gloated.

'You were right. So . . . ?'

'So I'm afraid I can't tell you. It's all very confidential.'

'How can it be, when you were practically shouting down the phone in front of all those people?'

'People who had no idea who I was, or who I was talking to.'

'Except me.'

'Exactly. Except you.' The smile grew even broader.

Thea was sitting across the table, leaning forward eagerly. 'Have you spoken to her again? Whoever she was.'

'I can't tell you that, either.'

As instructed by Doreen, Thea made a sudden grab for the bag on Thyrza's lap. It was a long way to reach and her grasp was shaky. But she succeeded in overturning the thing, so that several items spilt out onto the ground.

Thyrza grabbed fruitlessly at the tumbling contents, while Thea, leaning down to intercept as much as she could, caught an odd cylindrical object, covered with printed paper and quite heavy in her hand. She tilted it curiously and it emitted the same gruff bark that had first alerted her to Thyrza's presence at the Moreton cafe. She tilted it again, and it made the same sound. It was a toy of some kind, the picture on the outside that of a large brown dog with its mouth wide open.

She blinked, her mind stuck in thoughts of old-fashioned toys. Thyrza, with a sound like a hiss, reached out and snatched it from her. Thea looked into her face, and caught a flash of alarm. The expression then quickly changed to one that was half amused, half wary. 'Thank you,' she said. 'It belongs to my granddaughter.' She returned to gathering her scattered possessions.

When Thea's thoughts finally began to fire up, they were to confirm the theory propounded by Doreen.

'You've been playing with me,' she accused loudly.

Thyrza said nothing, still crouching under the table

and refilling her bag. Mobile phone, pack of tissues, purse, keys – the usual stuff. Thea waited impatiently. Finally, the woman straightened, again clutching the bag to her chest.

'That wasn't the ringtone on your phone, was it? It was this toy.' She waved the object under the woman's nose. 'So what on earth was going on?'

'Revenge,' said Thyrza. 'When I saw you arrive at the cafe last week, I just couldn't resist it. I wanted to teach you a lesson.'

'It was clever,' Thea acknowledged. 'But pretty childish. And I'm afraid it's going to rebound on you in the long run.'

She beckoned to the watching Doreen, who was at their table in seconds. She took hold of the barking toy that was still in view. 'Oh!' she said. 'I had one just like this, as a child.'

Thyrza gave her a sharp look, evidently realising who this sudden interloper was. 'It's you,' she said.

'I'm afraid it is. And I am surprised you were such a fool as to carry this around with you, once you'd stolen it from me. You used it in public to deceive this poor young lady.'

'You were there?'

'Unluckily for you, I was. But it was no coincidence. Having nothing better to do, I followed you that day. It wasn't the first time. I had a feeling I might catch you out eventually.'

'Hang on,' said Thea. Doreen had told her only the

barest facts, enough to convince her to arrange this lunch. Several details were still obscure. 'You were *following* her?'

'Didn't I tell you? But I had no idea she'd got one of my most precious possessions in her bag.'

'But you did think she might incriminate herself somehow?'

'Not even that, really. I don't really know *what* I was doing. Possibly preventing her from robbing anybody else.' She looked almost benignly at Thyrza. 'I have read *Crime and Punishment*, you'll be pleased to hear.'

What an adorable old lady, thought Thea.

It was all determinedly civilised. There was no sense of danger, no hint that anybody would behave with violence here at the respectable Cotswold pub. And that made it unreal. Thea had in recent years witnessed the worst of criminal acts – or at least their consequences. She had cradled a dead child in her arms and been terrified more than once. This was nothing – a silly game played by a woman with a grudge.

'Well, please yourself,' she said. 'I've had enough of this. Whatever you meant to do to me hasn't worked. It's all too convoluted for my simple brain. Thanks for the diversion, but I'd like to finish my lunch in peace from here on.'

Thyrza narrowed her eyes. 'Hoity-toity,' she said.

The elderly Doreen made a clucking sound of disapproval. 'You have been a very wicked woman,' she accused. 'Not just stealing valuable antiques, but teasing this harmless young person.'

Thea laughed at that, despite a certain turbulence in her insides. Thyrza had gone to considerable trouble to upset her, after all – and it had worked. The fictitious telephone conversation had occupied her thoughts for far too many days.

'A wicked woman, indeed,' she said. 'You deserve to be prosecuted.'

But Doreen was apparently of a different opinion. 'I'm just glad to get this back,' she said. 'As far as I'm concerned, we can just leave it at that.'

And Thea could hardly argue with her.

Humiliation

Thea had not anticipated the extent to which her social life would expand once she was living permanently in the Cotswolds. People made contact – people she had met so fleetingly during a house-sit in one or other of the small villages that she had quite forgotten them. Others came with painful or embarrassing associations. One or two had been strongly suspected of having committed murder. They phoned and emailed, and even showed up at the house. The establishment of a new natural burial service in Broad Campden had received a lot of publicity in the local media, making the Slocombes all too easy to find. Their new home was on the northernmost edge of the region, making places like Minchinhampton and Painswick seem a long way off. And yet here was a barely remembered voice from that area, phoning to invite her to lunch.

'You've probably forgotten me,' came the undisguisable London tones, with a metallic ring to them. 'Valerie Innes, from Frampton Mansell.'

'Oh.' Frampton Mansell, where Thea's sister Jocelyn had joined her and a boy had been killed, and people had felt strongly about the abandoned canal. 'Yes. Goodness me, that seems a long time ago.'

'It is, I suppose. A lot has happened, anyway. I read about your new venture. I have to tell you, I most heartily approve.'

'Oh,' said Thea again. 'Good.'

'So, listen. Would you like to come over for lunch one day? Is Friday any good for you? It'd be nice to talk over the old times, and now you're living here permanently, I thought we might see something of each other. What d'you think?'

'I . . .' Had she *ever* regarded this woman as any sort of friend? If so, she could not recall it. She had felt no inclination to send a card at Christmas or exchange emails or establish some sort of Facebook connection. As far as she could remember, she had rather disliked Valerie Innes.

'I was hoping to talk something over with you, actually. The thing is, I thought you'd be able to give me some advice. I remember how cool and objective you were when there was all that trouble. I don't want to sound mysterious, but it does need something more than a phone call.'

Must be a funeral, Thea supposed. A tentative exploration into what the burial ground could offer. Probably for an aged parent, given the woman's age.

'All right,' she said, trying to sound accommodating. 'I mean, yes, Friday looks more or less free. I'm not sure what Drew's doing, though. I might have to be back for when the kids come in from school.'

'Kids?'

'Yes, Stephanie and Timmy. They're going to school in Chipping Campden now, and we've managed to get them onto the bus. But someone has to be here when they get home. They're still very young.'

'Well, come about twelve. Do you remember where I live?'

'Not exactly.'

Valerie Innes explained, and Thea made a few notes. *Cool and objective* was still ringing in her ears. She'd thought herself to be almost hysterical at times during that particular adventure. Not to mention losing her heart to the detective conducting the investigations. There had been nothing at all cool about that.

She made no mention of the appointment to Drew. Partly, it slipped a long way down her list of priorities almost as soon as she put the phone down, and partly she hoped to surprise him with new business. Her role in the operation was still far from well defined, and there were times when she felt more of a dead weight than an active participant.

The entry in her diary ensured that she was prompt when Friday arrived. Driving into Frampton Mansell again was a strange experience. She even passed the property that she had taken charge of for a week or so, although everything there had changed in the past few years. One of the barns had been demolished, and where there had been a paddock full of poultry, with a small pond for the ducks, now there was a paved area with young trees encircling it. Thea stopped the car for a closer look, remembering moments of high emotion that had occurred on this very spot. Not a hint of them now, of course. New people, new lifestyle, and not a trace of the family that had lived there before.

Valerie's house was close by – a beautiful, large stone house set on rising ground – but was not at all familiar. The details of all that had taken place between them had become hazy over time, with so many subsequent dramas pushing it to the back of her mind. She had no idea of the impression she might have left on the woman, causing her to renew the contact now.

The door was opened with considerable energy, moments after her knock. 'Good timing!' Valerie congratulated her. 'Your hair's different, but I'd have known you anywhere.'

'You too,' lied Thea. She found she could hardly remember Mrs Innes at all. She was the mother of three sons and had a loud voice. Nothing else came to her.

'Have a drink. Gin. Martini. I might even have some sherry. Take your pick.'

'Better not,' said Thea, thinking of her driving licence. She looked around the house, wondering what had become of the husband she was sure she remembered. 'Is your husband here? I'm afraid I've forgotten his name.'

'We split up. Actually, it was falling apart before all that trouble. We were just waiting for the right moment.' Her voice had a choked quality that cast doubt on the airy words.

'I'm sorry. Have you got anyone here now? What about your boys?'

'They all moved out. It was horrible. Within three months the whole family had dispersed. I'm rattling around on my own, and I hate it.' She shivered. 'I'm one of those people who has to be with somebody – you know? Someone to greet me in the morning.'

'Get a dog,' Thea said thoughtlessly. 'They're great for greeting.'

'I loathe dogs. They smell and they chew things. We did have a cat, if you remember . . .'

Oh yes, Thea did remember the cat. A Siamese that shared its favours amongst various village residents. 'Jeremy was upset when it died,' she said. 'But it wasn't really yours, was it?'

'Never mind the cat,' snapped Valerie impatiently and slightly confusingly. 'I didn't ask you here to talk about that. It's *people* I'm concerned with.'

Thea waited, wishing she had been offered a soft

drink or a bowl of nuts. She had nothing to do with her hands, and there was some awkwardness developing between the two of them.

'Sorry. I'm not making much sense, I know. Let me go and dress the salad and we can talk over the meal. It's nothing special, but I love having somebody to eat with me. I'm really grateful to you for coming.'

Again, Thea just smiled and said nothing. It was beginning to look as if she'd been wrong in assuming there might be a funeral in the offing. It felt more as if she'd been some distance down a list of possible confidants for a woman who struck her as rather low on friends. There was to be an outpouring of some sort by a lonely individual badly in need of advice.

Flickering memories of the time in Frampton Mansell were returning: the conflict over plans to restore the abandoned canal; her sister Jocelyn's presence; a woman called Cecilia and another called Fran – or something like that. It had been horrible at times. Worse than that – much of it had been frightening and upsetting. But mostly she remembered Phil Hollis and how sweet she had thought him in those early days.

Valerie had only been in the kitchen a minute or two before she called, 'Will you come through now? It's all ready.'

'That was quick,' she said, following the call. A spread including smoked salmon, French bread, a perfectly arranged salad with slices of avocado, olives and cucumber, was laid out on the big table.

'I hope you're okay eating in here? The dining room's a bit formal. I hardly ever use it now. It'll be dusty, probably, as well.'

'It looks fantastic.' Thea found she was actually salivating at the sight of the food. It would have graced a professional cookbook with no difficulty.

'It's therapy for me. I enjoy it enormously.'

'Well, I'm honoured. I don't often get anything like this.' Snatched makeshift meals were the norm in the Slocombe household, with Drew often called to the phone, the children wanting to be somewhere else and Thea ashamed of her poor cooking skills.

They each loaded a plate and began to eat. Then Valerie asked, 'So what went wrong between you and the police detective, then?'

The question shouldn't have come as a surprise. Hadn't she been full of thoughts about Phil already? And yet it was so far from what she had expected that she was paralysed for a moment, in mid chew. 'Oh! It's hard to explain,' she managed. It occurred to her that she had never precisely summarised it for herself. She felt a degree of shame at the way she had behaved, along with relief that Drew had come along to teach her how a relationship could flourish in the right conditions. 'We never properly understood each other, I suppose,' she said. 'And I didn't know what I wanted. It was probably too soon after my husband's death.'

She noticed that Valerie had an avid, almost hungry look on her face, as if her words were of immense importance. 'And you do know now? What you want, I mean.'

'It's different.' She was not going to be drawn into talking about her new marriage. The way women habitually disclosed intimate details to each other had always repelled her. 'Why do you want to know?'

'I'm sorry. It must seem a bit odd. It's just that you always seemed so sure of yourself, and clever at getting out of corners.' She must have caught sight of the alarm on Thea's face. 'Don't worry – I'm not asking for advice. Not really. I know what I have to do.' Tears began to gather, which only increased the apprehension that Thea was feeling. 'I've been trying to come to terms with it for six months now, you see. And it doesn't get easier. Not much, anyway.'

'Did somebody die?' Why else would this conversation be happening?

'No, no. Although it did feel like that. I've been grieving as if he'd died, I suppose.'

'He?'

'His name's Paul. He lived here with me for over a year, after my marriage ended. It was wonderful. We were so happy. So in love. I never knew it could be like that.'

'He greeted you every morning.' She was unable to conceal the hint of scepticism. There was something uncomfortable about a woman in her fifties talking about being in love.

Valerie laughed. 'The mornings were glorious,' she claimed. 'He was always in such a wonderful mood, first thing.'

'Incredible,' Thea murmured. And obviously, it must have been incredible – or at least unsustainable – because Paul had gone, for whatever reason. She loaded her fork with salmon and waited for the sad story to come. How had she walked into this, she wondered. Wasn't she well known for the difficulty she had when it came to showing proper sympathy? Well, no, she supposed there was no way Valerie could know this about her. Something was being asked of her, and she ought to earn this lavish lunch by providing it.

'He was so sweet. But that wasn't the whole story.' Valerie's mouth drooped, but the tears had drained away, to Thea's relief. In the months with Drew, she had been cried on by people in the most extreme distress. People who had been widowed, or lost a beloved parent. And Drew had persuaded her that sympathy was not what they wanted from her. Simple acceptance was more than enough.

'Whatever you do, don't tell them it'll all be okay,' he warned her. 'Because it won't.'

At first she had been nervous of this approach, but it had worked miraculously well. The sense of liberation had overflowed onto the mourners, who had found themselves able not only to voice their sadness, but also to admit to relief and even occasional gladness. Not every death was a tragedy, Thea discovered.

But Valerie Innes was laying claim to some quite other kind of attention. 'Oh?' said Thea faintly. 'What happened?'

'It was just as if he was two different people. One was so loving and kind; the other was a real mess. That side of him made him tell lies to me. You see, he was starting up a new business . . .'

Uh-oh, thought Thea. *Here it comes.* She could predict the next part of the story, simply by a casual acquaintance with the many documentaries, consumer programmes, stories, plays that repeated it endlessly, with only minor variations.

'He swindled you,' she said.

'No, no. I wouldn't put it like that. He didn't mean to hurt me. He always believed it was money well invested. But everything went wrong and he didn't dare admit to me how badly it was going. In the end, of course, he had to. I didn't have a penny left to give him. I'm going to have to sell this house and find a full-time job. At my age!' The tears returned, and a few slid down her face.

'Where is he now?'

'Oxford. He's got some work and a tiny little flat in Headington. I still speak to him. But I couldn't go on living with him, could I? Not after that.'

'You should have put the police onto him,' said

Thea. 'He must have taken you for a soft touch, right from the start.'

'How can you *say* that?' Rage erupted without warning. Valerie dropped her fork and pushed back her chair. 'You don't have any *idea* what he's like.' Both hands were shaking, and her lips were drawn back in a snarl.

'You're right,' said Thea, certain for a second that she was about to be slapped or pushed backwards onto the floor. She put up her own hands as a defence. 'Of course you're right,' she repeated cravenly. 'I didn't mean it. Calm down, for heaven's sake.'

The woman stood there, breathing heavily. Then, 'Sorry,' she said. 'You caught me on a raw nerve. Nobody else has said anything like that. If you knew him, you'd understand it wasn't done deliberately. He's just unlucky, that's all.'

'Okay.' Irritation was simmering inside her now. Why was she here in the first place? What purpose was she supposed to be serving? She took a bite of bread and a sip of the apple juice that had appeared in a glass jug. 'So what happens now?'

'What do you mean?'

'Selling the house. Getting a job. Have you got any plans?'

'Not really. We bought this when I was pregnant with Jeremy. Twenty-two years ago. It's awful to think of starting again in a new place.'

'But it is yours, is it? I mean, what about your husband? Doesn't he get a share?'

'That's the problem. I have to split it with him if I sell. It'll leave me with enough for some hovel in Cirencester or Gloucester with no garden or garage.'

'That's dreadful.' Finally Thea experienced a genuine pang of sympathy. The current house had a large garden and handsome double garage. 'Although Cirencester's not so bad.' She realised that Valerie was still defending the rotten Paul, despite the catastrophic effect he'd had on her life. 'The people there are really nice.'

'I'm sure they are.' The tone was bitter. 'I'm sure I'll be a great success on the checkout at Tesco, as well.'

Thea was tired of being lost for words. It was an unusual state for her and she did not like it. Something was being asked of her and she was fairly sure she was failing to provide it. If she wasn't so afraid of being punched in the face, she might well say what she really thought.

And then Valerie said it for her. 'You think I brought all this on myself, don't you? That's what people always think. The homeless only have themselves to blame. Bankruptcy is just punishment for greed. Bad health is the result of smoking or drinking or eating the wrong things. I'm in this mess because I'm a lousy judge of character.'

'Well . . .' said Thea. 'Not exactly.' And yet it was partly true – her view of the world did have some elements that chimed with Valerie's accusation. Her father had embraced the philosophy of Sartre in his youth, and a doctrine that might be seen as somewhat heartless had still coloured a lot of his thinking in the years when his children were forming their own values. The whole family took it as a basic premise that people made their own luck.

'People like you are so *smug*.'

Again the accusation was not entirely wrong. Determinedly, Thea spread pâté on her bread and slowly consumed it, absorbing the insult along with the food, and trying to process it calmly. She swallowed, and said, 'What do you want me to say? Why did you invite me here?'

'I told you. I wanted your advice as to what I should do. Stupid of me, I see that now. You're all right, so everyone else can go to hell.'

Thea reminded herself that Valerie *had* said she wanted advice, when she phoned originally. And then, ten minutes earlier, she had contradicted herself, saying she wasn't looking for that at all. And when did anybody listen to advice anyway, Thea thought crossly. Surely there must have been a friend or relative a year ago who'd told Valerie not to give her bloodsucker boyfriend any more money?

'My advice, such as it is, comes much too late,' she said. 'And it's probably just stating the obvious. Salvage what you can. Cut your losses and learn from your mistakes. Clichés, I'm afraid.'

'Smug clichés at that.'

'I suppose so.'

'Have *you* put money into this burial business, then? Can *you* be certain your new husband isn't going to bleed you dry and lie to you about it into the bargain? Here you are, an independent widow, with a nice house somewhere, ripe for the picking. Don't tell me you haven't sunk all your capital into his scheme, without a second thought. Did you draw up a prenuptial contract? Of course not. Could you survive if the whole enterprise collapsed, leaving nothing but massive debts? I doubt it. So what gives you the right to be so disgustingly superior about it?'

It was humiliatingly clever. Every response she could think of sounded hollow and self-deceiving in her own ears. She could feel an overwhelming urge to stand up and stab Valerie with her fork. 'Touché,' she said with a painful smile. 'All I can say is that Drew never asked me to put money in. And I just *know* he wouldn't lie to me. Sounds feeble, doesn't it?'

'You met him – what? Two years ago? The same as me and Paul, more or less. Long enough, most people would say, to be sure they were trustworthy. Too long for a deliberate swindle, anyway. He hasn't made enough out of me to warrant that much time spent on it. You're saying he never loved me, never saw me as anything but a source of cash. Think about that – how do you think that feels?'

'Terrible,' Thea acknowledged. The realisations

were making her feel sick. She had trusted Drew the first day she met him, even though he was under suspicion as a murderer at the time. On paper, he was probably a worse prospect than Valerie's Paul. And nothing anybody could say would change that trust. The nausea arose from the insight into other people's situations. These people had felt as she would feel if Drew now turned into a swindling monster. Valerie had loved Paul – no doubt still did. Her anguish must be beyond bearing, now that he had so wantonly destroyed her.

'But *he* feels terrible as well. And knowing that only makes it all worse. He's lost all his self-respect. He's just crawled away into a hole, and can't see any future for himself.'

Well at least that fitted with an existentialist view of the world, Thea thought. 'Serves him right,' she said. 'You wouldn't want him to get away with it, would you?'

Valerie's eyes glittered with angry tears.

'Sometimes I just want to kill him,' she admitted. 'And other times I want to call him back and live with him again, even if he does lie to me all the time.'

'I'd just want to kill him,' said Thea. 'I could probably work out a way of doing it without getting caught, as well.'

'Don't tempt me.'

'That's not what you wanted my advice for, then?'

Their voices had both become light and jokey, Thea's

especially. She had come close to numerous murders since embarking on her career as a house-sitter, and while fully aware that it was not a matter for jokes, her experience had revealed a degree of dark humour associated with it.

'I could never kill anyone,' said Valerie with great solemnity.

'I expect you could, in the right conditions. They do say revenge is sweet.'

'He didn't do it deliberately. He got caught in a spiral of bad luck and desperation.'

'So why throw him out?'

'We couldn't bear to look at each other any more,' said Valerie miserably. 'It was all too horribly spoilt.'

The lunch trailed to a conclusion with neither woman saying very much. Valerie produced coffee, and Thea looked at her watch, making much of the need to get home for the children. No questions were asked or future plans discussed. Back at Broad Campden, she watched herself closely. *Was* she smug? Did she take Drew for granted, after only a few months of marriage? When he came in from visiting an old lady whose husband had just died, she gave him an elaborate hug.

'What was that for?' he asked.

'It wasn't for anything. Just checking that you're real. I've had a very peculiar day.'

But he was prevented from hearing about it when

Timmy demanded help with a school project, and the phone rang twice, and then Andrew came to the door to consult about the coming funeral. Valerie Innes and her miserable story were pushed aside by more urgent matters.

And yet the woman would not go away. She haunted Thea's dreams and unsettled her equilibrium, although not in any predictable fashion. Nothing to do with trusting Drew or worrying about money. It was more personal than that – more a case of regretting her lack of feeling and the assumptions she had made. There was an unfinished argument endlessly looping inside her head. She found herself assessing the relationships of friends and family in an attempt to demonstrate to herself that Valerie's Paul had been a far from typical example.

A week passed, and still she was unable to shake the obsessive comparisons. Strangely, she said nothing about it to Drew, after that initial moment had been lost in the whirl of family and work. It felt risky to talk about it before she could come to any firm judgement on the matter. And in order to do that, she needed evidence. It was a familiar situation, in some ways. There had been several mysterious crimes committed in the vicinity of her house-sits, which had prompted her to indulge in her own investigations, for her own inquisitive purposes. Something in her nature required that a story must always be finished, the questions resolved.

She wanted to meet the renegade Paul and see for herself what kind of man he was. For that, she would need his surname and current address. *A tiny little flat in Headington* was the only clue she had to go on. She needed to discover more than that if she was to stand any chance of finding him. And the obvious place to use for tracking anybody these days had to be Facebook. This was something she had managed to avoid until very recently. Only when Drew's daughter Stephanie had begun to show an interest in social media, starting with YouTube, had both the adults realised their obligations to acquire at least some knowledge of the subject. Drew had already accepted that his business would benefit from a Facebook presence, and had elicited Thea's help in setting it up. She could now navigate it, but still felt a strong emotional resistance to becoming personally involved.

Valerie Innes had a minimal profile, but two of her sons were much more forthcoming. The links and likes and friends and favourites swirled back and forth until anyone with the slightest diligence could formulate a picture of the whole family. And there was Paul Grover, with photos and boasts about his brilliant new venture into the world of instant displays of house plants. The postings dated back a year or so, and nothing was very recent. But a few more searches revealed an address in North Oxford where any creditors were invited to apply. There was something almost endearing about that detail. At least the man wasn't trying to dodge his debts. Did that not suggest that he wasn't actually a swindler, after all?

Oxford was not far away, although it was a place she hated to drive in. She always got lost and there was nowhere to park. There was no need to go there. Paul Grover was nothing to her. She was slipping back into the same bad old ways that had got her into trouble more than once. She had quite forgotten Valerie and Frampton Mansell and its canal until the woman reminded her. And yet here she was, indulging an itch that would not go away. Doubt had been cast onto much that Thea held dear, her assumptions shaken and her values undermined. If she could persuade herself that this Paul was an obvious scoundrel, everything would slot back into its normal pattern.

It was a quiet day, the children safely at school, the dog briefly walked around the field at the end of the lane, Drew on one of his visits. In fact, Drew's visits were increasingly reminiscent of the daily round of an old-fashioned village vicar. He would call in on lonely elderly folk, letting them reminisce about their lives and drinking their tea. 'They'll suspect you of touting for business,' Thea worried. 'It must look awfully bad. Isn't there some sort of protocol that says you shouldn't do this sort of thing?'

He looked at her from under his eyebrows, saying

nothing for a few seconds. 'You haven't paid proper attention,' he reproached her. 'Everyone I visit has been bereaved in the last year or so. Even if I didn't do the funeral, they know I understand. And they mostly came to me first, asking about the burial field. I'm not doing anything in the least bit dodgy.'

'Here I go again,' she'd apologised. 'Always thinking badly of people – even you.'

'I forgive you,' he said easily.

In some convoluted way, she felt she was correcting this failing in herself by seeking out Paul Grover. It would be good to find that he was nothing more than inadequate, and not a professional con man, greedily stripping vulnerable women of their assets.

So she took her little car to Oxford, using the satnav that she had long resisted, and quickly found the modest backstreet that was the address she hoped was Grover's home. It looked like an ordinary house, but nobody came to answer her knock. She stood there, undecided, thinking she might wait in the car for a while, before trying again. It was parked some streets away, on a meter. She was reluctant to waste the money she had shovelled into it, and had a book to read while she waited.

Half an hour later she was back. Coming in the other direction was a woman of a similar age to her own. It soon became apparent that they were both calling at the same door. 'After you,' said the woman.

Thea knocked, and again there was no response.

'I think it's one of those places that lets itself be used as an address,' said the woman. 'As a sort of cover.'

'How do you mean?'

'You know. All kinds of people are afraid of giving their true address, so they use a false one. Whoever lives here agrees to pretend to be the right name, if they're asked. They do it for dozens of people, all paying a bit, and it adds up to a nice little earner.'

'I see,' said Thea slowly, thinking she must have lived a more sheltered life than she realised, for such a service never to have occurred to her before.

'Who are you looking for?'

'A man called Paul Grover.'

'Never heard of him. I'm after an outfit called Blaskett Data Services. They owe me five hundred pounds.'

'Oh dear.'

'Could be worse, I s'pose.'

'How am I going to find him?' Thea wondered aloud. 'It's meant to be easy to find people these days.'

'Do you know where he works?'

'No idea. I think he's just got a new job, although nothing about him's at all definite. He might not even be in Oxford at all.'

The woman shrugged. 'Well, I guess you're out of luck, then. Same as me.'

'Can we be sure this place is what you think? That in itself would be a bit of a giveaway.'

A man was approaching them, his expression a mixture of curiosity and apprehension. He seemed to be in late middle age. 'Uh-oh,' he said, stopping beside them. 'Is this what I think it is?'

Neither woman answered him.

'A drop house,' he explained. 'False address, and all that.'

'Looks like it,' said Thea. 'Who do you want?'

'A bastard by the name of Baxter. Harold Baxter.'

'Not Blaskett?' asked Thea's new friend.

'Nope. Who's Blaskett?'

'The swindlers who did me out of five hundred quid.'

'There must be hundreds of letters in there, at this rate,' said Thea.

The others looked at her. 'Why?' said the man. 'Nobody writes real letters any more. All they need is an *address*. The house is probably registered to someone who lives abroad, just kept as a front. If there was someone living here, they'd never get a moment's peace, would they?'

A kind of collective shrug emphasised the futility of standing there, and they dispersed. Thea's car had ten more minutes of parking time, some of which she spent in thought. On the back seat was a map book, and she reached over for it, wanting to get an overall idea of just where she was. A satnav was hopeless in that regard, which was the main reason she had always disliked them.

A tiny little flat in Headington repeated itself inside her head. This address was not in Headington, which was a complication she had overlooked, but there could be no possible sense in going in any further search of the man, when she had no idea what Paul Grover looked like. Facebook hadn't offered a picture of him. In the olden days, there would have been the simple expedient of looking him up in the phone book. But even then, if he had only recently moved, he wouldn't be listed.

She would go for a look anyway. Having lived in Witney for many years, she was familiar with Oxford and knew that Headington was an expensive address. Even a tiny flat would set a person back considerably. Grover might be renting, unless the flat had been a bolt-hole he had kept up his sleeve while living with Valerie. *Think*, she adjured herself. Valerie had approached her for some specific reason. Was this madcap trip to Oxford a result of a deliberate plan? Was she so predictable? It seemed impossible. There had been far too little information provided to ensure that she came here to this spot on this day.

And yet, this North Oxford address had been easy to find. The nature of the building had quickly become apparent. The strong implication was that Grover was indeed a con man. Why else use such a place?

So what was Valerie's intention? Thea drove westwards with that question ringing loud in her ears.

So loud did it ring that she went again to Frampton

Mansell, zigzagging confidently via the A429 and then the 419. She was there in well under an hour, ignoring the fact that it was the middle of the day and lunch was going to be an issue before much longer.

There was a mud-splashed Renault outside Valerie's house. Thea parked behind it and walked up the short driveway to the front door. She could see movement through a window, but nobody answered her knock. This was annoying, and she tried the door. Plenty of people still left them unlocked, after all. But not Valerie.

Angrily, Thea went around to the back. There was a gravel path, and a flimsy garden door that she easily unlatched. The rear of the house had its own porch, full of plants and a chest freezer. She could faintly hear a shrill voice. But this door did not open, either.

She went to a window and pressed her face close to it. The interior was shadowy, but she recognised the kitchen she had eaten in a few days earlier. A woman was standing in the furthest corner, her arms raised. As Thea watched the arms came down, and the object held between them collided violently with the balding head of a man sitting at the table. He was facing Thea, slowly focusing on the surprising appearance of a face at the window. It was hard to be sure, but she thought he smiled at her, before slumping forward.

The woman leant over him, carefully placing the heavy iron skillet beside him on the table. Then she looked up and saw Thea at the window. Her lips drew back in a snarl, part horror, part triumph.

Thea's heart was thumping irregularly. She had just witnessed a murder. Valerie Innes had just killed the man who had ruined her life. A swindler who deserved whatever came to him – within reason. Hardly anybody deserved to be killed like that, though. And he had actually looked rather nice, in that final second. 'Hey!' she shouted stupidly. 'What have you done?'

The double glazing muffled all sound, but Valerie clearly understood. Then she looked up at a point above Thea's head, and her expression changed.

'Bad luck, love,' came a man's voice. 'In the wrong place at the wrong time, well and truly. You know what they say about cats and curiosity.'

She whirled round and met the face of a handsome man. Paralysed for a moment, the next thing she knew, Valerie had come out to join them.

'Roger – it's done. I did it. I never thought I would, but this woman helped me to decide that I had to.'

Thea simply stared from one face to the other, unable to find words.

Valerie went on. 'She's called Thea Slocombe, and she's the nosiest woman I have ever met.'

'Pleased to meet you,' he said, 'Val's play-acting worked, then? You swallowed the story she spun you.'

'She did,' said Valerie triumphantly. 'You should have seen us, arguing about whether a man could be trusted or not. Now, what do you think we ought to do with her? I never thought she'd come back here, I must admit.'

'Play-acting?' Thea managed to speak. 'That wasn't play-acting. Nobody could act as well as that.'

Valerie cast a nervous glance at the man she'd called Roger. 'It was. I made it all up.'

Thea's mind was in turmoil. 'But why involve me at all? I don't get it.'

Valerie gave her a complicated look. 'Credibility,' she said briefly.

'What?'

'If I could make you believe I'd finished with Paul, once and for ever, I'd know we could safely follow the plan through.' She grimaced. 'But you turned out to be even more nosy than I thought.'

'And now she's seen a lot more than she should,' said Roger grimly. 'This changes things you know, old girl.'

Before either woman could react, he had grabbed Valerie around the neck in a tight hold from behind. 'You'll be joining lover-boy in the old well, my darling. Sorry about that.'

'What about me?' Thea realised she could simply run away and report the entire episode to the police. But that would entail abandoning Valerie to her fate, which was clearly unthinkable. A phonecall was the obvious answer, but as usual her mobile was in the car, and time was clearly crucial. Roger could break his captive's neck in a second.

'You can go to hell,' said Roger calmly. 'I'll be off where nobody can find me before your thumb hits the first nine.'

'But Roger,' Valerie choked out. 'Why?'

'You've served your purpose, my pet. Paul was never a swindler. I was blackmailing him into taking your money. He loved you, every bit as much as you loved him. But he couldn't take the humiliation of you thinking so badly of him. He was doing everything in his power to get back on track and redeem himself. He'd have done it, too – which very much did not suit my plans. Not at all.' He tightened his grip on her, and Thea braced herself for some sort of ineffectual rugby tackle, which might at least slow him down. It did not occur to her for another fifteen seconds that she might simply scream as loud as she could.

'Lucky for me that it's true what they say – Hell hath no fury like a woman who believes herself scorned. Stupid bitches,' he added.

Thea launched herself forward, with a shout that was nowhere near as loud as she'd intended. Her face met Roger's knee, and came off very much the worse.

Then a voice came from the side of the house. 'Hello? Is anybody there? Hello?'

'Yes!' squealed Thea. 'Help!'

Round the corner came the man from outside the drop house in North Oxford. He was holding out some sort of card. 'Good afternoon, everybody. I'm Detective Sergeant Vernon. I'm conducting an investigation into a fraud, involving false addresses. I thought perhaps this lady might be able to help, so I followed her as she drove down here.'

Thea crumpled into a boneless heap. Roger began to run down the garden, before realising there was no way out. Valerie Innes simply wailed.

In Which Thea
Meets Tony Brown

Timmy was being petulant and Thea was doggedly trying to mollify him. 'So what *do* you want to do?' she asked him.

'Run round the woods with Hepzie,' he replied promptly. 'The woods look great.'

'Oh.' The reply was not what she had expected, and it placed her on the spikes of a dilemma. Stephanie and Drew wanted to look round the Roman villa. She herself was flexible. Chedworth still had several unexplored corners and she was happy to wander around any of them.

'But the villa's really good,' she tried. 'Aren't you interested in the Romans?'

'They'd have been in the woods as well,' he said quite reasonably. 'There are probably ruins of stuff they made in there.'

'I doubt it. And even if there are, we're not going to find them, are we?'

'You can leave me and Heps on our own, and find us later,' he said, without a vestige of hope. A boy of eight was regarded as barely more self-sufficient than an eight-day-old baby, in these anxious times. Even Thea couldn't remember being allowed to roam free until very much older.

'I'll come with you,' she said. 'I'm not crazy about Romans myself, to be perfectly honest.'

She left him in the shop attached to the villa, and went to find Drew. He and his daughter were waiting by the entrance to the site. 'What's going on?' he demanded.

'Tim's not sold on the villa. I said I'd take him and the dog for a run in the woods. Probably just as good for him, and definitely better for Hepzie.'

'But I bought a family ticket,' he said. 'That's a big waste of money.'

'Go and see if they'll change it.'

'They won't. Computers won't allow that sort of thing.'

She sighed and looked around. 'There's a man with a little girl, just going into the shop. I'll ask them if they want tickets. You can create a family somehow. Don't make it difficult, okay?'

'It's not me being difficult. It's Timmy.'

'He's only making his wishes known. That's not so awful, is it? Not everybody likes this sort of place.'

'Timmy does. He's being awkward on purpose.'

That was possible, Thea conceded, but it still felt

easier to go along with what the little boy said he wanted. She looked at Stephanie. 'Do you think he'll be sorry he missed it when it's too late?'

The big sister shrugged. 'He might,' she said. 'Where is he, anyway?'

'Over there, look. Let me go and talk to that man before he buys a ticket.'

She went quickly after the man and caught him as he queued at the counter. Timmy joined her, looking as if he was braced for being betrayed. Only then did it occur to her that the National Trust staff might take exception to what she was proposing, so she tried to speak softly, while making it appear that she was just idly chatting. 'Excuse me,' she began, 'but my husband has a family ticket with two spare places. If you and your little girl would like it, you're welcome.'

'For free you mean?'

His quick, almost greedy, response threw her. Of course, Drew would want some recompense. 'Well . . . less than you'd pay otherwise. Our Timmy changed his mind at the last minute, you see.' She put a hand on Timmy's shoulder, as he stood meekly at her side. The man dithered and Thea lost patience. 'Suit yourself,' she shrugged. 'That's my husband there, if you decide to join him.'

The queue moved forward and Thea became aware of suspicious looks from the woman at the ticket desk. 'It's up to you,' she repeated, and steered the boy out of the shop. Signalling to Drew to wait a minute, she went back to the car, some distance away, and liberated the spaniel. Let the men work it out in whatever way they chose. She'd done more than enough in her efforts to keep the peace.

The woods were magnificent. It was May and the leaves were unfolding on all sides, fresh and vivid in their new colours. Sunlight filtered through them, and a mild breeze gave them movement. 'You did the right thing,' she congratulated Timmy. 'This is lovely.'

Hepzibah thought so too, revelling in her freedom, sniffing into tufts of young bracken and then suddenly dashing at full speed down the path ahead of them. Thea resisted the urge to call her back. Hepzie never got lost. Or almost never.

'Have you been here before?' Timmy asked.

'To Chedworth, yes, but not the woods. We were too busy for any sort of exploring.' She had taken scant notice of the direction in which they were walking, or where they might find themselves if they carried on. The woods seemed to stretch extensively on all sides. There was no sound of traffic. 'Are we going north, south, east or west?' she asked him.

He gave her a bemused look. 'How would I know?'

'By the sun, or the shadows it casts. Or using a compass. I thought all boys knew how to work that out.'

'Not me,' he said firmly, implying that such arcane skills were far beyond the scope of what interested him.

'So what *do* you like about it here?'

'I don't know.' He looked around. 'I thought there might be conkers.' He scuffed through some decayed leaf mould.

'Wrong season, chum,' she said, wondering how this child of the countryside, born to a mother who had loved everything about gardens and growing things, could be so perversely ignorant.

'We're going east,' said a voice behind them. 'But you can't tell much from the sun in the middle of the day. You can look for mossy tree trunks. It grows more thickly on the north side, as a general rule. Or find a tree stump and have a good look at the rings. They should be wider on the south side, because that side, where it gets more sun, grows faster.'

Timmy and Thea both gazed at the newcomer in wonder. 'Thanks,' said Thea cautiously. 'I never knew that about the rings. And I can never remember which side moss likes best.'

The man was about forty, she guessed, tall and moderately handsome. He wore a brown anorak and jeans, and looked tired. 'Sorry to intrude,' he said. 'I couldn't resist it.'

'Do you work here?' she asked. 'For the National Trust or something?'

'No, no. I just came for a walk. I don't live around here. It was just somewhere to go,' he said vaguely. 'I just got in the car and drove.'

That sounded to Thea like a person running away

from something. Combined with the haunted look in his eyes, she detected the makings of a story.

'Can we find a tree stump, then?' asked Timmy.

'Good idea,' said the man.

But all they could see were small, half-rotted branches, left for insects and birds to enjoy. 'They probably don't cut trees down in these woods,' said the man. 'Oh, by the way, my name's Tony. Tony Brown.'

'Thea and Timmy,' said Thea, without adding their surname.

'All starting with a T,' said Timmy acutely. 'That's funny, isn't it.'

'Very,' said Tony Brown.

'Have you got any children?' Timmy proceeded to ask, making Thea wince. Wasn't he too old for this? Hadn't he learnt where the boundaries were by this time? Was there something the matter with the child?

'Well, no, actually,' said the man hesitantly.

Again Thea grasped the hint of a tragic tale just below the surface.

'Thea isn't my real mother, you know,' the boy prattled on. 'My mother died, and now Thea's married to my dad.'

At least he gave no suggestion of resentment or unhappiness, Thea noted. There was really no reason why he shouldn't explain the situation to anybody who would listen.

'I see. The truth is, I had a little baby girl, but she died before she was born. It was terribly sad.'

'How could she?' Timmy enquired. 'I mean – she couldn't die before she was alive.'

'That's enough, Tim,' said Thea. 'I'll explain it to you when we get home. I'm really sorry,' she told the man.

'It was more than two years ago now. I'm almost over it – as far as anybody ever can be. But it's had a few unforeseen consequences,' he added wryly.

Thea pushed down the eagerness to know more. The man had a neediness to him that rang warning bells. 'I'm sorry,' she repeated. 'Now we'd better go and find that dog.' Only then did she notice that Hepzie had been out of sight for rather a long time. 'Did you see a cocker spaniel?' she asked Tony Brown.

'No, I don't think so.'

'Come on, Tim. She might be miles away by now.' She hurried the child along, wondering whether she should be worried. '*Hepzie!*' she yodelled. 'Come on now.'

'You should whistle for her,' puffed Timmy. 'Dogs always come when you whistle.'

'I'm sure they do, but I can't. You know that.'

'Well I can,' and he emitted a reedy sound that no dog would take seriously.

'She'll be along here somewhere, digging under a tree or chasing a squirrel.' They followed the broad well-trodden path between the trees, hoping to catch sight of the plumy black and white tail waving up ahead of them.

The search was an unwelcome distraction from the easy mooching Thea had envisaged. 'Dratted dog,' she repeated more than once.

Timmy kept trying with his whistle, the improvement with each attempt worthy of comment. By the fifth repeat, Thea was optimistic that the dog might actually respond.

'There she is!' the child cried triumphantly. They had turned off the main path, for no good reason, stepping over dead branches and trampling new undergrowth. 'Over there.'

And so she was. In a small clearing, the spaniel was sprawled at the feet of a large woman who looked displeased at the attention. 'Damn it, Heps,' snapped Thea. 'Why don't you come when you're called?'

'It's yours, is it?' said the woman. 'Honestly, she wouldn't leave me alone.'

'Sorry,' said Thea. 'She doesn't usually behave so badly.' She looked around, thinking it was a funny place for a woman to be by herself. 'She might have thought you needed to be rescued.'

A harsh laugh was the response to this. 'Don't tell me she's that clever.' An expression of despair briefly crossed her face.

'Why? Are you saying you really are in need of rescue?'

A slow shake of the head indicated a refusal to continue the conversation. Timmy was cuddling the dog, and Thea was more than willing to abandon any further interaction with strangers. 'All right. Thanks for . . . well, thanks, anyway.'

'I didn't do anything.' She was a buxom individual, in her thirties, with a pale indoor complexion. She wore unbecoming, cheap-looking clothes, and spoke with an accent that suggested the softer, more western reaches of the Midlands. Her brown hair was curly.

'Come on then, kids,' said Thea, eliciting a laugh from Timmy. It was a running joke that the reconstituted family included Hepzie as one of the children. Drew winced every time it occurred. For Drew, a dog was a dog and a child was a child. Timmy and Stephanie had embraced the spaniel with considerably more enthusiasm than they would a stepsibling.

They had been in the woods for half an hour or so, first walking eastwards if the man called Tony could be believed. Then the search for Hepzie had taken them in another direction – south, Thea calculated with some difficulty. The village of Chedworth was in front of them, invisible apart from brief distant glimpses through the trees. From past experience, she knew it would take a lot of time and effort to walk it from end to end, and had no intention of trying.

Drew and Stephanie would start lunch without them in the cafe attached to the villa, if they were late back, but they wouldn't be very happy about it. It was not yet twelve, however, and Stephanie was a child who insisted on reading every word of every information sign in a museum or historic site. 'We should turn back,' she decided. 'But there's no great hurry.'

Timmy was showing signs of inner conflict. 'What's the matter?' she asked him, expecting him to confess to a need for a lavatory. It would not be the first time he'd been caught out in the open countryside, and until very recently he had adamantly refused to pee behind a tree.

'It's boring in the woods,' he complained.

'So you wish you'd gone to see the villa after all?'

'No-o-o. Not really. I wanted to talk to that man. He knew things. He must be a teacher, do you think?'

'I'm not sure. He seemed a bit too outdoorsy for that.'

'Outdoorsy?'

'Think about it.'

'Right. I know – a person who works outside a lot. Like a farmer.'

'Exactly. Perhaps he's a farmer.'

'Do farmers go for walks in the woods?'

'Why not?'

'They'd be too busy.'

'That's probably true. Well, wouldn't you like to be an outdoorsy person? It's fun to grow food, and understand how trees grow and watch birds. Lots of things like that.'

'I don't know.' He looked around him. 'The birds wake me up really early, with all that singing. It's annoying.'

She laughed. 'I love it. The blackbirds are fantastic.'

'Mm.'

She was keeping a close eye on the spaniel as they walked, fearful of losing her again. When they came within sight of the road that led up to the villa, she attached the lead. 'Well, we didn't get lost,' she said.

They were on a wide track with trees on their left and a small river to the right. 'That's the River Churn,' she said, proud that she remembered the name. 'Not much of a river, is it?'

Timmy barely glanced at it. Then he brightened. 'There's that man again,' he said. 'Look!'

The man was walking ahead of them in the same direction, going unnaturally slowly. He turned back as they watched him, and took a moment to recognise them. Thea thought that strange, suggestive of a mind deeply preoccupied with other matters. He smiled faintly, and then evidently decided to turn back on himself. 'Didn't mean to come this way,' he explained in a low mutter, as he passed them.

Thea and Timmy exchanged a look, with raised eyebrows and questioning eyes. 'Funny,' she whispered. 'Maybe he got the direction wrong.'

Timmy giggled. 'Don't think so,' he said.

'Maybe it's us that's wrong. Is that building over there real or just a mirage?'

'A mirage is actually a refraction of something real, but in a different place from where you think,' the child told her earnestly. 'It's not just imagination.'

'Is that right?' She frowned. 'I don't think I ever knew that.'

'The building's real,' he assured her. 'But it's not the villa.'

'I know, but it's the one we passed on the way up to the car park. So that means we're almost there. It also means we're heading north,' she added proudly. 'Because the woods and the village are south of the villa. Easy-peasy.'

'It doesn't seem easy to me,' said Tim.

'It will. It's the same as left and right. You just have to remember which is which. East is right, if you're facing north. And it's always a good idea to face north, especially if you've got a compass.'

He asked a few more questions, much to Thea's gratification. They stood in place while she talked him through the points of the compass, and he connected them with references in familiar stories. 'Now I get it!' he exulted, finally. 'Thanks, Thea. I bet Stephanie doesn't know where east is.'

Thea again looked at her watch, and realised they were almost late. 'Hey – we'd better—' She was interrupted by a loud scream somewhere in the woods, south-west of where they were standing. It sounded quite close. 'What was *that*?' she said.

Timmy didn't answer. He was gazing raptly in the direction of the sound.

'We should go and see,' she said, before realising she might be taking a vulnerable child into a scene of horror or danger.

'It must have been that man. Phone Dad,' he urged her.

'Yes. Good thinking.' The existence of a phone in her pocket was still nowhere near as obvious and familiar to her as the existence of a thumb was to most people. She extracted the gadget, while automatically trotting towards the source of the cry, ears straining for a repetition. There had been great pain and shock in the sound, but nothing to hint at what might have caused it.

Drew took his time answering. 'Hi,' he said cheerfully. 'Are you lost?'

'No, we're just down the road a little way, on a path that runs between the river and the woods. Listen, we just heard somebody cry out . . . scream . . . and I should go and see what's happened. But Timmy . . .'

'Leave it, for heaven's sake. We want our lunch. I don't suppose it was anything important – just someone messing about.'

'No, it wasn't. We saw a man. We talked to him. It's probably him, hurt himself somehow.'

'Surely the woods are full of people? Someone else will have got to him by now.'

'I'm going to see, Drew. Stop arguing. And come and fetch Timmy. We'll come to the corner, where the track meets the road. There's a big gate. Hurry up. When we see you, I'll send him up to meet you, and run back on my own.'

'What about the dog?'

Good question. 'I suppose she'll come with me,' she said. The pressure to go and investigate was building by the second. She danced restlessly on the spot, wishing Drew would understand the urgency. 'He might be *dying*,' she shouted, careless of the effect this could have on Timmy.

'All right. Calm down. It's not your problem,' said Drew unfeelingly. 'Have you called 999?'

'No. I have to see what's happened first.'

'Okay – if you must, we'll come and get Tim. How far are you from that gate?'

'About one minute's walk.'

It was all accomplished in under five minutes, during which no other sounds came from the woods. Where were all the other weekend walkers? Having lunch somewhere, she supposed. If she and Tim were the only people to have heard the scream, that made it even more incumbent on her to go to the rescue, call an ambulance, stem an arterial bleed, apprehend an attacker . . . She increased her pace, unsure of which little path she should take into the woods. Too much time had passed; she was no longer at all certain of quite where the cry had come from.

'Hello?' she called, trying not to feel self-conscious. Shouting in the open air, where any stranger might hear her, was embarrassing. When there was no response, she couldn't manage to do it again.

She was thinking about giving up, and persuading herself the scream was of far less significance than first supposed, when she heard a kind of panting somewhere nearby. Rounding a curve in the path, she at first could see nothing of interest. But the sound came again, and she located a shape in a hollow, some four or five yards off the path. Expecting to see a prone human figure, she had to adjust to the strange sight of a man on his hands and knees, rocking and panting like an animal. Her first feeling was of self-righteousness at her decision to investigate. Nobody else was anywhere in sight. She fumbled for her phone, and had already keyed 999 by the time she got to the man's side.

'Hey! What happened?' she demanded. 'I'm calling an ambulance.' Then the call was answered, and she did what she could to explain how to find the casualty. When asked the nature of the injury, she was at a loss. 'He can't breathe properly,' she began.

The man – who had become easily identified as Tony Brown – twisted his head round to look at her, stark panic in his eyes. 'Knife,' he choked. 'Back.'

Bewildered, Thea leant over him, her feet sinking into the leaf mould. There was no sign of a weapon, but she could see a splash of blood on his brown anorak, halfway down his left side. 'Were you stabbed?' she asked in horror.

The woman at the end of the phone was listening. 'Stabbed?' came a tinny voice. 'Where?'

'His back, I think. There's a bit of blood. Not much. At a guess, I would say it's just a little way below his heart. Probably got his lung.'

'Is he conscious?'

'Yes. But he can't really talk.'

'An ambulance is on the way. It'll be coming from Cirencester. I estimate it'll take twenty minutes at least. Can you stay with him?'

'Yes, I suppose so.' The call was refreshingly easy compared to some she'd attempted on other occasions. 'I don't know what to do, though. He's on his hands and knees.' The position was worrying her, making it very difficult to see Tony Brown's face, and preventing her from performing any of the procedures she'd heard about. He was sagging at the knees, too, his back sloping at a more acute angle.

'Oh.' The woman could be heard tapping a keyboard. 'Yes, that's probably a good idea, if he has a ruptured lung. How's his colour?'

'Rather blue,' Thea reported, peering at the face that was now hanging lower. 'I can't see very well, but his lips look a sort of bluey-grey.'

'Just talk to him. Reassure. Don't ask him questions. Is there any blood on his face?'

'I don't think so.'

'Is he breathing through nose or mouth?'

'I'm not sure. His mouth's open, so it must be that.'

The time passed quickly, with every breath a small triumph. The solid reality of the damaged body in the incongruous position consumed all her attention. When she looked up to see two girls staring at her in consternation, she had no idea how long they might have been there. 'Go away,' she told them. 'Unless you want to meet the ambulance and show it where to come.' At that moment, she heard a siren, and waved more urgently at them. 'Go!' she urged. The girls stumbled arm in arm towards the sound, their faces pale.

Tony was breathing more slowly, and she hoped that indicated a calmer, less painful, development. 'Sit,' he gasped. 'Legs sore.'

She helped him twist gradually onto his bottom, both arms holding his shoulders, trying to keep him upright. It seemed to improve his condition, and he looked into her face. 'Stabbed,' he said, with wonder on his face. 'She stabbed me.'

'Who? Do you know her?'

He nodded, looking like a kicked dog. 'Geraldine,' he said, with a drunken-type slur. 'My love. Why?'

The effort weakened him, and he gave a sort of squeal of pain.

Thea waited for the spasm to pass, resting one hand anxiously on his shoulder. His question still reverberated. 'You mean – why did she do it, I suppose.' Thea experienced a moment of cynicism. Why did a beloved stab the man she was supposed to adore? Because he betrayed or damaged her in some emotional way he might not even have been aware of. Because most men were annoying, some beyond endurance. Or perhaps the woman was a psychopath and the man the sweetest individual alive.

Then the ambulance came, and Thea was instantly

superfluous. It had happened before, the almost rude elbowing aside by self-important paramedics. She had learnt not to take it personally, and willingly stepped away, looking around for her dog. Hepzie had been entirely forgotten in all the drama.

She called, already mildly concerned that the dog had got bored and pottered off yet again into the woods. It would not be so easily forgiven a second time. Thea was hungry and thirsty, and rather shaky. The stabbed man would probably survive, and tell his story much more coherently to the appropriate authorities. But if he didn't, she was privy to a name that would probably be enough to justify arresting and charging his girlfriend for murder.

First she ought to phone Drew. It was surprising that he hadn't tried to contact her, although he was not in the habit of making unnecessary phone calls. Presumably he would wait patiently for her to update him.

She felt in her pocket for the dog lead, and then remembered that it was still attached to the animal. She must have unthinkingly dropped it when called upon to administer whatever aid she could to the injured man. That meant Hepzie was at risk of getting caught in brambles or undergrowth, which would be bad. But she would also be slowed down, which was probably good.

'Hepzie!' she carolled, losing all former inhibitions, and trying to second-guess where the dog would go. She might retrace their steps back to where they met with Drew, and then follow him up to the villa. That would involve trailing her lead along a small road, inviting someone to apprehend her, and even possibly steal her. Would anybody *want* a muddy, middle-aged spaniel? Or would they think, in some misguidedly public-spirited fashion, that they were doing a good deed?

It was a great effort to trudge around in search of her pet and therefore very tempting to simply assume she'd found her way back to the others, and the car, and was patiently waiting for her mistress to catch up with her.

'Hepzie!' she shouted again. 'Come here, will you?'

The ambulance was loaded and moving steadily back towards the road. The two bewildered girls had long since disappeared. A fresh group of walkers came into view, striding along purposefully with sticks and boots and pink cheeks. They waved one or two sticks at the incongruous vehicle, asking each other what might possibly have happened. Thea inwardly noted that if Tony Brown had been killed, there would now be legions of police people crawling all over the woods. As it was, he had been brutally attacked, and there ought actually to be officers combing the scene for evidence of the attacker. Somebody ought to be questioning her, and assessing the facts as far as she could provide them.

'What happened, love?' asked a man who appeared to be leading the walkers.

'A man was hurt,' she said carefully.

'Badly?'

'Yes.'

'Is that a police car up there?' He waved his stick again.

'Looks like it. I should go and speak to them, I suppose. I was the one to find him. But I've lost my dog. Have you seen a cocker spaniel, trailing her lead?'

'Sorry. She's not down that way. We've walked up from the Yanworth road. Skirted the southern side of the woods. How long's she been gone?'

'Half an hour or so, I think. I sort of forgot about her.'

'They're coming to you, look.' He indicated two police officers walking down the track towards them.

'Oh, yes. So they are.'

She hurried to meet them, rehearsing the briefest way she could explain what had happened, and remembering again that she should phone Drew. A flicker of resentment made itself apparent that there were so many things she should be doing, when nobody else was showing the slightest trace of concern. Resentment led to defiance and she pulled out her phone. She would speak to Drew before she did her civic duty.

'Hey – you've been *ages*,' he complained. 'We've had our lunch. What's been happening? We heard a siren.'

'Have you got Hepzie?'

'What? No. Haven't you?'

'She's off in the woods somewhere. And now I have to talk to the police. Could you take the kids and go and search for her? Get Timmy to whistle. That might work.'

'Well, all right. But I really need to get home soon. Did you say police?'

'You know I did. A man was stabbed. I need to tell them some things. Phone if you find the dog, okay?'

The police officers were standing eighteen inches from her, their eyes on her face. The moment she disconnected the phone, one said, 'Stabbed?'

'You took your time. The ambulance has been and gone. I can give you names, that's all. I have to go and find my dog.'

'There's been some other trouble that slowed us down. We've spoken to the paramedics. The man's in a bad way. Lost consciousness, apparently. You know who he is?'

'Only his name. Tony Brown. Nothing else. I met him about two hours ago, or less, walking in the woods. He said his girlfriend stabbed him. Her name's Geraldine. No, wait – he said "my love", not girlfriend. Probably the same thing.'

'Probably not, if she was angry enough to do that to him. Where did all this happen?'

'Over there. Down this little track.'

'What was he doing there?'

She began to say *How should I know?* when she

paused. 'That's a good question. He seemed to be heading back to the road, and then suddenly turned round and came back down here. It was quite odd, actually. As if he'd forgotten something.'

'Was he on his own?'

'Yes. Both times. We saw him first over there.' She waved into the heart of the woods. 'I was with my stepson, and we had a little chat.'

'And then you saw him again here?'

'Exactly. Now, I really don't think I can help you any more. I've got to go and find my dog. She could be anywhere by now.'

'Just give us your contact details. Then you can go.' He threw a frustrated glance at the point in the woods where the man had been stabbed. 'Not much there to go on,' he muttered.

It had not been conducted according to any textbook, Thea suspected. But she assumed that reality never did follow the rules, anyway. The ambulance had been priority, and the interests of the police came well behind the need to save a life. Her own statement was probably the best lead there was to who had plunged the knife. A woman called Geraldine, known to the victim, wasn't likely to be difficult to trace.

'Thanks,' she said, and trotted off into the heart of the woods, calling again for her dog.

She zigzagged along small paths, with some idea that Hepzie might have retraced the route she had taken with Thea and Timmy. The trouble was, she didn't quite remember what that route had been. It was an old wood, with some big trees, as well as plenty of young undergrowth, fallen branches and tangled brambles. Evergreens mixed with those boasting tender new leaves, several had unusual twisty trunks, which she did not recall from earlier in the day.

'Hepzie!' she bellowed. 'Where are you?'

'She's here,' came a voice, and Thea was thrust right back to a repeat of the scene of two hours ago. The same large woman was receiving lavish attentions from the spaniel, again. But this time she was sitting on the ground, her back against a tree. Hepzie was cuddled up close to her, apparently rather more welcome than otherwise. 'What is it about me that she's so obsessed with? What do I do to make everything follow me about like this?'

'I have no idea. She's not usually like this. But I'm extremely glad to see her, I can tell you. I was beginning to think she was lost for ever.'

'Where's the little boy who was with you? Have you lost him as well?'

The jokey words were not echoed in her face. She looked ill, even paler than before and dishevelled.

'No, he's with his father. There's been some trouble. I . . . I got distracted and the dog ran off when I wasn't looking.'

'We've been here a long time.' There was no reproach in the voice. 'A few people passed by, but nobody noticed us.'

'Are you all right? You're not, are you?'

The woman gave a tight smile. 'That trouble you talked about. Was it a man? Is he dead?'

Thea's mind gave an almost audible click. 'You're Geraldine, aren't you?'

The woman nodded. 'He's not dead, then? I suppose I'm glad about that. I just hope it's enough to make him stop persecuting me.'

'What?'

'He's a stalker. I've been stalked by him for two years now. Ever since the baby. His baby was stillborn. I was the midwife. He went to pieces and I was the one to mop him up. I suppose I was too kind to him, at the exact moment when he was most vulnerable. He came back to talk to me a few times, and I never saw any harm in it. Then his wife left him and moved away, and he just fixated on me from that time on. He *follows* me. Like today. I've got the weekend off, and thought I'd come here for a little break, staying in a B&B. He's been hacking into my emails, which is how he knew I was here. He knows my car. It wasn't hard to find me. When I saw him early today, I just flipped. I deliberately led him here, into the woods, determined to make him understand, once and for all.'

'Taking a knife with you?'

'That's right. That'll count against me, I suppose. But I can prove he was harassing me. I've reported it to the police twice, but nothing ever came of it. He's absolutely convinced that I'm the love of his life, and that I feel the same as he does. It's the weirdest thing, you know. His wife was so sensible and sweet. They were just a normal couple.'

'What was wrong with the baby?'

'Nothing. It was placental failure. No reason for it. It just happens sometimes. A nightmare for the parents, obviously. They called her Edith. Isn't that a nice name?'

Thea was clutching her dog to her chest, partly to prevent any further escape and partly as a sort of protection. There was madness in this story somewhere, although she was less inclined to attribute it to this Geraldine, the more she listened to her.

'I'll give myself up, of course. They'd catch me anyway. How do I do that, I wonder?'

'Best to go to Cirencester police station, I would think.'

'All right, then. I deliberately missed his heart, you know.'

'But he had his back to you.' There was something viscerally treacherous in attacking a person from behind, an impression gleaned perhaps from all those westerns where you were meant to shoot a man while looking him in the face.

'That's true. He was looking for me, pacing around amongst the trees, and I jumped him. He saw me, though. I'll never forget the look on his face.'

'Come on, then. Let's get back to the car park.'

Geraldine stumbled heavily as she got to her feet. 'God, I feel terrible,' she said.

'You've had quite a day of it.'

'And more to come.'

'They'll be okay with you. They're all quite decent. I know a few of them.' She refrained from mentioning Tony Brown's lapse into unconsciousness, with the implication that he might yet not recover. 'He seemed such a nice man,' she burst out, instead.

'What? Who?'

'Tony. He chatted to me and Timmy, and was perfectly ordinary and pleasant. He didn't look as if he was searching for you, or obsessed at all.'

'No, I don't suppose he did. He'd have been happy to think I was engineering a meeting with him. He turned everything around to suit his own delusions. And I don't mind admitting that I often wondered if I was the crazy one, and not him.'

Instead of reassuring her, this remark gave Thea grounds for concern. Wasn't it more likely that the overweight, overworked midwife would conceive an excessive passion for the bereaved father and abandoned husband? Had she pressed herself on him, offering the sympathy and medical information that he craved, and mistaking gratitude for adoration?

'I have to phone my husband,' she said. 'He'll be worrying.'

Geraldine said nothing, so she made the call. 'Hey, love,' said Drew. 'Did you find the dog?'

Love. Tony Brown had said Geraldine was his love and she had denied it. Which was all Thea or anybody needed to confirm the woman's version of events, because it was not really love if it went unreciprocated. Obsession, delusion, whatever else you called it, it was definitely not love. Throwing Geraldine a smile, she said to Drew, 'Yes, and someone else. We should be in the car park in about fifteen minutes. Sorry to keep you waiting.'

'That's okay. Timmy says he's glad he didn't go to the villa, and he had a great time with you in the woods. Now he's playing with one of those balsa wood planes. He bought it in the shop.'

'I've made you awfully late,' she persisted. 'You must be fed up with hanging about.'

'I don't mind. And I know you'll have a fascinating story to tell me when you get here.'

'You can't even begin to imagine,' she said.

The Moorcroft

Den Cooper was finding the responsibility of parenthood more of a worry than he had expected. The finances especially were of concern. His job as security officer at Bristol Airport paid modestly, and Maggs was never going to earn much working for Drew Slocombe. In fact, during the year or so she was taking off, she earned nothing beyond what the welfare system allowed her. Baby Meredith was equipped with second-hand or borrowed items, and their food was both simple and repetitive. 'I need to find some way of getting more cash,' he said, every few days.

'You can't. You haven't got enough spare time,' Maggs always argued.

It was Maggs's mother who made the fatal suggestion. 'What about buying and selling on eBay?' she said, having overheard one of these conversations. The new grandmother spent a great deal of her time at the Coopers, proving to be alternately useful and infuriating. 'Maggs and I could do the parcels, if you handle all the computer side of things.' Den was no computer wizard, but his skills far outstripped those of his wife or her mother.

'I have no idea where I'd start with something like that,' he objected. 'How do you get the stuff in the first place?'

'And what sort of stuff would it be?' wondered Maggs. 'You probably need to specialise.'

'And you have to do all that business with pictures. I haven't any idea how to do that. My phone can barely make calls, let alone take photos.'

'I don't think it's very difficult,' said his mother-in-law. 'All sorts of very ordinary people seem to manage it. For that matter, I've got very attached to Twitter myself. You do read such very amusing remarks there, not to mention all the funny pictures.'

Den was not persuaded. 'I'd have to buy a new phone, at the very least. And there'd be no certainty of making a profit. I need something more reliable than that.' But he had a thoughtful expression that was not lost on Maggs.

'Well, what are you interested in?' she pursued. 'I've never noticed you bothering with antiques, or old books or models. You're not the type for collecting war medals or spoons, are you? You need special knowledge if you're going to start dealing.'

He looked at her from his considerable height, impressed at the way she had detected the most subtle manifestation of pique in his tone. Because his attention had been snagged by the idea, despite the many objections. His words had been dismissive, but his eyes had widened a little, gleamed a little, at the images of auction rooms and flea market stalls that had flickered into his head. Not eBay, no, but something more immediate and controllable could be the answer.

'Maybe we could go to that antique place in Bristol at the weekend,' he said thoughtfully. 'Get a few ideas. I do rather like china,' he finished unexpectedly. He had surprised himself just as much as he surprised Maggs and her mother.

'It's a flea market,' said Maggs. 'If you mean the one in Corn Street.'

'Even better,' smiled Den.

'China? What – plates and vases and all that? Since when?'

'Ages ago. When I was about sixteen, I had an aunt who ran a stall in a market in Exeter. She did car boots as well. I went round with her sometimes. She showed me a few tricks.'

'What sort of tricks?'

'How to spot fakes, or damage that'd been covered up. I remember the marks – some of them, anyway. It'd probably come back to me with a bit of effort.'

'Which aunt was it? Have I met her?' Maggs frowned. 'Doesn't sound like your dad's sister. She's Auntie Chrissie, isn't she?'

'The one I mean has died. She was Aunt Pauline.

She had cancer when she was only fifty-four. Nobody talks about her any more.'

'Until now. What day is the flea market, then?'

'I forget. Let me find out tomorrow. Someone at work's sure to know.'

And someone did. Leslie Perkiss, well past retirement age, and moved sideways again and again, still clung to his position at the airport. He was currently being paid to channel travellers through the security gates, where they removed shoes and laptops, placed heavy luggage into plastic trays and walked stiffly through the archway that scanned them for unauthorised metalwork. Leslie Perkiss had a ready smile and never tired of the tedium. He had long ago abandoned any hope of discovering a machine gun inside a baby buggy's frame or a hand grenade in a sponge bag. He regarded the procedures as pure nonsense as far as actual security was concerned. He had worked out for himself that it was actually designed to pacify the passengers and make them believe they were safe. And that was fine with him. He chucked children under their chins and made sure the elderly weren't jostled in the queues.

Den liked Leslie, and often sat with him in the canteen. They had chatted about a thousand subjects over the years, including the joys of treasure hunting in junk shops. Leslie collected militaria and old postcards. He had a profound understanding of the ways of eBay. 'I wondered whether I could do a bit of buying and selling,' Den ventured. 'China, probably.'

'China from China and Japan?' quipped the elderly man.

'No, no. Strictly British. Worcester, Royal Doulton, Poole. I like Poole particularly.'

Leslie cocked his head. 'Bit girly,' he said. Leslie had a horror of anything girly, never suspecting that his fondness for small children might qualify. 'Wouldn't be my choice.'

Leslie's choices had all been made decades ago, but Den refrained from pointing this out. 'Any hints for me, then?' he asked. 'I wondered about the flea market they have in Corn Street.'

His friend pulled a face. 'Never find anything good there. They know the exact value of everything to the last penny. Best bet's a car boot, or charity shop. Same as it's always been. People that don't know what they're doing. Mind you, there's not so many of them any more, with all this antique stuff on the telly. Everybody's an expert these days.'

'Thanks.' Den nodded to himself. The advice was good. 'I think I'll have a look at the market, even so. Just to get an idea of prices and whatnot. It's been years since I went to anything like that. What I'm thinking is maybe getting a bit of stock and then putting it all into an auction in the Cotswolds or somewhere, with plenty of rich people, and seeing how that goes.'

The face was pulled again. 'Have to pay seller's commission, remember. Eats into any profit, that does. You'd do better to have a stall in one of those posh towns up there. They do big fairs in the town halls . . . Stow-on-the-Wold – isn't that one of them?' He pronounced the name slowly and roundly, as if there was something comical about it. Then he said it again. 'Stow-on-the-Wold. What a name!'

'I might manage that,' said Den slowly. Plans and possibilities were filling his head, although he knew perfectly well that he lacked the capital to buy anything but the most cut-price bargains at either charity shop or car boot sale.

They made it a family outing, driving through Somerset to Keynsham, near Bristol, in the ageing car that was in urgent need of new tyres and a thorough clean. As a former police officer, Den was in agonies of worry that they would be stopped and chastised for the bald treads. 'It's actually rather dangerous,' he told Maggs.

'Only if we skid, and that won't happen,' she reassured him. 'It's not icy or wet. We'll be fine.'

'The first thing I spend any profits on will be the car,' he promised.

'Profits!' she scoffed. 'You haven't even bought anything yet.'

He had in mind a raid on a small emergency fund for outlay, if it seemed worth the risk, but was not proposing to buy anything immediately. First he had to try to get an idea of how it all worked, twenty years or more after he had last shown any interest. The flea

market was not the one in Corn Street after all, but a
different monthly operation, which was actually easier
to reach from their side of Bristol. 'It starts at ten,' he
kept saying. 'I want to be there from the beginning.'

They arrived precisely on time, thanks mainly to
Maggs's ineffable efficiency. Well trained by Drew
Slocombe, she could estimate times and distances
with great accuracy. Even though not constrained
by a crematorium's inflexible schedule, a burial had
to be punctual. Everything had to be in place at the
exact moment promised. 'Otherwise they think we're
unreliable,' she had explained to her husband.

They followed a small queue of cars, and parked
easily. A huge, half-derelict building filled the view,
until they turned and identified the new centre,
hosting the market. There were a few stalls outside,
but almost everything was inside. They went in, and
all three were instantly delighted by the scene that
met their eyes. 'It's like a fairy tale,' gasped Maggs.
Meredith kicked her heels and crowed aloud. Den
quickly felt overwhelmed by the sheer quantity of
objects on display. How would he ever work out any
sort of plan? There were two big spaces filled with
stalls offering antique, vintage, collectable, junk and
kitsch. *Shabby chic* was yet another category, and one
he barely understood. What might it be like to have a
stall in this place? Could such a venture possibly bring
in enough money to justify the time and outlay?

He stopped at a stall near the entrance densely

stocked with ceramics. He identified Staffordshire and Worcester at a glance, and then paused over three very nice pieces of Limoges. He picked up a small lidded jug and turned it over. It felt creamy and cool in his hand, and he found himself wanting it with a startling passion. The sheer luxury of porcelain hit him between the eyes. He leant down to show it to his little daughter, to the palpable alarm of the stallholder.

'Careful!' he yelped. 'That's a genuine chocolate pot.'

'Oh?' Den examined the translucent object with increasing interest. 'I had no idea.'

'Pouyat, about 1860,' said the man carelessly. 'Lovely thing.'

'How much?' asked Maggs, who had been slow to notice the exchange. She had drifted towards a stall full of toys, all in original boxes with prices that stunned her.

'Hundred and fifty,' said the man promptly.

'Thought it was English you were after,' came another voice close by.

'Les! What're you doing here?' Den was flustered. Too much was going on for clear thinking. Meredith was reaching for the pot, assuming her father had intended to give it to her, and making loud sounds of desire. Maggs was shaking her head in disgust at the apparent impossibility of affording anything on offer.

'I come here most months,' shrugged Les. 'Makes a good day out, if there's naught else to do.'

'You know a bit about china, after all,' Den accused him.

'Enough to tell French porcelain when I see it. Doesn't everyone?'

Den put the pot down with infinite care. It was the loveliest of the three, but the others were still gorgeous. 'Porcelain,' he murmured. 'Imagine the first time anyone made something half decent with it. Getting it really thin and firing it just right. Maybe colouring it with something. Then realising you could see through it. What magic it must have seemed.'

'God, listen to him,' sighed Maggs. 'Who are you, might I ask?' She smiled at Les, as if at an ally.

'Sorry,' said Den. 'This is Les Perkiss, from work. He knows a lot about antiques and collecting.'

'I see. So it's all your fault, is it,' she said cheerfully. 'And now you've got Merry all excited about it as well.'

'Out of my price range,' said Den to the stallholder, with a regretful shake of his head. 'But you're right – it is a lovely thing.'

Over the lunch that Maggs had prudently brought with them, she asked several probing questions. 'What exactly do you think you might achieve?' was the gist of most of them. 'These people all know what they're doing. There isn't a single bargain in the whole place. They know just what everything's worth.'

'That's true. The question really is – where did they

get these things from? Did they pay a couple of quid for something worth a hundred? And if so, where?'

'Don't ask me.' She bit into a thick ham sandwich. 'But it's a nice cheap day out,' she acknowledged. 'I like looking at all this stuff.'

'Meredith's bored, though,' he noted. 'Not being allowed to touch anything or toddle about where she likes.' The child had learnt to walk at thirteen months and was constantly eager to practise.

'Pretty much the story of her life,' Maggs agreed. 'We could find a park for her, if it's not too cold.'

It was March, with the appropriate chilly wind. 'We have to check out the stalls by the entrance,' he said. 'There are four or five of them. You can let Merry toddle on the grass out there, look.'

'Like a dog,' said Maggs. She sounded tired and at the end of her patience. 'And there's probably the muck to prove it.'

'Not these days,' he argued.

He got his way and that was what they did when all the food was finished. Meredith appeared bemused by her sudden freedom after so long in the buggy. Her unsteady walking skills were unequal to navigating the many obstacles in her path, as Maggs chivvied her around the stalls and towards the patch of grass. She fell head first onto a hand-embroidered tablecloth that concealed a prickly wicker basket with sharp edges. The stallholder feared for her embroidery, and the child wailed at the pain caused by the bruise on her cheek. 'We'd better go,' said Maggs. 'I think we've seen enough, haven't we?'

Den begged ten minutes in which to thoroughly explore these final stalls, which in the arcane scheme of things struck him as composed of mixed junk, most of it in large bins labelled 'Everything £2' or sometimes 'Everything £1'. There was something forlorn and unhopeful about these overflow tables, cast into the inclement outdoors where few buyers paused on their way in or out.

He rummaged in two of these bins, bringing out a small blue lustre jug, and a larger orange lustre vase. He looked up at the person sitting in an incongruous deckchair, who appeared to be half asleep. 'I owe you four pounds,' he said, proffering the right money.

'Thanks, duck,' said the woman. 'You have a good day, now.' The accent was North Country, the smile exhausted. 'D'you want a bag?'

'No, thanks. I've got one.'

'What have you got there?' asked Maggs.

'I'm not sure. I just liked them. They're nothing special, but she was virtually giving them away. And I felt sorry for her.'

'That's no way to do business,' she reproached him.

'I'm not doing business. These aren't for resale.' Only then did he turn the orange vase over and look at the mark on its base. Saying nothing, he glanced back at the stallholder, who was paying no attention. 'Hmm,' he said, rubbing his cheek. 'Now that's a surprise.'

'What is?'

'Let's go. Can you remember where we left the car?' He carefully put the china into a canvas bag he'd brought with him. He felt furtive, as if he had stolen something, which Maggs was quick to observe.

'Of course I can,' she said. 'Can't you?'

'Not exactly.' His lack of observational skill was a standing joke with them. How he had ever functioned as a policeman remained a mystery. His current work seemed equally inappropriate, but he had taught himself to take note of any anomalies in the behaviour of air passengers, and he was good at following them unobtrusively. Most of the time he was simply responding to other people's requests, without any need to show much initiative, anyway.

Since Meredith had been born, he seemed to be suffering from a kind of fugue state that was commonly associated with new mothers, rather than fathers. He found himself dreaming of the future, where his daughter would share all her thoughts with him and be willingly instructed in the ways of the world by him. He was also eagerly pressing for a second child. 'She'll be well over two at this rate,' he worried. 'She deserves a companion. I hated being an only child.'

'I don't believe you. I loved it, personally.'

'Well, we should have a try. It'd be a waste otherwise.'

Maggs sighed. While not actively opposed to the idea, she was in no rush to repeat the whole process.

It would upset Drew, apart from anything else.

They found the car, and Maggs demanded an explanation for Den's behaviour.

'It says "Moorcroft" on the base,' he told her. 'You've heard of Moorcroft?'

'I'm not sure. Vaguely, maybe. So what?'

'It's usually covered with art nouveau-type patterns. Flowers mostly. I never knew you could have plain ones. The shape seems right, though.'

'Not sure I like the colour.'

'Don't you? I think it's lovely. Like a sunrise. Or a ripe mango.'

'Never seen a mango that colour,' she objected.

'Yes, you have. Inside, not the skin.'

'Oh. Okay. You're probably right.'

'I should really try to sell it. It might be worth as much as that Limoges.'

Maggs gave him a sceptical look and concentrated on strapping Meredith into her car seat. 'That'd be real beginner's luck,' she muttered.

Den was inspired. He spent an hour that evening googling the subject, trying to find the very item he'd bought so cheaply and establish a value for it. He found the orange lustre, but not the exact shape. He was bemused by all the different marks that denoted the Moorcroft factory over the years. He took a magnifying glass to his purchase, fearful of finding a hidden crack or chip. At the end of his researches, he was very little the wiser.

'Well, if it's that unusual, some collector might want it,' said Maggs, looking over his shoulder. 'If you could just track such a person down.'

'I should have asked Perkiss, I suppose. But I think he'd gone.'

'No, no. You want to keep it quiet. Don't tell him anything. That's too close to home.'

He angled his head so he could see her face. 'Suddenly you think this is a good idea?'

'I never said it wasn't. I just didn't think it'd work. I'm still not convinced. It can't be as easy as this.'

'We'll have to see then, won't we,' he said. 'I'm going to the local car boot sale next weekend, and maybe one or two charity shops in Shepton Mallett. I'm on early shift this week – I can pop in on the way home.'

'Just don't spend much money,' she warned him.

Ten days later, Den had spent forty pounds on an assortment of ceramics, including a small Limoges plate that had caught his eye in a Cancer Research charity shop. 'Three pounds,' he said triumphantly.

'Now what?' said Maggs.

'We find out where there's an antiques fair or auction, preferably in the Cotswolds or thereabouts. We can ask Thea and Drew if they know of anything.'

When Den phoned the Slocombes, Thea instantly thought of an Easter garden party she had seen advertised in Snowshill. She riffled through a pile

of papers by the phone and found a leaflet. 'It says
"indoors if wet",' she read out. 'Which it probably
will be. Anybody can have a stall and donate ten per
cent of their proceeds to the cause. Which appears to
be something to do with donkeys. And they have a
hashtag on Twitter. You ought to tweet about it.'

'That's my mother's department,' said Maggs,
who was listening in, with the phone switched to
speakerphone. Then, 'Where's Snowshill?'

'Not very far from here. It's got a big National Trust
place right in the middle of the village, full of weird
and wonderful objects. The owner was an eccentric
collector, and he filled the whole house with rubbish.'

'You did a house-sit there. A kid was killed.'

'That's right,' Thea said tightly.

'So – is this garden party anything to do with the
collector chap? I assume he was some while ago?'

'No and yes, roughly speaking. It's a typical
Cotswolds event, fundraising for somebody's pet
charity and Snowhill gives it added appeal, because of
the associations. You'd get some well-heeled customers.'

Den was both enthusiastic and apprehensive. 'I'm
not sure I've got enough for a whole stall.'

'The trick is to imply quality not quantity. Give
everything its own stand, with spotlights and velvet
cloths.'

'*What?*' he spluttered. 'Did you say spotlights?'

'Well, it might not work outside. But you must have
seen the way people make everything look so sparkly

and special. When you get it home, it turns into a dull, ordinary bit of tat.'

'You'll have to help me,' he pleaded.

'I'd be delighted,' she said.

'Thanks.' He still sounded doubtful. 'It seems like an awfully big job. Maybe I should go to an auction house instead.'

'Up to you,' said Maggs. 'But I think it'll be fun.'

Thea agreed. 'Easter Monday's always dreary,' she said. 'Just another annoying bank holiday. This'll brighten it up for you.'

'All right, then. I'll phone and ask if I can have a stall.'

They had almost two weeks to prepare, during which Den went to two more small towns and spent a further eighteen pounds on a jug, two plates and a rose bowl, all from charity shops. One of the plates was Royal Doulton, but the gilt had largely rubbed off and the decoration was a somewhat unappealing shade of green. 'Nobody's going to buy *that*,' said Maggs decisively.

He washed every piece with care, wiping them dry with the softest cloth he could find. The small blue jug that had come with the Moorcroft vase was an exquisite thing in its own right. The impressed mark on the bottom left him none the wiser as to its origins. It was full-bellied, the lip in perfect proportion, and it was in mint condition. He practised pouring milk from it, and could have sworn he was channelling the rich lady who might once have owned it.

He told Leslie Perkiss about his plans, unable to restrain his eager anticipation. 'I really don't think I can lose,' he said. 'Largely thanks to your advice, I might say.'

Perkiss waved this away. 'Naught to do with me, mate,' he said. 'This is your very own baby.'

'Don't be modest. You obviously know more about the business than you let on.'

The man bristled. 'What d'you mean by that, then?' he demanded.

'What's up with you? What did I say?'

Perkiss subsided. 'Sorry. Thought you might be implying something, that's all. Sensitive business – you'll find out. Nobody's what they seem. All out to get one up on each other.' He cocked an eyebrow at Den's open face. 'Don't know as it'll suit you, to tell the truth.'

'I'm not going to become a fence for stolen goods, if that's your worry,' he laughed.

'No, mate. That's not my worry,' said Perkiss with a weak smile.

Den was reminded of his aunt's tuition concerning fakes and damage and hard bargaining. 'I'll be careful,' he said. 'Don't worry about me.'

The morning of Good Friday was blustery with spiteful little rain showers, which Maggs's mother said was exactly as it should be. 'Never want a sunny Good Friday,' she said. 'That wouldn't be right at all.'

She was spending the whole weekend with them, along with Maggs's father. They insisted on keeping Meredith at home with them on the Monday, while Maggs and Den went off to sell antiques. 'Nowhere else we have to be,' they said complacently.

'And look at the lovely weather, all of a sudden,' said Maggs provocatively, pointing at the rapidly improving sky.

Snowshill was quite a long drive away, but the garden party did not begin until two o'clock, so there was no great rush to make an early start. Den fussed over the details of the display, worrying that the folding table they were using would look amateurish and insubstantial. 'They'll all be amateurs,' said Maggs. 'It's only a little local fundraiser, after all.'

They were met by Thea in the centre of the little village, and together they went to the big house that was hosting the event. It was impossible to miss, with balloons and bunting festooned around the entrance, and a pair of smiling children standing there to welcome stallholders. They were given directions for parking, unloading and setting up. It was organised with military efficiency. The three of them set about unpacking the delicate wares and setting them out on the rich red brocade that had once been a curtain. Maggs's mother had unearthed it from a box that she had still not opened since moving house six months previously.

The clear sky was a real bonus, spring sunshine reflecting off the gilding that adorned some of Den's pieces. He and Maggs admitted to each other that it was good to be free of their daughter for once, enjoying an adult pursuit without worrying that she would break something. Thea heard this and laughed. 'She'd be a real liability amongst all this china,' she said. 'You should probably have chosen something less breakable to specialise in.'

'It chose me,' he said.

Maggs rolled her eyes. 'He's come over all whimsical about it,' she told Thea. 'I blame Auntie Pauline, even if she has been dead for ages.'

The lady of the house floated by, smiling at everybody indiscriminately and asking if they needed anything. She paused at their stall, her gaze resting on Thea, who was trying to straighten a stand holding the Royal Doulton plate. 'Hello,' she said, with a little frown. 'I'm afraid I can't recall your name, but I know I know you.'

'Oh, I don't think so,' said Thea, who had already made it clear to Den and Maggs that she had every hope of remaining unrecognised. It was over two years since she had spent a week in Snowshill – but the associated scandal had drawn considerable attention her way, and she knew it was a gamble. 'I live quite a distance from here.' This was not true. Broad Campden was barely five miles away. Maggs made a low hiss of surprise at the blatant lie. 'I just came to help my friends.'

The woman did not press the point, but cocked her head in an attitude of scepticism. 'I see,' she said, which to Den's ear sounded slightly ominous. 'Well, I hope you find plenty of buyers. You've got some very nice things.'

'Thanks,' said Den. He walked a few steps away and looked back at his table. Something wasn't right. Not enough objects; the red cloth totally wrong; too formal; not formal enough. He didn't know what it was, but the whole thing made him nervous.

'Five minutes to go,' said Maggs. 'Stand back and wait for the hordes.'

'Nobody else is selling the same sort of thing as us,' Thea pointed out. 'At least, not nearly so well displayed.' She had spotted a stall crowded with a chaotic jumble of stuff she supposed was bric-a-brac – candlesticks, bowls, boxes, plates, mugs, bookends, small china figures and a lot more. People would enjoy rummaging through it, singling out something they might think special. With Den's way of doing it – which she admitted had been at her own suggestion – there was no chance of a surprise. It was more like a shop than an open-air bazaar. *We got it terribly wrong*, she thought unhappily.

But the first customers showed an interest that belied her thoughts. Wary of picking up the goods without permission, they were soon encouraged to hold them to the sunlight and turn them over to inspect the marks. 'I know someone who'd like this,' said a woman of the Limoges. 'She'll be along later. Can you keep it back for her?'

Den was immediately torn. 'Well, I don't know about that. If I get a definite buyer, I'll have to let it go.'

'How much do you want for it?'

Den had been given conflicting advice about putting prices on the things. His instinct was strongly to avoid the uncertainty and potential irritation associated with a lack of labels, but he could see the sense in assessing the level of interest and charging accordingly. Besides, Aunt Pauline had always enjoyed a vigorous haggle.

'I'd say fifty pounds,' he said.

The woman's eyebrows rose and her chest heaved. '*How much?*' she choked. 'You must be joking!'

He held his ground with difficulty. 'It's a genuine piece. Look at the mark.'

'What did you pay for it?' she demanded, unexpectedly. 'Less than a fiver, I'll bet. I'll give you fifteen here and now, and you should think yourself lucky.'

He was unnerved by her accurate guess, but he knew it had much more value than fifteen pounds. He looked to Maggs for rescue. She did not disappoint.

'No deal,' she said. 'This is quality, not just any old rubbish. We might be new at the game, but we know what things are worth.'

'Well there's no way you'll get fifty for it,' said the woman with finality. 'You need to understand that right away.'

'We'll see,' he told her. 'Come back in an hour, and if it's still here, I'll let it go for thirty.'

The woman moved off across the extensive lawn, and all three sighed with relief. 'She'll remember who I am,' said Thea.

'She'll keep an eye on us, and what sells,' predicted Maggs.

'We're doing it all wrong,' Den agonised. He caught Thea's eye, and was in no way reassured by the look on her face. It was close to fear, he realised with alarm. 'What's the matter?' he asked her.

'Nothing, really. I just made a connection between all this breakable china and what happened when I was last here. It's stupid. Take no notice of me. I hadn't realised how much of an effect it would have on me, that's all.'

Den knew only a little about what had happened, and this didn't feel like the moment to enquire. 'Nobody's going to break anything,' he promised her. 'Look at them!'

He and Thea both looked around at the decorous garden party going on around them. There was something quite Edwardian about it. One or two women wore long skirts; another had gloves on. The children were well behaved, as were the dogs. The stalls were offering home-made fancy cakes, pickles and jams, as well as handicrafts and *objets d'art*. There were watercolour paintings and big framed photographs. It was a triumph of local enterprise.

People were arriving in small clusters, but the garden was more than big enough to contain them all.

There was a gazebo supplying food and drink, and the door into the house stood wide open. 'How brave to offer your house like this,' said Thea. 'I can't imagine doing it.'

'You must be having all sorts of people in and out for the funerals, aren't you?' he asked. 'The same as Drew and Karen did.'

'That's different,' she said quickly. 'We only use one room, and the people are there for a specific purpose.'

'So are they here.'

They were interrupted by a potential customer. A very young woman wearing a woolly hat seized hold of the orange lustre vase with startling violence.

'Hey!' said Maggs. 'Careful with that!'

Thea was suddenly moving away, her back turned, but it was evidently too late. 'Thea Osborne,' said the girl. 'I remember you. I'm Ruby. Janice's daughter.'

Reluctantly, Thea faced her. 'So you are. Hello,' she said.

'What are you *doing* here? I would think you'd never want to see china or glass again, after what happened.' She waved the Moorcroft for illustration. Den reached out and firmly took it away from her.

'Careful,' said Maggs again.

'I'm just helping my friends,' said Thea. 'I didn't think anybody would spot me, in such a different context.'

'I don't think we'll ever forget you,' said Ruby with youthful emphasis.

'Oh dear. The lady who owns this house seemed to know me as well. I don't remember her at all.'

'You *were* rather famous,' said Ruby. She waved at the Moorcroft in Den's hands. 'And I recognise that pot, as well. I'd know it anywhere.'

'What?' Den stared at her. 'I don't believe you.' He waited in dread for her to prove the object had been stolen and that he was therefore in deep trouble. He should have asked the stallholder in Keynsham for documentation, provenance – all that stuff. But when you only paid two pounds for something, that would be ridiculous.

'Can I see the bottom?'

He turned it over and pushed the base towards her, still keeping hold of it.

'There!' She grinned delightedly. 'I knew it!'

He held his breath until it hurt. The girl was lovingly stroking the lustre. 'I'll give you eighty pounds for it,' she said. 'It's worth around that. I do know about these things,' she added. 'I'm working with the Wade collection now, while doing a degree in fine art.'

He came very close to dropping the fragile thing. 'Pardon?'

Beside him, Maggs and Thea both made little shrieks.

'It was made by my great-great-uncle,' Ruby explained. 'And we've been searching for this exact piece for ages. Look, those are his initials.' She indicated a squiggle on the base. 'It fills a gap in our collection. My mum will be thrilled.'

Den laughed with relief. 'Good God – I thought you were going to accuse me of stealing it.'

'No, no. I'm sure it's perfectly kosher.' But then she lightly touched the blue lustre jug. 'Although I know for a fact that this one – or something exactly like it – was nicked from a house in Taunton not so long ago. I'd be careful who you show it to, if I were you.'

Den sighed and turned to Maggs. 'You win some, you lose some,' he said.

Blood on the Carpet

The blood was appalling. It gushed out, thick and red, making a ghastly vivid puddle under the woman's head. Sheila Whiteacre stood there, frozen beyond any emotion or thought. The saw was still in her hand. Blood was flowing around her shoes. Elizabeth was going to die, right there on the ground, and she, Sheila, had killed her.

It wasn't possible, obviously. Elizabeth and she had known each other for decades; they'd been at school together. Old school friends didn't kill each other. It was all some bizarre mistake, or a dream, or a very clever joke.

But the blood was dreadfully real. Colour, smell, movement, even a faint sticky sound as Sheila moved her foot. Could a dream or a joke or even a mistake conjure such complete sensory authenticity?

She had studiously avoided looking at her friend's eyes, ever since Elizabeth had sunk to the floor clutching her neck. The pumping blood was more than enough to fill her view. But now she inadvertently let her gaze drift up the face, to be freshly appalled by what she saw. The eyes had become glassy, entirely lacking in feeling. No fear or accusation, no pain or panic. Just blank, like those of a doll. There were no signs of emotion anywhere on the face, either. Just a smooth flawless expanse of skin, with a nose and a mouth approximating to those of a human being. Already it had ceased to be Elizabeth in any meaningful sense.

They were in the living room. The blood was on the carpet. The grubby, hairy carpet that should have been replaced ages ago, or at least better cared for. It would certainly have to go now, thought Sheila. And she didn't suppose the insurance people would pay for a new one. There was sure to be a tiny little clause somewhere that excluded damage wrought by criminal activity on the part of the householder. Besides, if she was serving a life term of imprisonment, the carpet would be the least of her concerns.

Slowly, her thoughts were reviving, like little seedlings finally watered after too long a period of drought. She had to *do* something. Make a phone call. Go outside and shout for help. Fetch a bucket of soapy water and try to remove at least some of the congealing blood. She nudged a dollop of it with her foot, finding it revoltingly spongy as it thickened. Like a living thing, it was changing as she watched. There was so much of it that it looked more like a bodily organ than a pool of fluid. A chunk of tissue, like liver or lung, wobbling and glistening and making her feel sick.

But much worse was the body itself. Five foot five inches, eleven stone, wearing quite a lot of clothes – Sheila couldn't hope to move it without assistance. And why was she thinking of so doing anyway? What was she planning to do? Take Elizabeth outside and bury her in the garden? That was, after all, what people in films often did. Or bundle it into the car, drive to a remote clifftop and chuck it over the edge. Or put it in a bath of acid and wash all the resulting greasy sludge down the drain.

No, none of those strategies was possible, even though they were surprisingly tempting to think about. She could actually envisage one or two of them taking place – the favourite being the garden burial. There was something almost feasible in that one, if it wasn't for Art, due back next week and sure to want to catch up with his digging.

She had barely moved since the sudden violent blow that caused the injury. She still held the bowsaw in her hand. She had been cutting up logs, out on the patio, before running in and swiping blindly at Elizabeth's neck, with no conscious thought of what the consequences might be. The saw had very sharp teeth; she had cut her own hands with it once or twice, simply from the lightest touch. One of those teeth had snagged into Elizabeth's jugular, ripping it open and allowing her precious blood to escape. Such a simple, effortless way to kill somebody! All the safety measures in the world could not have prevented it. A young child could have done it. And yet nobody told you to lock saws away in a secure cabinet, like a gun or a knife. The world relied on universal common sense to prevent such an injury as Elizabeth had just suffered. It assumed that nobody would ever wantonly wave the thing around in proximity to bare, vulnerable skin.

The truth of the matter was that, at that moment, she had actually *wanted* Elizabeth to be dead. Or at least she had wanted to stop her in her tracks, force her to listen for a change, and generally take a stand against her friend's infuriating behaviour. Elizabeth always knew best. She took it for granted that the way she lived was the only acceptable or reasonable one. She told people where they were going wrong, warned them they were in error and gloated when proved right. She did it all in a friendly fashion, smiling and then rolling up her sleeves to take an active role in whatever she believed had to be done. Sheila had often asked herself why she maintained the friendship with regular emails and occasional phone calls. They followed each other on Facebook, commenting and sharing and taking an interest in each other's lives.

But having Elizabeth to stay was never easy. Sheila had hoped that when her friend moved to the Shetland Isles to live, there would be no more face-to-face contact. Everything would be a whole lot easier then.

But all that happened was that the visits became more prolonged. Not quite once a year, they still seemed to come around all too often. Both women having reached the venerable age of sixty, they had developed independent habits financed by substantial incomes, supplied mainly by their husbands. Sheila had Art and Elizabeth had Malcolm. Until recently, Sheila also had two children still living at home – Tiffany and Ricky. Both had moved out a few months previously, and Art had suddenly announced he was going to America for a month to catch up with long-neglected elderly relatives.

Malcolm was contentedly monitoring seabirds on the remoter islands, while his wife flew south to visit various old friends. Not only Sheila, but Diana and Jackie and Stella. She stayed three or four days with each one, making a cheap and varied holiday in the process.

Sheila had been left in charge of the big house near Cirencester. She had promised to give it a comprehensive clean, once they had all suddenly noticed how scruffy and dilapidated it had become over the years. When it was full of children, that hadn't seemed to matter. Now, it was a source of shame.

All this filled Sheila's mind, as she deliberated on what was to be done. *At least I haven't panicked*, she congratulated herself. Which meant, in reality, that at no point had she screamed. It had been a very quiet murder, all things considered. She might have shouted 'Stop!' half a second before wielding the saw, but other than that, not a sound had been uttered.

Elizabeth only had one last friend to favour with her presence, and that was Stella, who lived in Carlisle. It was all very cleverly worked out, with a flight home from Newcastle at the end of the week, all her friends suitably corrected and advised for another year or so.

Sheila's Cotswold house was a favourite with Elizabeth. On the outskirts of Cirencester, the whole area had always been popular with people of means. The houses were handsome, the gardens extensive. It was close to numerous quiet villages with lovely views, walks, gardens, pubs. All this meant it saw its share of visitors, despite Sheila's reluctance to provide hospitality. For twenty years she had welcomed little friends of her five children, producing endless meals and a reliable smile. Since events of a few months earlier, she had no longer wanted to be seen as an ever-open door. It had not been particularly difficult to deter most would-be visitors. Her local friends had busy lives, and Sheila herself had a job that took her to Cheltenham three times a week, and kept her at the keyboard for much of the remaining days. She was the proud owner of two large dogs and a cat – each one of whom shed hair generously on all the furnishings. She had taken time off to be with Elizabeth – time that she quite deeply resented. But friendship dictated that she make no objection, prepare meals, sweep away some cobwebs and forego her favourite TV programmes.

The first day began well. It was a Friday, the sun

shining patchily, perfect for a long walk. Both women took pride in their physical robustness, striding along in amicable competition. Elizabeth insisted on paying for lunch at The Plough, on a bend in the minor road that ran between Stow and Stanway. The food was more than either of them needed, and weighed them down on the walk they took afterwards, during which a wind sprang up and made Sheila irritable. Back in the house, she was acutely aware of the half-hearted job she had made of cleaning in preparation for her guest. There were greasy streaks on the kitchen cabinets, dust along the tops of pictures, and general grime on the skirting boards. But she had done her poor best with the hairy carpets, and brushed the animals in the hope of reducing their shedding. When Elizabeth lowered herself onto the sofa for the evening, the grimace of distaste at the presence of Jenny-Cat and Baxter the big Labrador on the cushions beside her was impossible to miss.

At least Bert remained on the floor. He was quite a large creature, and didn't really fit on the sofa. There was mastiff in his ancestry, if the size of his head was anything to go by. For a short-haired dog, he made quite a lot of mess.

'Do you want me to move them?' said Sheila, in a voice tight with challenge.

'No, no, of course not. I wouldn't dream of it.'

'You knew what it would be like. Why can't you just relax? The hairs brush off easily enough. You're not going to catch anything.'

The glance that her friend threw around the room implied that this might be in doubt. Sheila laughed. 'I've always been a rubbish housekeeper. I'm lucky Art doesn't mind. He always thinks it's fine, so long as there's enough light. He's always polishing the mirrors – have you noticed?'

Elizabeth smiled. 'The mirrors are dazzling,' she said.

'They've dulled a bit since he went off on his jaunt – not up to the usual standard, I'm sorry to say. It never even occurs to me to clean them, however much I agree it's a good thing to do. I'm never going to change. And quite honestly, I'll never understand why it matters.'

'It doesn't, of course,' said Elizabeth. 'Are we going to play Scrabble or Canasta?'

'I rather fancied Boggle. Art gave it to me for Christmas. I'm not very good at it.'

'All right, then. But bags we play Scrabble tomorrow night.'

The games had gone well both evenings, once Elizabeth had ostentatiously blown the dust off the Scrabble box. The dogs had got the measure of her by then, and kept their distance.

The dogs! Now, with Elizabeth in a heap on the floor, white and still, the moment the dogs came in from the garden, they'd be all over her. Sniffing, wondering, getting blood on their paws – they would present yet another insuperable complication. Quickly, Sheila went to the back and made sure the door was firmly closed. She remembered rushing through it, ten minutes earlier, without a thought of shutting it behind her. She had no idea what Baxter and Bert had been doing. They had half an acre to do it in, and she saw no reason to constantly monitor them.

Of course, there had been no need at all to cut up firewood. It was July, and the shed was already full of logs, in a jumbled heap with no concession to the usual ritual of neat stacking. The log pile was a significant element of Cotswold life, a thing of beauty in its own right. But very few sixty-year-old householders cut and split their own fallen branches, as Sheila did. Approximately a quarter of her outdoor area was devoted to trees, the little copse punching above its weight, with willow, ash, cherry and sycamore crowding together. She had planted them all herself, twenty years earlier, much to the consternation of neighbours. The trees had blocked the view, but also formed a cosy shelter against the wind and a much-loved playground for the dogs. Where Sheila Whiteacre might be a slipshod housewife, she was a deeply attentive gardener, and the trees had flourished magnificently. There were trilliums and ferns and bluebells growing at their roots; birds and squirrels favouring the upper regions. 'It's my own little patch of genuine wildness,' she would say. 'Amazing how much you can do with an eighth of an acre.' The temptation was to expand it to twice the size, but the neighbours had pleaded with her not to do that. Many people, she discovered, regarded trees with scant enthusiasm.

The willows grew outrageously fast, needing to be strenuously lopped every autumn. So Sheila lopped them, using an electric chainsaw only for the thickest boughs. Then she set up her sawhorse and used the bowsaw to render them into logs, with Art standing by making worried comments. His talents ran more to vegetables and making wine. Sheila had been determinedly cutting up logs on that third day, as a way of showing off to Elizabeth.

The pile of branches awaiting her attention was still quite a size when Elizabeth came to the back door. 'Enjoying your lumberjacking?' she asked. 'How much longer will you be?'

'Twenty minutes or so,' Sheila estimated. 'Are you all right?'

'Fine. I'll go and read the paper.'

Sheila suspected nothing, as she set her saw to another length of willow.

She relived those moments now, standing there unmoving over the body of her friend. Her own rage now seemed insane, pathetic, inexcusable. Nobody would understand or forgive her. She would be deservedly cast out of normal society, locked away and forgotten. And the pity of it. The terrible finality of death was beginning to filter into her thoughts. Elizabeth was gone for ever. Her family would never see her again. The husband would be bereft, alone in the far north with his birds.

Her two sons would be at first disbelieving and then furious. They would persecute and prosecute and make perfectly certain that Sheila got her full punishment. She had committed the ultimate sin, broken the one commandment that every society on earth regarded as unassailable. And for something so banal, she could not even articulate it to herself. Never could she even attempt to explain it to anybody else. If they weren't disgusted, they'd be amused. There were some, she feared, who would laugh at her.

Humiliation was a subtle and far-reaching thing. It led to loss of self-respect, a plunge downwards of one's status rating, becoming the object of scorn and ridicule. In the Cotswolds, it would be even worse than that. In the Cotswolds there were stricter standards than in most other places. Respectability was essential, although eccentricity was acceptable as an alternative. Sheila knew what it was to sail close to the cold wind of disapproval at times. The trees, for one thing, had made people wary of her. The strategy of seldom asking anybody into her house served only just adequately to damp down any criticisms of her dust and cobwebs.

All of which meant that she could never, ever, tell the truth of why she had killed her friend. That, she decided, was Point Number One. After that, things fell into place surprisingly easily. It could not be more than ten minutes since Elizabeth's blood first began to gush. In a frenzy of efficiency and focus, she threw the saw down in the thickened blood, went out to call the dogs in and ushered them through the kitchen to investigate the object on the floor. 'Sorry, lads,' she murmured. 'This is the only thing I can think of to do. Don't worry, old chap. I won't let anybody harm you.' She grasped Baxter's front left paw and dabbled it in the blood. Then she pushed his head right down to the floor, so he got streaks of red on his neck. After a short pause for thought, she plunged both her hands into the gore and wiped it down the dog's chest as well. He resisted, with a puzzled whine. When Baxter resisted, nobody could gainsay him, but the job was done. 'Now you,' she told the other dog. 'For good measure.' She did the same again to him, but with lighter daubs. Then she stood back for a look. Would the police see what she wanted them to? How closely would they examine the animals?

It was important to keep blood well away from their faces – which she had successfully achieved. 'You'll do,' she told them. 'Good boys.' She watched as they slunk warily back to the kitchen, showing considerable concern at this strange turn of events. She pushed the vacuum cleaner into a corner, and gave the room a quick inspection. Then Sheila Whiteacre dialled 999 and asked for the police. 'A woman is dead, in my house,' she said, in a thick whisper. 'It was a dreadful accident. I am *so* sorry. The blood . . . there's so much blood.' British women did not wail and scream or go into hysterics. They clung to the illusion that by staying calm everything would be all right. Sheila's mother, born in 1928, had rigidly upheld this approach to her final breath.

'Are you certain she's dead?' asked the young man on the line who had been passed to her by the original responder. Why a young man, Sheila asked herself. How could he get the right tone without a lifetime of experience? Wasn't it usually a woman, anyway?

'I'm afraid so. I have a bit of medical knowledge, and I'm fairly sure it was her jugular vein. Artery, I mean. Or is it the carotid? It absolutely *flooded* out. I know I should have called sooner, but I was so shocked. I just couldn't believe it had happened. I did try to stem the flow myself, but there was nothing I could do. And, quite honestly, I don't think anybody could have got here in time, anyway.' She allowed herself to prattle, as a small concession to a hysteria that these days might be expected.

'Please give me the address. Your name. We'll have somebody with you as soon as we can. I can stay on the line until they get to you, if you'd like me to.'

'Thank you. I don't know. Poor, harmless Elizabeth. I absolutely can't believe it. She looks so *awful*.' Rising voice, choked breath. Dawning awareness of implications. It was not difficult to convey, being close to the actuality.

'Will your people find the house? It's quite simple, really. You have to find the gateway, beside a big tree. Perhaps I should go outside and wait for them.'

'You're on a landline, I see. Is it cordless?'

'Oh yes. I'll take it with me.'

She kept talking, sticking to her feelings of shock and disbelief and horror, never mentioning what had caused the death. Time enough for that when the relevant people turned up. There would be a recording of this conversation, and any inconsistencies might well be noted. She was immensely proud of her clear thinking. After those first minutes, she had pulled herself together magnificently.

A police car arrived with remarkable speed, the officers assuring her that an ambulance was right behind them.

'I don't think they'll be needed,' she said, waving a shaky hand towards the house. 'I'm quite sure she's dead.'

It was a man and a woman, the latter apparently the senior partner. Her uniform jacket was buttoned tightly across a generous chest, and the black trousers strained to enclose substantial buttocks. Sheila reproached herself fiercely for such outdated observations. The woman could be any shape she chose, and still be excellently good at her job. Obviously. But the man was lean and good-looking and sharp of eye. It was to him that she addressed herself.

The dogs were shut in the kitchen, which made them bark much more than they normally would. 'Poor things,' she crooned. 'They've got no idea what happened. They were only playing. But Bert really is awfully big.'

This was not intended to make any sense; she was simply preparing the ground for the story that was yet to come. A story that ran itself through her head repeatedly, despite her awareness that it was not to sound rehearsed. Broken sentences, pauses, backtracking – incoherence was key.

The woman crouched over Elizabeth, wearing latex gloves, and performed a few basic checks. 'You're right,' she told Sheila. 'I'm afraid she's gone.' She had approached from the top of the body, avoiding the blood that had flowed in the other direction. She looked up. 'How long ago did this happen? The blood is drying already.'

'Oh, I don't know. I did try to stop her bleeding. She was so terrified, poor thing. And the dogs kept getting in the way. They've got blood all over them. And they were only playing. She should have known that.'

'Did the dogs do this?' asked the man.

'Oh no. They would never hurt anybody. That's what I'm *saying*. No, it wasn't them. It was me. With the saw. Look.' She pointed to the tool, where it lay half in the puddle of blood. 'Of course, I didn't mean to.' She stopped, afraid she was sounding rather too coherent.

'Better not touch it,' the woman said. 'Till the others get here. I'll call it in.' She gave Sheila a long look that revealed suspicion, confusion and a dash of fear. Was this a madwoman, to take a saw to her friend's throat? *Well, yes*, thought Sheila. *Possibly so.*

'Better do the basics,' said the handsome male officer. 'The name of the deceased.'

'Elizabeth Humphries. She has a husband . . . oh, God! Poor Malcolm! However will we tell him? Oh . . .' A stifled sob, readily produced by allowing the image of the desolate husband on his windy island.

'How are you spelling Humphries?' he asked carefully.

'What? Oh . . .' she stumbled it out. 'She lives on the Shetland Islands. She was visiting me. We've been friends all our lives.' The tears welled in some profusion. 'What's going to happen now?' she wailed, before reining herself in. The question, however, was a good one. How much punishment would she get? How much did she *deserve*?

The dogs were still noisy in the kitchen. The female officer was speaking into a phone, her back turned, voice subdued. Sheila couldn't hear what was said. The smell of blood became suddenly acute. Metallic and organic, all at once. She'd never experienced it so rich and thick before. There was a dreadful fascination to it.

'I can explain what happened,' she offered, with a gulp. 'I'm sure I should.'

'Of course, Mrs Whiteacre. But best to wait for the ambulance, maybe. And the doctor.' He frowned. 'Or should we send the ambulance back? Lettie? What about that? It's not needed, is it?'

Lettie? Was that a first or second name? Or a nickname? In any case, the woman had finished her call and was considering the question.

'Police doctor comes next. Then she'll have to go to the mortuary.'

This didn't directly answer the question. Sheila blinked at her. 'Will they take her away in it? The ambulance, I mean?'

'Not immediately. Sometimes it's an undertaker who does it. Depends.' She did not reveal on what it depended. 'They're all on their way,' she added, brandishing the phone that she'd used for the summoning. 'Ambulance ought to be here by now.'

'Perhaps it can't find me,' Sheila suggested diffidently.

'They'll see our car. It's not difficult.' And then it was there, obedient to Lettie's expectations. Sheila began to understand that here was a woman of power, who felt comfortably in control nearly all of the time. Except that she was not quite sure, even now, that she was dealing with a comprehensible situation.

Closely behind the ambulance came two more cars, causing a commotion that was sure to attract attention from anyone present in the village that day. Each car contained a single man, which struck Sheila as wasteful. 'The DI, and the doc,' murmured Lettie, not so much for Sheila's benefit as for her own purposes; a sort of mental checklist.

The DI was a detective inspector named Higgins,

who took Sheila into the kitchen, having given the dogs a good long look. 'That's blood on them, is it?' he said.

'It must be. It was everywhere.' She rubbed absently at Bert's shoulder.

'Better not do that. We need to photograph him.'

'What? Why?'

'Well . . . for evidence.'

'The *dogs* didn't do anything. At least, I suppose they started it, but it wasn't their fault. They were just playing.'

'I think we ought to go back to the beginning. And in the light of what the other officers tell me, I'm afraid I'll have to caution you formally. And record everything you tell me.'

She had been prepared for this, but was careful not to let this be seen. 'Oh! Do you mean I'm being interviewed? Here? Now?'

He paused. 'I suppose technically I ought to take you to the station. I will, if you prefer. And you're entitled to have a solicitor present, of course.' He looked unhappy, his fatherly features sagging. 'Perhaps if you just give me the gist of what happened?'

'Yes. The thing is, Elizabeth was nervous of them both, but Bert especially, even though she's known him for years. And sometimes he gets a bit boisterous. I was outside, cutting up some firewood, when she shouted for me to come and get him off her. He was jumping up, because I think she must have taken the lead off its hook, so he thought they were going for a walk. I'm not sure if she did. Something set him off.' She paused, reminding herself that she ought not to sound too lucid. But prattling was good. 'And then Baxter must have joined in. He's not so big, but he's heavy and very dim. He just does whatever Bert does. But it was too much for Elizabeth. She wasn't scared, really. Just cross with them. They never believe that anybody could dislike them, you see.'

'So she called to you. Where were you?'

'Out on the patio. You can see where I was sawing. It's all still there, just as I left it. I came in holding the saw. Stupid. Ridiculous. *Why* did I do that?' This was a genuine question, which she would continue to ask herself to her dying day. 'I suppose she sounded quite urgent. I was worried they might push her over. So I came in, and Bert was being rather a pest, I must admit. I shouted at him, but he just kept on trying to lick her face, and get her to play with him. And then . . .' her voice cracked, tears began to erupt '. . . then I hit out at him, with the back of the saw. The smooth handle part, not the blade. Not hard, just to get his attention. And I must have swung it back, towards Elizabeth, to clout him again, and the teeth got her neck. She was bending over, fending Baxter off. And Bert was dancing about, around our legs. They are awfully sharp, you see – the teeth of the saw, that is. I cut my own hand last week.' She showed him the scab. 'And it seemed to *catch* in her skin, right under her ear. She squealed, and the dogs still didn't get away, and suddenly the blood started. That's it, really.' She wiped her cheeks with bloodstained fingers. 'All my own idiotic fault. I will never forgive myself.' This too was true. The truth smacked her hard, for the first time. She would have an enormous albatross of guilt around her neck for ever, now. 'Sorry,' she gasped. 'I think I'm going to be sick.'

And she was, fifteen seconds later, having managed to reach the downstairs lavatory just in time.

When she dragged herself back into the kitchen, Higgins was sitting very still, not making notes or attempting to speak. He had gone pale, she noticed. What luck to get a man so human for her interrogation. He was on her side, she knew.

She did have to go to the police station, but no arrest was made. They requested that she stay in the village, and be prepared for further questions. They let her wash the dogs, and herself, eventually. The post-mortem on Elizabeth, the following day, comprehensively confirmed her story. Every detail fitted like magic. An inquest was opened, and then adjourned to some far-distant date. Detective Inspector Higgins told her that the verdict, when it finally came, was almost sure to be Accidental Death, on the advisement of the police. Her carelessness was reprehensible, and many people would believe that punishment was appropriate.

'I believe that myself,' she said humbly.

But Higgins pointed out that no good would be done

by sending her to prison. They had bigger criminals to apprehend than her. She had smiled and thanked him, and hugged her maligned dogs.

Only Elizabeth's ghost – which never materialised – knew the truth. How Sheila had heard the vacuum cleaner going, after she had explicitly requested Elizabeth not to do any cleaning. She had heard humiliation, criticism, even disgust, in that whirring engine. She had heard her friend thinking she was a slut, incompetent, lazy, slovenly. She, Elizabeth, would show her how it was done, gathering up the dog hair and dust with easy efficiency.

Sheila had paused for perhaps three seconds, during which a great rage swelled and blossomed within her. The very *rudeness* of it infuriated her, but bigger than that was the sense of shame and inadequacy that she had devoted her whole life to conquering. She ran through the kitchen, saw in hand, and struck out without any other thought but to make the woman stop.

It worked.

Key References to Novels in the Cotswolds Series

'In Guiting Power'	*Death in the Cotswolds*
'With Slaughter in Mind'	*Slaughter in the Cotswolds* and *A Cotswold Ordeal*
'Making Arrangements'	*A Grave in the Cotswolds*
'When Harry Richmond Sold His Cottage'	*A Cotswold Killing*
'Little Boy Lost'	*Trouble in the Cotswolds*
'The Stone Man'	*Shadows in the Cotswolds*
'The Blockley Discovery'	*A Cotswold Mystery*
'Ladies Who Lunch'	*Deception in the Cotswolds*
'Humiliation'	*A Cotswold Ordeal*
'In Which Thea Meets Tony Brown'	*Guilt in the Cotswolds* and the Lake District titles
'The Moorcroft'	*Malice in the Cotswolds* and the Den Cooper titles
'Blood on the Carpet'	*Revenge in the Cotswolds*

To discover more great books and to
place an order visit our website at
allisonandbusby.com

Don't forget to sign up to our free newsletter at
allisonandbusby.com/newsletter
for latest releases, events and exclusive offers

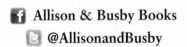 **Allison & Busby Books**
@AllisonandBusby

You can also call us on
020 7580 1080
for orders, queries
and reading recommendations